Precious *little* Secrets

Michelle R. Nickens

This is a work of fiction. All incidents and dialogue, and all characters with the exception of some well-known public figures, are products of the author's imagination and are not to be construed as real. Any resemblance to persons living or dead is entirely coincidental.

Text copyright © 2013 by Michelle R. Nickens
Cover photography copyright © 2013 by Michelle R. Nickens

All rights reserved.

Visit www.michellenickens.com for information about the author.

ISBN-13: 978-0615851648
ISBN-10: 0615851649

DEDICATION

This book is dedicated to my mother and father, whom I love and miss more than words can say.

I also dedicate this to my husband. His support, love and help during this process made this book possible.

CONTENTS

Chapter 1	*1*
Chapter 2	*7*
Chapter 3	*17*
Chapter 4	*24*
Chapter 5	*32*
Chapter 6	*41*
Chapter 7	*46*
Chapter 8	*49*
Chapter 9	*58*
Chapter 10	*65*
Chapter 11	*73*
Chapter 12	*78*
Chapter 13	*84*
Chapter 14	*90*
Chapter 15	*98*
Chapter 16	*106*
Chapter 17	*111*
Chapter 18	*116*
Chapter 19	*123*
Chapter 20	*128*
Chapter 21	*138*
Chapter 22	*145*
Chapter 23	*152*
Chapter 24	*157*
Chapter 25	*160*
Chapter 26	*163*
Chapter 27	*173*
Chapter 28	*176*
Chapter 29	*183*
Chapter 30	*188*
Chapter 31	*191*
Chapter 32	*197*
Chapter 33	*207*
Chapter 34	*218*
Chapter 35	*222*
Chapter 36	*228*
Chapter 37	*234*
Chapter 38	*238*
Chapter 39	*242*
Chapter 40	*246*
Chapter 41	*250*
Chapter 42	*255*

CHAPTER 1

I don't remember how I got to my car, yet I found myself driving the two-lane rickety road. Massive trees whipped past and the illuminating moon guided my way home. Bits of the evening flashed through my mind like speeding headlights blurring the landscape. I'd lost the last couple hours of my life.

Dried tears caked my cheeks. My heart sank somewhere deep in my gut. Although my eyes ached, I opened them wide, pushing myself to keep driving. The thought of my mother's face upon discovering I'd wrangled with an oak, forced me to stay alert.

A text popping up on my iPhone caught my attention. I grabbed it. Scott's name appeared on the screen. Disgustedly, I tossed the cell phone onto the passenger's seat.

Seconds later, my foot pressed firm on the brake pedal. A screeching sound cut the silence. And then, nothing.

I raised my head. Blood smeared the steering wheel. A pounding erupted in my forehead. Lightheaded and nauseous, I struggled to balance. I drew in a huge breath and examined the situation. The car sat slanted in the other lane. *What the hell?* All the air escaped from my lungs, fogging the windshield. *Did I hit something?*

I wiped the glass with the back of my hand. Through the

streaks, I saw a boy standing a few feet in front of the car. He held his arm out, his palm up, like he was telling me to stop. His dark green eyes cut into me. A chill worked its way up my spine. I closed my eyes tight. When I opened them, the boy had vanished. *My imagination.*

But, what made me stop so suddenly? I got out of the car. I don't know why. It was so unlike me. The car looked fine. It was quiet, only the wind shuffling the leaves in the trees. I glanced at the moon, noticing that the sky had more stars than usual.

"Natalie?" a voice whispered against my neck.

Without a second thought, I turned straight toward the car, opened the door, fell onto the driver's seat and smashed the lock button. From behind the glass I waited, expecting someone or something to appear. The road remained deserted. The engine roared and I peeled away. *No one will need to be told about this, especially mom.*

Ten minutes later, I found myself running up the stairs, my apartment in sight. With it locked behind me, I slid down the door and collapsed. Every muscle in my body beat with exhaustion. Stress had taken its toll.

Random thoughts streamed through my mind. One of my father, Frank, and I playing kickball. I never liked sports. I preferred watching dad arrive at a marathon's finish line than to compete in one myself. Yet, my heart pounded as if I'd just run a race. My thoughts flashed to my mother, remembering her sitting on the edge of the bed, holding an old photo and rosary.

I am way too tired.

After struggling to push myself up from the floor, I managed to clean the cut on my forehead, brush my teeth and change into my ratty nightie. I crawled into bed at 2:23 a.m. My head hit the pillow, possessing no strength left to lift it. I looked like a tattered old shack that had weathered a violent storm, but the worst awaited—the healing.

I curled up in my bed, covering my head with my beloved yet bedraggled blanket—the last one my mother had given me.

Its scent reminded me of cuddling with her on my parent's bed, watching old movies.

I tried to block out the evening, but like puzzle pieces taking shape, memories returned. The incident in the street confused me. Scott's cruel words left me cold.

I should have realized after four years of him not mentioning the *M* word. Every man I date turns into a huge *M*istake. I thought Scott might be the one. I loved his playful and clever personality. He made me laugh. He was sexy and good in bed. *The best sex ever.* At least as far as I'd experienced. Scott had no inhibitions. After a while, I caught up, succumbing to his anytime, anywhere attitude. His convertible, the stairwell of his apartment building, the ladies room at Pasha's, the rough jetties leading boaters back to the harbor—were all fair game. The jetties—the walk out to the farthest point was worth the wait.

The thought of him wanting someone else turned my stomach and rattled my chest.

He had dressed too nice for dinner and a movie. *How did I miss the signs?*

"Lisa will be at that meeting in Denver. Kinda happened that way. Didn't know." He lied. "I'll probably sleep with her," he announced, like our relationship was just a Jr. Cheeseburger and a small fries. *Fried, for sure. How could he possibly want to sleep with Lisa? After all this time.*

Lisa was a bitch, with a distinct desire to claw her way through life. I met her once in a bar. She had no redeeming qualities, but I remember her breasts were like small countries. She looked like a burned out stripper. *What did Scott want with her?* At thirty-nine, I thought he had grown up. But, inside his manly shell still lived a horny teenager.

The last time we broke up, he followed me for weeks. He bought me flowers and professed his love in notes, voice messages, emails and on a billboard on 54th Street. I took him back. But, this time our relationship was over. I couldn't help wonder when he had stopped loving me, or what I did wrong. *Nothing.* I just had not found 'the one.'

I closed my eyes and repeated—relax, rest, inhale, exhale. I breathed deeply into my blanket, the smell of my parent's house squashing my anger.

The piercing green eyes of the little boy appeared in my mind. Yet, now, they seemed so innocent. The icy grip clutching me earlier had faded. My body loosened, easing me into sleep.

***

Hundreds of people surrounded me. Friends and family were smiling, hugging and kissing. Droplets of sweat hung to the tip of my nose and drizzled down my legs. Birds chirped in the distance. Music mysteriously filled the room. My parents waltzed on a small portable dance floor. Cocktail tables sat dressed in lilac satin, with beautiful bouquets of lilies neatly centered and tied with eggplant dyed ribbons.

Gripped in my hand was cold steel—a long sharp knife. I stood next to a table, cutting a large cream colored cake, its icing in a basket weave and adorned with flowers. A much stronger hand cradled mine. White lace, satin and small white pearls covered my body.

My wedding day.

Muscles I never used before contracted, and a smile extended across my face. I pivoted to behold my groom. *This is the man I'll marry.*

When I stared up at him, hoping to glimpse my future lover, horror spread throughout my body. A faceless man stood before me with no eyes or mouth, no features, just a blur of skin, stretched across a shadowy skull. I screamed, dropping the knife and slashing both of my hands. Blood spilled onto the velvety cake, the lilac cloths and my precious gown. In slow motion, I ran through the crowd, out from under the tent and into the dominating sun.

After running a few yards, I stopped dead. My bloody hands hung to the sides of my gown, soiling it dark red. I spun around, eyeing what stretched in all directions. I stood in the center of a cemetery. Tombstones for miles.

The tent had disappeared. There were no dancers, no guests flirting with the bartenders and no anonymous groom. The music had stopped, and the silence was interrupted only by the hard and erratic beat of my heart. A race had begun deep in my chest as the smell of decay filled my nostrils. I bent over, gasping. I was alone.

***

Scratchy, on-again, off-again music, crackled through the air. I woke up and whacked the radio with the palm of my hand to silence the noise. *What on earth?* I had not dreamed about the cemetery since I was a child.

I stumbled into the bathroom. An unforgiving reflection stared back. I covered the blotches and dark circles. From one room to the other, I shuffled like a slug, tossing my nightclothes on the floor and yanking on black slacks and a purple polyester blouse. My hair flipped up in the back, but it was not supposed to, and I had no time for a shower. I desperately smoothed my untamed strands with my $24 useless sculpting gel. I swept my bangs to the right covering the scratch on my forehead. From my jewelry box, I dug out my gold hoop earrings. I dabbed on some lip gloss. *That's the best I can do under the circumstances.*

Thirty minutes later, I tiptoed up to my office, inched behind my desk, sunk into my chair and turned on my computer. I waited for the Windows logo to appear on the screen, the silence filling the hole in my chest. I grabbed a pencil and began rolling it back and forth on my desk. Reliving Scott's selfish diatribe and waking from my bizarre nightmare left me anxious. Even though my eyes stared blankly at the monitor, fireworks exploded within the confines of my head, trying to recreate the dream.

I jumped when Darren, an intern, waltzed into my office. We exchanged empty looks as he pulled the mail cart behind him. As the CEO's grandson, Darren's arrogance soared. A permanent smirk painted his patronizing face. I bit my tongue on numerous occasions when confronted with Darren's lack of skills and poor attitude. I forced myself to be cordial, but questioned whether he was a spy planted in the company to report secrets up the chain.

"Here," he said, tossing the rubber-banded pile of mail on my desk. "Same as you always get. Must be pretty boring, day-in-day-out. I guess it's better than the rest of the losers in this place. If my grandfather only knew. Well, at least there's a few things interesting to look at. Sara sure is something I'd like to—"

"Thanks for the mail." I wanted to tell him to go to hell, but more important matters rushed through my mind than sparring with a bully.

He grinned, his mouth warping into a wicked curve, and quipped, "Ah, have a super day, ma'am." He chuckled, pushing his cart to the next office. *What a twerp.*

I sat the pencil on my desk. A humming resonated from my purse. I grabbed my buzzing cell phone and I stared at the number. My hand automatically stuffed it back into my leather bag. My mother would reiterate the I-told-you-so monologue. *My wonderful crazy mother, Sybil.* She never liked Scott and regularly referred to him as 'a snake that just crawled out of the muck.'

She was right, but I didn't want to hear her lecture now. And, even though I wanted to tell her about my dream, I had never mentioned them before. She had enough worries.

CHAPTER 2

I turned just in time to see the fluorescent pencil roll off the side of my desk, thumping as it hit the floor. I rolled my chair to the corner of my desk to retrieve it, stretching my arm, struggling to grab it with my fingertips. Defeated, I got up from my chair, sighing as if it was the most labor-intensive chore and bent over to pick it up. I thoughtfully moved to the window, tapping the pencil against my palm. I examined my office, as though searching to find kind words to say about a bad piece of art.

A floor-to-ceiling window overlooked a small park where the smokers gathered during breaks and the friendless sat at lunch. Azaleas, oak trees and the occasional iris surrounded the park. *I should be grateful. At least I've got an office.* Most of the staff sat isolated in cubicles for eight hours a day, getting lost in the mazes to and from the bathroom. But I could close my door and block out the hallway chatter, the humming copy machine and the trickling water fountain.

My decorating would suffocate even the worst interior designer, but my organizational skills would help solve world peace. Every staple, rubber band, sticky note and pencil had a home. Not a speck of dust lay on my polished desk. A coat rack stood nestled in the corner, stowing a burgundy sweater and a Monet print umbrella. My degrees hung level on the wall. Two plants clung to life on my credenza. I did not inherit the green thumb that my mother proudly exhibited. A fault she so openly criticized.

A Salvador Dali print—*Swans Reflecting Elephants*—rested high behind my desk. The art reminded me there were more to things than just the surface. Everything has a side, an angle. If you turn it over and look beyond the obvious, beyond oneself, you'll find truth and humility—whether you want to or not. This morning, I stared at it and thought about Scott. *There must be someone better than him. No games. More than these four drab walls, annoyed clients and paper pushing. Where is the fantasy, the excitement that all the movies make you believe in?*

I had not lived out any fantasies working at Jameson Research and Marketing, Inc., but businesses sought our help and mine in particular. I've never understood it. My boss calls our success the 'it' factor. I think *it's* a bunch of bullshit. Say what they want to hear and all is good. I'm acting, switching roles constantly depending on whom I'm talking to. It's natural for me to change my personality to serve the need at the time. Anyway, I've gotten this far, so I can't really complain. Okay, I can complain. Eight years at Jameson equals permanent detention. I move through the days, working hard and doing all the things expected of a professional woman. Secretly though, I yearn for a new beginning.

About four years ago, Suzie Mott spread a rumor that I had slept with Mark from accounting. Completely false. And disturbing. If there was going to be a rumor about me, couldn't it have been with some hot guy like Nate. Anyway, since then, avoiding office gossip is a top priority. I rarely share my personal life with anyone, not even friends. I guess you could say I'm paranoid. Seems extreme, but after people point and giggle at you for 18 months, it has an impact.

"You keep your feelings inside twisting like a knot," my assistant Sara nags constantly. She's right. The strings that pull me are strong, and I'm restless and confused. A broken pendulum contains more balance and stability than me. Fighting to survive in the dog-eat-dog world of marketing and Miami's madness creates obstacles, especially for a single woman in desperate need of a mental and physical makeover.

The pencil in my hand stopped its relentless tapping on my palm, and I stared mystified at my surroundings. The green tweed guest chairs sat positioned as if they had just arrived from the factory. My mahogany desk, a barrier between me and the world. I turned toward the huge window that in the afternoons warmed my office with the soothing sun. Movement in the landscaped square distracted me. I peered down at the smokers, chatting absentmindedly. *There must be more than this, and the dream is a sign of something to come.*

My stomach growled as I noticed my screen saver zooming in the window's reflection. I had not worked a second since I arrived. I felt mildly guilty.

I leaned my forehead against the sheet of glass, my eyes scanning the green space. I observed each flower, the squirrel waiting for leftovers, even the nest of baby birds hungry for their mother's return. Then, I spotted Joanne Messer sitting in the far end of the park. She sat by herself, as usual, eating her customary turkey sandwich, carrots, two Fig Newtons and a Diet Dr. Pepper. Every day, Ms. Messer sat in the same spot, ate the same lunch and read a magazine. She only emerged from her cubicle to eat, visit the bathroom and go home.

As if I witnessed a car crash, I gawked at the scene. Ms. Messer nibbled at her bland rations, like a hamster. She cut her sandwich in four squares, ate a square then a carrot. An anxious squirrel waited for her to toss unwanted crust. Afterward, she ate one Fig Newton, put the other one in a zip lock bag and placed it in her purse.

What a dreary prospect—to sit each day in the same spot, eating the same food. Ms. Messer's expression never changed. Her mouth turned downward and her eyes looked sad. She resembled a bronze bust in a forgotten monument. I wondered if she had a husband or children, whether she had a life beyond this building. *I hope.* But maybe not. Maybe she had no family, no friends and the highlight of her day was that second Fig Newton tucked away so discretely.

A sour taste rose in the back of my throat as I contemplated that someday I would transform into the vague lonely lady in the park, feeding the birds and blowing second hand smoke away with a smirk. I swallowed, breathed deep, closed my eyes and looked back down in the park. Ms. Messer was struggling to get her tree-trunk sized legs over the picnic table bench. Her plump frame waddled as she collected her empty brown paper bag and soda can. She lazily walked to the door and disappeared.

I am an idiot. Here I am allowing a person I've barely talked with to influence how I feel about myself and my future. What does Ms. Messer know? I am supposed to be independent, but I grow less independent each day.

I returned to my desk, sat in my leather chair, turned to my computer and opened my email. *Eighty-nine emails! Are you kidding?* It's a never-ending battle. *Do elves visit nightly to re-supply me with fresh new emails?* I wrinkled my nose and clicked the first one, which was from my boss, John Beatler. Before I could begin reading, Sara poked her head in around the door.

Her natural, young and honest face was exactly what I needed to see after a night of pure hell. Her hair sparkled with strands of light blonde and strawberry, floating over her shoulders, past her turned up little breasts, barely reaching her waist.

Sara acted much better than I, although she would not admit her secret talent. She regularly used her puppy-look to get what she wanted. But, our relationship was genuine. I knew her whole life story, from when her dad lost his job and her family was forced to move from their home, to the moment she fell in love and married Victor. A romance that would make any woman sprout goose bumps.

As best friends go, Sara was the one. A true friend and the only person at Jameson I confided in. I often wondered if Sara pitied me, for being thirty-eight and single. No matter whether people say its okay to be single, they are secretly wondering what is wrong with you. *Well, of me.* I watched Sara's hair swing back and forth, and waited for her to speak.

"Um—" Confusion filled her face as she struggled to figure out why she entered the room. "Oh, yeah, I remember now." Before she formed another word, Mr. Beatler squeezed his round short frame around Sara.

The roots of his remaining hair seemed grayer than last week. He painfully tried to ignore the slivery locks and bald spots. Rumor claims he had purchased every hair product on the market trying to grow new hair, but nothing worked from what I detected.

He squashed past poor Sara, pushing his thick glasses higher on his head and dabbing the sweat from his brow. *Thank goodness our offices are close. If he had to walk much further, he may collapse.*

Stopping short at the edge of my desk, he started, "Listen, Natalie, I've got a huge favor to ask you. There is a ton going on and you know when I need something, you are the first one I turn to. You have 'it' you know. You really do."

He spoke so fast, his words sounded garbled. He had no intention of taking a needed breath between sentences, so before he continued, I interrupted with an embellished, "Good morning, John." He rolled his eyes and sighed. "Yes, good morning, Natalie. Hope you had a pleasant day so far," he answered with his usual sarcastic tone. "Actually, I have," I said. "What can I do for you?"

"Well," he started a bit shaky, looking over at Sara, who still had her head awkwardly poked around the corner of the door. "You know the problems we've had with the West coast office?" he asked, as his overgrown mustache twitched. I shrugged and nodded. "Well," he continued, "it's worse than we thought and clients are walking."

"What happened?" I pressed, my interest piqued.

He stepped toward the door, and yelled, "Sara, call Maria for me. Tell her I'll be a little late to the meeting."

Sara seemed to get the point, surprisingly. "Yes, Sir. I'll call her right now." She didn't leave immediately. She sorta nodded toward Mr. Beatler. Before I processed their exchange, Mr. Beatler turned back to me and started to spit his words.

"Well, apparently," he began, looking back at the empty doorway, "Barry Thorton, the San Francisco VP, has been having an affair with one of his subordinates, Jessica Mason. According to Mark, the acting manager, Jessica tried to break it off and Barry lashed back. He's been following her all over town, leaving notes on her car, giving her the worst assignments, constantly calling her house and most recently sent her a threatening email on the company's computer. Long story-short, in the middle of all that, he's let things slide. Clients are stirred up like a flock of hens at feeding time. They've been billed wrong, no one has returned their calls and some have never even received a contract. It's a damn nightmare. Some clients are original, with us from the beginning. The only reason they haven't left is because they have loyalty to the people. But, I think, and so does Mark, that some of the clients have just about had it. His phone's been ringing off the hook. We fired Barry, and Jessica is on extended leave."

After a labored sigh, Mr. Beatler tilted his head and in a fatherly manner said, "Now, I understand you're more on the creative side, but we need someone to go out there and straighten this mess out. You've got a real knack for smoothing the rough spots, building a consensus, staying calm and, you know, looking at the issue from the customer's point of view. So, I told Mark," he coughed, "you'd be arriving later this week."

My stomach had left the building. It faced a semi traveling at 45 miles an hour on 23rd Street.

"Wait, wait, wait a minute. You told him I would come without asking me? I don't want to go to San Francisco." I stood eye-to-eye with him. "You know I don't like to travel. Not to mention, I am clueless when it comes to accounts and billing."

"I know this is different but you're the only one I trust with this. You can salvage it."

"Why can't Mark handle this?" I huffed.

"His wife is due with their first child, and apparently, she is having some complications. He's going to be out quite a bit. Anyway, he doesn't have the 'it' factor that you do. You can make 'it' happen."

My glare hardened. *There's the 'it' factor excuse again.*

I tried to hide my frustration, but my arms were crossed firmly, wrapping my body, as if I was trying to hold a tight ball of wire so *it* wouldn't spring.

I'm bored, but the truth is maybe I don't like change. *Hell, maybe I'm afraid to fail.* Breaking up with Scott, the dreams returning and Mr. Beatler's plea—all left me angry, vulnerable, reluctant and uncertain. *I can't believe Mr. Beatler did not consult with me prior to committing me to this trip.*

Built up energy exploded inside my chest and catapulted me around my desk over to the window. The park was empty. I began contemplating how to get out of this predicament. Mr. Beatler moved closer.

"Nat, I'm sorry I did not come to you first. I thought you might want to go and get out of here for a while. You're the best. You have what it takes to get us through this. It's a new opportunity."

He trusted I would go. But for a moment, I strategized on how to circumvent the trip. *I have to take care of a sick parent, or there is no one to watch the dog or I'm committed to volunteering at a shelter.* Mr. Beatler knew that if one of my parents were sick, I would have told him. I didn't have a dog, and I wasn't sure where any shelter was located. No legitimate reason came to my mind.

It may be good to get away. Perhaps it could be the new start I need to move past Scott and experience what the world has to offer.

"Well, I guess, if you think it's best," I surrendered. Mr. Beatler appeared pleased and scooted over to the door. *Funny.* I had not seen him move that fast since his wife stopped by the office unexpectedly.

"Sara," Mr. Beatler bellowed, "would you contact Marcie in

the San Francisco office. She's preparing a briefing package for Natalie's first meeting on Friday."

"Friday? Are you crazy?" I asked, much louder than I'd meant. My lips puckered as if I'd swallowed a lemon. "Sorry. But, that's only two days away, less than forty-eight hours from now. I'll need to leave tomorrow."

"Yes, right you are," Mr. Beatler said, as he eased his chunky bottom away from the door. "I guess you better ask Sara to make your flight arrangements and get home early tonight and pack," he added in a jovial tone. I hoped that he could feel the daggers behind my eyes. They wanted to leap out and gouge him.

My body trembled, my temples ached and everything turned black. My thoughts landed in a repressed childhood memory. I remembered hiding in a stairwell, hanging on every word.

"Can't you see what we're doing to her?"

"She's eight, for God sake, Sybil. Why are you always so overdramatic?"

"Do you love me?"

"What? Yes. Yes. Why do constantly ask me that?"

"Like you used to before all this?"

Even at eight, I accepted that my parents didn't love each other anymore, not like they did before I came into their lives. The young me curled up on the step, tears filling my eyes.

"Natalie. Natalie? Are you alright?" Mr. Beatler's voice brought me back to the present.

"Oh, yes, John. I'm fine. Sorry, just lots rattling around in there," I said, as I jokingly waved my hands over my head. "Oh, yes, um, you were saying?"

"I was talking about your flight arrangements and you stopped listening."

"Oh." I turned away from him and prayed that my exterior did not exhibit the war eating my interior. *I hate to fly.* A golf ball seemed to lodge itself in my stomach along with the lemon still lingering in my throat. The last time I'd flown was ten years ago to attend my grandmother's funeral. The queasiness in my stomach continued to grow and my throat constricted as I remembered that dreadful flight. *This day is not getting any better.*

Trying to pull it together, I asked, "Who am I meeting with on Friday?"

"Um," he started. "I think the company is Voeltgin Software."

"What? John, I don't have a clue about computers. You know that. I'm lucky I can turn this thing on," I exclaimed, as I flung my hand in the direction of my computer, which sat on my desk, as if it had just been taken out of the box.

"You don't have to know anything about computers. Just make the clients understand we value their business and we've taken care of the problem. Listen to them and convince them they made the right choice with Jameson. No computer talk is necessary. Not to mention, that's only the first meeting. Marcie will send a copy of the schedule and a profile of each company so you can review them on the plane."

Mr. Beatler came closer and leaned against the wall. He stared at me and said, "Look Nat, I know this isn't your favorite thing, but it might be good for you to get out of town for a while. You'll enjoy it once you get there."

"I got it, John. I just don't want to let you down," I said, as if it were my first day on the job. "I may not be able to fix all of this."

"I'm confident in you. And," he continued, "you'll be there over the weekend. So, have some fun, see the sights. You deserve a break," he winked. "The redwood forest is beautiful and Alcatraz is always a fun time," he laughed, his cheeks turning rosy, as though he carried a secret.

"So, when exactly will I be returning from this adventure?" I asked curiously, as I made my way back behind my desk.

"Well, I think the last meeting is scheduled for next Wednesday. So, how about a Thursday wrap-up with the staff and back on Friday."

"That's over a week!" I exclaimed. I felt put-out, but nothing surprised me now. He could have told me to fly to the moon.

"Yes. Well, think of it as a mini-vacation." He leaned against the door jam.

"Well, I guess I'll be doing laundry tonight. I'm not sure I own enough clothes for such a trip," I teased. "Good thing I don't have a pet."

"Maybe you need a pet."

"What?" I blurted, placing my hands on my hips.

"Well, pets are good companions. God knows Charlie's been there for me. Together we've shared the doghouse. Anyway, get your arrangements in order. Come by my office before you leave."

I nodded yieldingly, the wisps of my hair barely shifting against my neck. Mr. Beatler warped his wobbly torso, his belly the last part to twist around and started out the door. He crooked his head back, accentuating the double chin resting comfortably on his chest and barked, "I appreciate this, Nat." He disappeared into the endless grid of hallways, leaving me to fight the inner battle brewing inside my stomach.

CHAPTER 3

Stress needled my veins, tightening my chest as my breaths shortened. I worked furiously. Hours passed. I realized I had forgotten to eat lunch. I found myself in front of the snack machine hunting for anything that wouldn't taste like sawdust. Mr. Beatler's words looped over and over in my head. The last twenty-four hours reminded me of the first, and last, time I rode Space Mountain—not seeing the road ahead, speeding off into darkness. A scream amassed deep in my gut, ready to explode.

Without realizing the cheese and chive crackers had disappeared, the empty wrapper lay crumpled in my hand. I hovered over my desk, using its strength to balance. Like a crutch, the desk supported me, until I made my way around, throwing the wrapper in the garbage, and fell into my chair. I grabbed the pad of sticky notes and started doodling feverishly. Nerves bounced off the walls of my insides, like a thousand balls were tossed in the air. *Why do I let myself get this way?*

The flight was only one part of my self-induced torture. I feared the unknown, worried about meeting new people and stressed about possibly losing clients. The dream coursed through me like a disease. Scott was surely having a grand time with his old flame.

I had to get the hell out of there, or I was going to lose it. *Pull it together!*

I didn't.

I grabbed my purse and started to head down to the park. Smoking even crossed my mind. And I don't smoke. I dashed to the door. My cell phone buzzed against my hip, buried deep in my massive purse. People scoffed at the size of my bag, but it helped me win a number of scavenger hunts at bridal and baby showers. I hoarded an entire drug store in that leathery cave. I dug desperately for the phone, finally spotting it stuck between my makeup case and emergency kit. I debated. Mom's picture stared at me from the small screen.

"Hello," I answered, in a fake chipper tone.

"Don't you ever answer your phone?" my mother squealed. She sounded like a chipmunk munching on Cracker Jacks. I pulled the phone from my ear, my mother's voice vibrating.

"Mom." I sounded like a scolded little girl.

"Yes," she replied. "I've been trying to call you."

"I turned it on vibrate. Sorry. What's up?" I sulked back to my desk, threw my purse on the floor. I ripped the sticky note off its pad, crumbled it up in a wad, tossed it in the garbage and started doodling on the next sheet.

"Your father is driving me nuts," she barked, between the crunches.

I chuckled, like the only one laughing at a dirty joke. "How can he drive you nuts, when he lives in a different state?"

Instead of a snide remark, silence cut the air. The crackling stopped. I waited for a reply. Shallow sniffles seeped through the phone and then full-out crying. No longer sunken in my chair, my body stiffened, sitting tall and alert.

"Mom," I yelped. "What's wrong?"

"Well, he called to tell me," she started breaking up, "he's getting married."

I wondered when this day would smack me in the face, when the fantasy of my parents finding each other again would be lost. I worried about it, tried to plan for it, but when she spoke, the words sounded foreign to me. I didn't know either of them. Alone and deflated, the balloon carrying me since my parents' divorce popped and whizzed around my office spurting a mocking laugh.

"Natalie? Are you still there?"

This moment was not about me. I had to put my selfishness aside and focus on what mattered—my mother. The news surely struck a hole deep inside her.

"Oh, mommy," I shrieked in a high-pitched voice. "I am so sorry."

"I know I shouldn't be upset. We haven't been together for years. Still," she hesitated, "I suddenly feel very alone. I guess I thought as long as we were both single, we could be friends. It's worked okay up to this point. Hasn't it? We don't need to live together, but he's still in my life."

I crept over to my office door and closed it gently, not speaking again until I heard the lock click. "You can still be in his life."

"Oh, sure, Nat. Your father is not going to be thinking about me when he's got some young thing running around. Look, I have always loved him. I never stopped loving him. Even though he made the last few years of our marriage, well...I just can't get past some things. We couldn't live together anymore.

"Nat, I understand you don't want to talk about marriage and you've told me a thousand times that you'll find someone when you're ready, but let me tell you this, find a person that loves you as much as you love them, or more. Otherwise, you'll fight an internal battle every day. No matter what, you must know that the love is strong enough to get you through anything. Anything! I don't want you to ever feel, like this. Alone. Like me."

The sorrow and bitterness in her voice reminded me of the past. I could only remember a few times when my mother seemed truly happy. An underlying gravity always tugged the lines around her artificial smile.

My office grew warm. My polyester blouse stuck to my back. I grappled, searching for words to comfort her. I could not count the number of times my mother had called in frenzied despair.

"You're right," I replied. "I will find someone."

"And, not that Scott person. He is no good for you," she said, blowing her nose resolutely. The sound of crunching resumed.

She read my mind. I thought the same thing.

"We broke up last night," I blurted, although I had not intended to tell her. I'm sure she thought, "You broke up again. Right."

"This time we are done. I promise," I added, before she could comment. "Right now, I want you to know that daddy is lucky to have you in his life. He always has been. He's a fool to think that anyone could take your place."

"Well, I not sure," mom said sarcastically. "Apparently, she's some bigwig attorney with a fancy firm in California."

"California?" I interrupted. "Wait a minute. Will daddy be moving to California?" My nostrils flared. Steam began to brew behind my eyes. "He is, isn't he?" My mother did not respond.

I threw the entire pad of sticky notes across the room. It thumped against the wall and landed on the guest chair.

"Well," mom started, cautiously, "he hasn't come right out and said anything, but what's keeping him. I would imagine he'd move."

The sticky pad was not potent enough. I wanted to toss the phone through the wall and topple my desk over. *Why do the men in my life bleed all the spirit and energy from me?* I shook my head. *I can't stand it anymore.*

I never recovered from my parent's divorce. Their daily fights and hateful words stung deep. I didn't understand all that had happened. I just knew that I loved them both. If my father moved to California, how often would we visit? Wouldn't it bother him, too? Being thousands of miles away, on the other side of the continent?

"Well," I began cynically, "I guess he wants to get as far away from us as possible." I grabbed the yellow pencil and shoved it into the sharpener. Buzzing resonated, and shavings peeled out the corners.

"Now, Nat, don't say things like that. He loves you and he will want to see you as often as possible. And, what the hell is that noise?" I yanked the pencil out of the sharpener, breaking the freshly shaved point.

"Why is it that he makes you mad and then when I say something about him, you immediately defend him?" I interrogated, as I threw the pencil across the room.

"I think I answered that earlier," mom said, as she blew her nose again.

"You love me too, right? So, I'm upset about this, okay?" My persona became unrecognizable, like a schoolgirl, flustered and disappointed.

"Okay," mom replied. "I love you more than anything. I just don't want you to have bad feelings toward your father."

"I don't. I'm hurt. It doesn't matter." I tapered off, realizing that fighting would only add to the day's trauma. Besides, I had never won an argument against my mother. Disheartened, I leaned back on my chair and stared up at the fluorescent lights.

"Yes it does," she responded.

"I guess I've just had a bad day. Don't worry about me." I pushed away from the desk. I lifted my right leg over the left and it started jiggling uncontrollably.

"The most important thing is for you to believe that this woman cannot compare to you."

"You are sweet, Nat. But," mom hesitated, transitioning her tone to a grave monotone hum, she continued, "I am old, worn out. Saggy and as plump as a rotten pear. Too tired to worry this much." My mother complained about growing old regularly, but this time seemed different. Her voice had changed over the years, from a cheerful spirit to a glum groan.

As if my chair had caught fire, I jumped out of my seat and shouted, "She doesn't live in San Francisco, does she?"

"Who?" my mother asked, as if she truly did not remember whom I was referring to.

"The other women. The bitch daddy's marrying!"

"Oh, her. I don't think so. I'm not sure where in California she lives. Why do you ask?"

"Mr. Beatler asked me to go to the San Francisco office for a week to help out. I should be back next Friday, probably late."

"You don't like to travel," my mother commented.

"Right, but, there's nothing I can do about it. It's all set. I'm leaving tomorrow." I sat back down in my chair and said, "Hey, I have an idea. Why don't I drive up on Saturday after I get back and we spend the day together? Go shopping. Have lunch?"

"No. No. I don't want you to come up here because I'm too pathetic to get over a man that obviously has lost all feeling toward me. Plus, you'll just be coming back into town."

"Mother," I interrupted, "if I did not want to come, I would not have mentioned it. Really, sometimes I don't understand why you say the things you do. You're my best friend in the whole world, yet I don't think you know it."

"I do. I say stupid things. Don't mind me."

I spun my chair around, sitting on its edge, studying the Dali. "I will call you when I get settled in San Francisco. Meanwhile, try not to let daddy upset you. You are wonderful and I love you."

"I love you too. You are my precious little girl, no matter how old you are."

"Mom," I said with a mixture of shyness and amusement, "you're embarrassing me."

"How? Is your phone tapped?"

I walked to the window, picked up the note pad, sat in the guest chair and smiled. A memory surfaced of my parents together, happy.

"Natalie, Natalie. See them? Do you see them?

I chased the fireflies wildly on the shore's edge, the twinkling lights escaping my little hands.

"Try to catch one, Nat. Go slow."

I caught one and held it gently. The small creature twittered against my palm.

"Now, let it go, Nat." When I opened my hands, it flew higher and higher until the speck of light vanished. I turned and faced my parents. Their eyes sparkled in the moonlight. They held hands as we walked together along the beach.

"Well, no matter how dark my life gets," my mother started, "there's always that little light reminding me of the one awesome thing I did—have you."

I tried to listen to her, but my thoughts lingered on that beach.

"Be careful on your trip," I think she said, "and call me. Oh, and don't let Scott talk you into getting back together. He's bad for you."

I pictured her shaking her index finger toward the phone.

"Yes, I will call you. Don't worry."

I rested the phone in my lap, longing to recall more memories like the one on the beach. But, recent, tedious thoughts occupied the corners of my mind.

The sunlight moved across my office and began to fade as the end of day approached. As I pondered the conversation with my mother, my stress multiplied and radiated outward, filling the room and leaving me empty.

I glanced at my watch. *I can't believe it is 4:00.* Sweat seeped from my anxious palms. An adventure lay before me and I was unprepared and scared.

CHAPTER 4

I opened my office door and called, "Sara can I talk to you for a minute?"

Sara appeared instantly, as if she had anticipated my request.

"Hey, Mr. Beatler might be right," Sara, declared jovially. "It will be fun."

I narrowed my eyes and scanned her. "How did you know he said that?"

Sara tugged her right earlobe and replied, "My ears are like dog ears—they can hear up to at least a mile and a half on a good day. And these walls are paper thin." I chuckled even though I didn't find it funny.

"Maybe you're right."

"I also couldn't help hear about Scott. Is it really over?" Sara questioned. Since I tortured myself over this hopeless relationship, I'm sure she wanted confirmation that the on-again off-again romance had finally died.

"Yes. He is definitely not the one." *Right?* "I mean, there's got to be a nice, single, somewhat attractive guy out there that's right." I smiled, faking optimism.

"There is, Nat." With one brow arched, Sara pulled her hair up in a huge twisted knot. "Oh, and I know it's none of my business, but I hope your mom is okay."

"Damn, Sara, are you sure my office isn't bugged? I'll have to watch what I talk about in the future. Can't have any secrets around here."

Sara babbled on about San Francisco and stressed that I would love every minute. She described Fisherman's Wharf and recommended places to eat, none of which sounded appealing. I pretended to listen to Sara's rant. My attention was lost with other thoughts—the trip, Scott's selfishness, mom, the odd little boy and my morbid fantastical wedding. My hand pushed my hair behind my ears, and my foot tapped under the desk. It took every nerve in my body to hide my desire to jump straight through the window. A masterful dive onto the picnic table. Grass stains stretched across my face. *Would anyone notice?*

"Most of the details are ready for your trip," Sara interrupted my reverie. "You'll be staying at the Harbor Bay Inn. Marcie emailed the schedule and profiles. Here they are." She laid them on my desk and continued, "Your flight will leave at 6:35 a.m.," Sara's face recoiled. "I am so glad you're going, 'cause I'd be missing that flight."

"Well," I frowned, "I guess I better get to bed early tonight, huh? I haven't seen 4 a.m. since college, and that's because we stayed up until then."

"At least you'll gain three hours." Sara noted, overly positive, flinging her hands in the air.

"Wonderful. So, when it's nine, it will feel like midnight. I'm sure I'll be ready to paint the town."

Sara's focus shifted to the picture of Scott sitting on my bookshelf. She whispered, "Listen, maybe you'll meet some new people out in California. With all the clients and everything. You never know," Sara winked.

"I think that would be extremely inappropriate. I have no intention of meeting a client except in the conference room, where we will be discussing matters related to their continued relationship with Jameson. You know me, I don't do that."

"Yeah, but you're allowed some fun. Never hurts to keep

your options open. You know what I mean? It might help you get your mind off of Scott." Sara eyed the picture again.

"Look Sara, I appreciate your concern, but I'm fine," I lied. "Going out with a client isn't professional and how can I possibly trust anyone I barely know. I'm just leery about, well, everything."

"Hey, after that fiasco a few years back with, ah, what's his name? That bartender turned transvestite? Your defenses went up. Sometimes I'm shocked you actually went out with Scott, or that it lasted this long. You have to take a chance. Maybe fate's knocking at your door."

"The only thing knocking is a boatload of laundry, a ridiculously early flight that I dread and a bunch of annoyed clients that hate us. My goal is to be the perfect Jameson employee. And, just so you know, Scott has completely vanished from my mind."

"Okay, well, I believe you," Sara said, glancing a third time at Scott's picture.

"Here," I said, grabbing the photo from the shelf, "would you discard this on your way out?"

"With pleasure," she cheered triumphantly, as she snatched the picture. "You know what? Any normal person would kill for the chance to go to California and have some fun. Let things go, Nat. You are way too hung up. You know I love you, but don't waste any more precious time."

Sara left with Scott's photo tucked under her arm.

As requested, I headed down to Mr. Beatler's office, sticking my head through the narrow opening of the door. He chatted boisterously on the phone, making everything seem more complicated than it actually was. He began winding down, using his regular speech all new clients received. He moved the phone away from his ear, covered the receiver and whispered, "Come in, Natalie. I'll be a minute."

He continued, "Walter, yes, we can make that happen for you. Send me your thoughts, and we will draft up a proposal for you. Yes. Yes. All right, say hello to Melinda. Yes. Bye." Mr. Beatler laughed at himself, enjoying another closed deal.

"Natalie," he began, "I've asked a lot of you. I didn't realize how many people respect you. I'm not saying that because I don't. I do, very much. It's just when your name was mentioned, I thought, of course, she'd be perfect. So, everything works out in the end, you know?"

What? I didn't know. *Who had mentioned me and why?* I should have asked, but Mr. Beatler kept blabbing on and I stopped paying attention. The next thing I knew I was in my car sliding the key into the ignition. David Bowie's "Changes" seeped through the speakers. I tapped my foot as I waited for the light to turn green. I was annoyed with myself for not questioning Mr. Beatler. But, it was too late now.

My thoughts turned to Sara and how I wished I could tell her my true feelings. Seeing Scott's picture removed finalized the situation. It was over. He did not love me.

As I opened the door to my apartment, my mother's words rang in my ears, "He's bad for you." The chalky pigment covering the walls screamed dentist office. Items sat like stocked soup cans at the grocery store. I may have had the 'it' factor, but my apartment had the 'eek' factor.

I opened the sliding door leading to the balcony. It overlooked the community pool, which I visited when the apartment manager gave me a tour four years ago. "Oh, you'll love the pool," she said. "It's great for entertaining." I haven't been there since, just an occasional glance when I come out for air. I sat in one of the dusty wicker chairs and leaned my head back, wondering what tomorrow would bring.

"Nat," I recalled Scott saying. "I'm sorry if I'm being an ass. You knew what you were in for when you said yes on our first date."

"So, it's my fault? Fuck you, Scott."

"Nat, I still want to be with you."

Stupid idiot. *What does he think I am?*

On my way to the bedroom, I peered down my nose at Scott's paintings leaning against the wall. Even though I hated him at that moment, I should have put them up, but I couldn't. The accumulated dust must have been permanently affixed to the acrylic.

Staring into my so-called walk-in closet, I pulled the shoebox labeled, "Black Pumps," opened the lid, slid my shoes off and nestled them inside. I placed the box next to the one labeled, "Red Satin Heels." Like Scott's art, dust had settled on that box, too.

"Hmm, let me see," I said, as I started to flip through the clothes choices. "Not very exciting." I grabbed pieces and threw them on the bed, dumped my pile of dirty laundry onto the floor and picked out my favorites.

As the washing machine rumbled, I searched for something to eat. *How pathetic.* My refrigerator resembles something from a frat house—a half full bottle of ketchup, two sugar-free Jell-Os, a red onion, some old bread, a flat diet coke and a beer. The only edible thing was a frozen dinner, sitting there since Thanksgiving. I popped it in the microwave and pulled my suitcase from the foyer closet.

When I finally crawled into bed, I could not go to sleep. At two in the morning, I waddled out from under the sheets like a crab emerging from a hole and wandered back into the kitchen. Like a patient in the doctor's office waiting for results, my nerves flared under my skin. I grabbed the beer, sat on the couch, popped it open and had a sip.

"Oh, God. Maybe I am Ms. Messer. I feel like a toad crawling along the edge of a mucky pond. My house resembles a walk-in clinic. My kitchen is more like a morgue than a social setting. And, I am talking to myself."

I propped up one of the pillows from the couch for my head and thought about my life with a half empty beer bottle sitting on the coffee table. My eyes started to blink and close.

***

I stood in the soaring tent. The band played a waltz. Everyone danced. I searched for someone I recognized. Finally, I spotted my parents, arguing in the corner behind the groom's cake. I walked toward them, but the mysterious man, still faceless and disturbing, intercepted me. I broke free from his hold and started to run again, until I found myself alone, surrounded by the gruesome tombs.

The cemetery swallowed me like a ferocious monster, forcing me to run through the maze of graves. Exhausted, I stumbled and landed inches away from a small marble marker. Grabbing the edge of the stone, I cut my hand. Blood spattered on my virgin white dress, its heat seeping through the frail cloth.

I leaned over and squinted, trying to read the name on the marker. The freshly dug grave transformed into a pool of water. When I looked up, all of a sudden, I was balanced at the edge of a swimming pool. Scott stood along a chain-link fence. His hair wet, as though he had emerged from the water. He hummed a tune and seemed completely unconcerned that I just sat there. On the other side of the pool, a group of people congregated. I recognized one as my mother, but a much younger version. The group hovered over something, but I could not make out what. It must be something bad. Like a rash, panic spread across my mother's face. Mom began to talk, but no sound came from her mouth.

Scott walked past without acknowledging me. Annoyed, I jumped up on to the deck and screamed, "Scott. Scott! Look at me!" He did not respond. His selfish demeanor and smug grin angered me. I started to follow him. I wanted to tell him what I really thought. But his long strides outmatched mine. I peered up at him. Way up. He towered over me. *What is this about?* I reached my hand out toward him, preparing to make a last plea for his attention. My hand caught my eye. It was tiny. Miniature feet supported an equally small frame. *I am a child, maybe ten year's old.*

Scott disappeared. I watched the spot where I last saw him, but grew distracted by the crowd, huddled in the corner, still standing over the object. I slipped through the adults and to my surprise, on the ground lay the older version of myself, drenched and unconscious. I screamed and stumbled backward, crashing into the pool. My body fell. *How deep was this pool?* I kept sinking, until the light from the sky beyond the pool had vanished and only the silent blue water surrounded me.

The need for air only entered my mind when I reached the bottom, but I could breathe perfectly. I blinked a few times and refocused. Children floated around me, laughing and playing. A small group in the corner of the pool played Ring Around the Rosie and a couple of girls danced, drifting through the water like ballerinas.

"Excuse me," I said, my voice muffled. No one responded. "Excuse me, where am I? How do I get out of here?" I waited for a response.

A young boy swam towards me. As he came closer, he seemed to be suspended in mid-air.

"You're new." Bubbles floated up from the corners of his mouth. "What's your name?" he asked, swimming around me, like a detective at a crime scene.

"Natalie," I answered. "How do I get out of here?"

"You don't," an impish smile transformed his face. He drifted past me toward a group of giggling girls.

I kicked my feet hard, moving to the nearest wall. I worked my way around the entire pool, until I reached the point I started. I swam up and up toward the top, hoping to find the entrance. Hours seemed to pass. My legs never tired, but my hope vanished and finally I stopped. My body sank down to the bottom, and bounced on the hard concrete.

A circle of children formed around me. Their anger spewed outward, their screams deafening.

"How dare you try leave here! Don't you understand what we've suffered? Traitor!" they yelled. "You are an evil little child that left your parents, just like the other one. You will be punished." The circle of children narrowed, closing in on me. They walked on the bottom of the pool, eyeing me like sharks seeking pray.

***

I woke, gasping for air as though I had held my breath under water for a long time. My nightgown clung to me. I felt dizzy and disoriented.

I ran to the kitchen and turned on the light. *Thank God!* It was only two-thirty. My heartbeat slowly returned to normal. *Wonder if I'd missed my flight? That would make a good impression.*

"Why are the dreams back?" *They had been gone, but why come back? Why now?* "I must be going crazy. Who would hold their wedding in a cemetery? No one could survive at the bottom of a pool for eternity with a bunch of psycho children."

I sat on the couch. *Did one of those whacked water kids say something about "the other one?"* I tried so hard to remember, my head pulsed, the pain forcing a tear. For the rest of the night, I remained alert, waiting for the alarm to signal my imminent departure.

CHAPTER 5

At the airport, I sat at the gate for what felt like an eternity. My nerves stood on end. During the last half hour before boarding, I considered every possible thing that could go wrong. *Isn't being independent supposed to make you stronger?* I wasn't sure anymore. I wanted to get on the plane, get there, do what I had to do and come home.

We finally boarded. I burrowed anonymously in seat 15D waiting for takeoff. I listened intently to the flight attendants as they demonstrated how to use the seatbelt and the oxygen masks. I located the exit closest to me. The man across the aisle snored, and the mother with the small child struggled to control the youngster. I pulled the security information card out of the seat pocket and read it cover-to-cover.

Once airborne, I tried to breath and relax. When the flight attendant announced we had reached our cruising altitude and that a beverage service would be offered, I assumed all went fine. We were up there. No going back. I drank my diet coke, munched on my stale pretzels and hoped that we would arrive quickly and safely.

I fought my way through the herd of rolling laptop cases at the Atlanta airport. Then the adventure began again. By the time I arrived in San Francisco, I felt like I had walked from

Florida to California. All I wanted was a glass of wine and a shower. But I'd probably hit the bed and pass out. I walked along the terminal and road the escalator down to the main entrance where the conveyer belt was spitting out the arriving baggage. When searching for my purple bags, I saw a young lady with bright red hair, holding a sign that read, "Natalie Swan." I approached her.

"Um, hello," I began. "I am Natalie Swan."

"I'm Marcie." She reached out her hand to shake mine. "It's nice to meet you. Did you get the briefing package okay?" Marcie turned to the nearest trashcan and absentmindedly tossed the sign in.

"Yes. Thank you." I responded.

"We've got a lot of work to do in short order and we're so relieved you're here. We really need all the help we can get," Marcie explained.

"I appreciate you coming," I said. "I have never been to San Francisco."

"Really?" Marcie said surprised. "Well, there is a ton to do and since you are staying for a while, you will probably have an opportunity to check out the sights."

"I hope so. My luggage is coming. I'll be right back." I returned swiftly pulling my two bags and carrying my purse and laptop case.

"Here, let me help you," Marcie offered.

"Thanks." I handed her one of the suitcases.

We walked out of the sliding doors, entering a world of chaos, with people and cars and buses zooming in every direction. For what seemed like miles, we hiked to Marcie's car. Her cinched waist and tight bottom walked a foot in front of me.

"I'll drive you by the office. Don't worry. We won't go in. We'd be expected to work," Marcie winked. "But at least you'll be able to see where it is in relation to your hotel. Then, I'll drop you off. Everything should be in order. If you have any problems or questions, my cell phone number is in the briefing materials."

"Great. Thank you. I appreciate all you've done."

"I'm here to help. Anyway, our first appointment is tomorrow morning at ten. It was supposed to be with that computer company, uh, Voeltgin, but they had to reschedule for Monday afternoon. So, we will be meeting with Duncan and Cohn." Marcie sighed softly and rolled her eyes. "Anyway, as it said in the briefing, they specialize in accident law. Well-respected apparently, but in my opinion, they are cheesy assholes. Anyway, we've supported their account for years. They've also got connections. If we can keep them, they'll spread the word. So, I'll pick you up at 8:30 tomorrow morning. You'll have time to meet the rest of the staff and ask any questions before Duncan and Cohn arrive. Sound okay?"

I tried to listen, but Marcie's driving distracted me. The little Honda Civic weaved in and out of the lanes, flying by the other cars.

"Yeah. That sounds fine." My eyes ping-ponged between Marcie's lips and the street ahead. "Did Voeltgin say why they had to postpone?"

"Well, apparently their Marketing Director had a family emergency. He found out today and needed to leave."

"Oh, okay. That's fine. Has anyone else re-scheduled?"

"Only that we moved Jenkin and Associates from 12 to 1 on Monday. We wanted to make sure we had enough time with Voeltgin."

"You've done a lot of preparation. That will do us good. It's a shame it's come to this."

"I agree. Everyone is going nuts. I mean rumors are swarming like seagulls fighting for that last piece of bread, you know? Anyway, here is the office."

The tinted windows shimmered against the sun. Huge marble steps led to a glass entrance. The building's grandeur eclipsed the smaller, yet approachable Miami office.

The hotel was equally stunning with two circular turrets flanking the building. It was comforting to have a safe place to stay close to the office. I didn't plan on leaving often, perhaps on Sunday to visit the ocean. *I might as well seize the opportunity.*

It would probably be my last time in California, but then I remembered my father's move here with what's-her-name would force me to return at some point.

After the bellhop retrieved my luggage from Marcie's trunk, I thanked her profusely.

"See you at 8:30," Marcie shouted from across the car, as I followed the porter through the doors.

After checking in and reaching the room, I perched on the side of bed and analyzed the space. The beauty of the hotel's exterior had not found its way inside. The room was clean and well appointed, but lacked personality. *It feels like home. Oh God, my apartment is a hotel room! I've got to do something about that when I get back.*

A sitting area and desk blocked the sliding doors leading to a balcony. I slid the glass open and stepped onto the small landing where a single chair sat smushed against the railing. A large atrium decorated the center of the hotel. A tiki hut bar sat tucked among the foliage. Trees and green ferns completed the landscape. Guests splashed in a nearby pool.

My thoughts switched from admiring the details of the greenhouse to savoring the smell of a glass of Shiraz. *I should review the Duncan and Cohn file. But I really want that wine and some food.* A small volcano had erupted in my stomach about an hour ago. I left the room and headed toward the elevator.

A long and narrow hallway guided hotel guests to their rooms. On the cream colored walls hung magnificent paintings of distinguished Dachshunds, English Bulldogs and Rottweilers dressed in suits and ties. A soft drone hummed inside the walls.

I waited for the elevator a few minutes. I turned around and stared into a grand gold-rimmed mirror. A cherrywood buffet, with sharp bronze inlays edging the corners, sat underneath the mirror. Heavy brass handles dangled from each drawer. Squarely on top, a huge arrangement of lilies and soft green leaves adorned the table. Paintings of royal dogs flanked both sides of the mirror. I swayed back and forth, my purse moving from side-to-side. My eyes blurred and visions of the underwater children haunted my mind.

The elevator beeped and the doors slid open. Startled, I emerged from my trance and swung around straight into a man exiting through the metal doors. My purse flew off my shoulder, raining cosmetics on the floor and into the elevator.

The man jumped up and down hopping as if on a pogo stick. He clenched his right foot, his face pained. The elevator doors started to close but I leapt between them, stretching my arm to grab my $16 Clinique lipstick, determined to deny the elevator the pleasure of swallowing it.

"Oh, God! I am so sorry. I wasn't paying attention. Oh, my," seeing him clutch his foot, "are you okay?" He did not answer right away and I suddenly thought I might need to meet Duncan and Cohn for more ways than one, to save their account and to save my ass.

Still holding the door open with my foot, I grabbed the last item from the elevator and released the doors. I sighed, threw the items in my purse, tossed it aside and ran over to him. He had made his way to a chair. I knelt down by him and watched him impatiently, waiting for him to say something.

"Sir, I am so sorry," I started. "Are you all right?" I asked again.

Finally, he inspected me, his eyes peeking through his tousled hair. His face looked like a fire on a cold winter night, warm and as tender as an old love song.

He pushed one of his lazy locks away from his forehead. His square face, with its slight dimple in the middle of his chin, looked smooth as ice. As his deep blue eyes peered into me, he broadened his smile.

"Yes, I'm fine. You stepped on my foot. Those heels you're wearing are lethal. You don't need a weapon for protection, just use those." His voice, like a drug, stole my focus. It was soft, sensual and strong.

Nothing emerged when I parted my lips and attempted to respond. I forgot to breathe. Dizziness whirled in my head, shifting my balance. A memory of kissing Tommy Iggybotham under the bleachers flashed in my mind. His jaw locked. We had to get the school nurse. *Totally embarrassing.*

This time, a bewitching sense encapsulated me. The world disappeared. Everything vanished from my thoughts. I saw only this man, his face. I heard only his voice. The walls could have fallen away, the streets could have crumbled into the earth and the sky turn dark forever. But, nothing could interrupt this moment. Everything made sense. Nothing made sense. My total attention fell on him.

He seemed to study me too, his eyes flickering down my body. In his presence, I became filled with warmth. A new fervor invaded me. My insides felt ripped. One part insane with happiness, the other afraid and nervous. I did not feel like myself. Something new had entered my heart, my mind, maybe my soul. I had never experienced this before. It made me crazy and I didn't care.

"Did you get all your items?" he asked.

I didn't answer. I knelt beside him, frozen like one of the precious figurines in my mother's curio cabinet, and peered at him like I had been granted the greatest prize in the world. He stared back. He must have wondered what I was thinking. He repeated, "Miss, did you get all your belongings from the elevator?"

"Oh," I muttered, broken from my daze. "Yes, I did. Thank you."

As we both stood, he chuckled as he tapped his foot gently like he was testing whether it was okay to walk. I retrieved my purse, which I had crammed against the elevator and yelled toward him, "I am really sorry. Is there anything I can do?"

"Well, actually, I'd love to buy you a drink downstairs in the bar, if that would be okay?"

It took me a moment to comprehend what he'd said. Once I processed his words, I understood the offer and began internalizing every thought and feeling flowing through me. Part of me wanted to go. An unfamiliar sensation stirred, starting from the top of my head to the bottoms of my feet. My insides pulsed at the sight of him. I was scared but intrigued.

The practical and cautious side of me said, "Not a good idea." I did not know this man and my mother would not be pleased.

"Oh, sir, that's very, ah, kind. I'd really love to, but I have so much work to do before tomorrow," I fibbed.

"You don't have to call me sir. My name is Derek. Derek Voeltgin."

"Voeltgin?" I asked. All the bliss that ran through me stopped when I heard his name. I walked to the chair and sat my purse down. I closed my eyes tight and tried to remember.

"Yes. Have we met before?" he asked but quickly added, "I can't believe I would forget such a meeting." I opened my eyes and he smiled. I felt like a high school girl that had a crush on a teacher.

"Um, no. I don't believe we have," I said. "But, your name sounds familiar. What do you do?" I took a step closer toward him.

"I work for a small software development company."

Oh, shit! He is Derek Voeltgin from Voeltgin Software. That company I'm supposed to meet with on Monday. Just great. I am flirting with this amazing looking guy, thinking maybe there's something here and he turns out to be a client. Shit! Why is he a client? Why am I so damn ethical? I can't go have a drink with him. But, at least he IS a client. He's probably not a serial killer. Right?

As if an alien took control of me, I stiffened and the "business" Natalie, the one with the "it" factor, materialized.

"I am Natalie Swan." I stretched my hand out ready to shake his, but feared his touch. "With Jameson Research and Marketing. I am supposed to be meeting with you next week to discuss your account and services." A foreign, high-pitched voice flowed from my mouth. It sounded perky, as if I was recruiting for a sorority. I shook it off.

"Ah, really?" He studied me up and down, his hand rubbing his chin. He nodded, his mouth curling into a smile, and said, "So, you're the hell on wheels that is supposed to change my mind about Jameson, huh?"

I stepped back a little and analyzed him. *Do I actually have a reputation? Is that the one I want? Maybe he isn't a decent guy after all.*

"Well, I certainly wouldn't consider myself hell on wheels." The perkiness died as my body collapsed into a bag of disappointment.

"I was just kidding." He reached over and touched my shoulder. "I hear you're the best. I've actually been looking forward to meeting you," he said a bit slyly, stroking my arm. My eyes darted toward his knuckles. His touch had the power of hours of massage. When his hand fell to his side, I immediately missed the comfort.

"So, how 'bout that drink?"

I turned away. I did not want him to see me reach for the spot on my shoulder he had touched. "Oh, that would be inappropriate. You're a client."

"Please. There isn't any reason why we can't have a drink. I can give you a breakdown of my company and we can talk shop if that makes you happy. But, I don't really know anyone in San Francisco, and I'm not ready to watch reruns till I fall asleep. So, how about it?"

He stood like a warrior prepared for battle, yet his touch told a softer story. I wanted to go. A fire blazed within me. Overcome with the desire to explore this unexpected opportunity, I gave in, "Well, only if we pay for our own tabs."

"Deal," he said. "I just need to run to my room. So, why don't we meet down at that tiki-looking place in about fifteen minutes?"

"Okay," I agreed.

I watched him until he turned the corner. While picking up my purse, I stopped to look in the mirror that had captivated me earlier. I questioned whether to go but justified the decision. *As a client, I need to know as much about his company as possible. We're paying for our own bills. I did run into him and almost break his foot. The only right thing to do is to be gracious and accept his invitation. I'll have one drink. One.*

The mirror showed a beaten down rag doll with mangled hair, no lipstick and a black smudge on my sleeve, probably from holding the elevator door.

"Oh, no," I said out loud. "This will not do." I half-ran to my room. I didn't want him to think I had gotten all dolled up. But I also didn't want to look like a slob. I wore the same clothes, but added a simple gold necklace and hoop earrings. I powdered my face, replenished my lipstick and rubbed the mark off my sleeve. After giving myself a once-over, I grabbed my purse and room key and headed toward the atrium.

CHAPTER 6

Guests filled every corner of the quaint hideaway, complete with a straw roof and rattan walls. A stream flowed under the bridge that led to the watering hole. Gigantic gold, white and black koi glided through the shallow water. Bamboo flanked the sides of the bar and willows drank from the water's edge. A reggae band, crunched tightly in the corner, jammed some tunes. Two ladies line-danced on a makeshift dance floor. I felt like I'd just gotten off a cruise ship in the Bahamas. The entire bar looked haphazard, but every detail was obviously designed and placed strategically.

I peered across the room seeking an empty table. My eyes were drawn to the farthest point, opposite from the band. Derek caught me glancing in his direction and, as if drawn by a magnet, I found myself standing in front of him. He immediately walked to the other side of the table and pulled out the chair. I smiled pleasantly, surprised by his chivalry.

Derek had freshened up too. He wore a crisp white cotton shirt and faded cobalt jeans, which fit him perfectly. His bangs were brushed straight back offering a clear view of his face. A crease sat angled on his forehead. Stubbles shadowed his chin.

"Hello and welcome to The Bamboo Hut. I'm Sherika. Our special tonight is the Blue Bamboo shooter. And house wine is a $1 off."

"A glass of Shiraz, please."

"Wine drinker, huh?" Derek asked. "I'll have a Bombay Sapphire martini, straight up with a twist." The waitress walked away looking annoyed that we did not try the shooter.

Derek looked me in the eyes. It was hard not to look away, but then his focus moved down to my mouth and then my neck. "What are you doing?" I asked.

"I was noticing your skin. It's perfect."

Are you kidding? This guy must be a real pick-up artist.

"Oh, it's that three-step process: clean, tone and moisturize," I said, rolling my eyes.

"You think I'm just saying that? Fine. I completely understand. A strange guy bumps into you in the hallway, asks you to have drinks and pours on the compliments. Tacky, I know."

"I actually bumped into you."

"True. So, let me have some fun. I mean, if I want to give you a compliment, let it go. You're balled-up, aren't you? A guy says you've got icy blue eyes and a soft little turned up nose, and a tidal wave of mistrust and self-doubt crashes on you," he said, as the drinks arrived.

His mouth twisted like the perfectly twirled lemon over his martini. *I don't know how they do that or why it's needed, but it looks pretty.* And he looked confident tossing the peel into the glass.

"I am not balled-up, or whatever. I'm cautiously optimistic. And, you don't even know me, so maybe we should stick to work," I remarked, a bit more direct than intended. My nerves flared as if my skin crawled with hives.

"By all means," he said, straightening up like he was called out by the teacher.

"So," I started, "I don't think we are meeting with your company until next week. Why are you here so early?"

"Well, we were supposed to meet tomorrow, but one of my colleagues had an emergency and couldn't make it. I didn't find out until last night, and I could've bought a private island with what it cost to change my flight. So, I thought I would come up and spend some time here. I've only been a couple times and have never gotten to see the sights. I've got my laptop and can keep up with emails. So, I'm going to enjoy a mini-vacation." He leaned back in his chair, grinning like he knew something but was sworn to secrecy.

"Sounds nice, but lonely," I teased. "You don't know anyone here?" I sipped my wine while I conducted my own investigation.

"Ah, well, now I do," he paused. I maintained my composure, controlling my desire to flirt back. "How long are you going to be here?" he continued.

"Forever," I answered sarcastically. "Ah, no, not really, sorry. Just until next Friday. We have a number of meetings scheduled throughout the week."

"So, you'll have some time to get to know the city as well?"

"Yes, I do plan on seeing some things. Everyone tells me there is a lot to do. Something for everyone," I added.

"I think that's true. I'm not sure what to do first. So, how long have you been with Jameson?"

"Eight years." I swirled the red liquid around in my glass.

"Do you like it?" he asked.

"Sure. I mean I always wanted to be a PR person and hey, now I am one, right?" I began tapping my foot to the beat. The wine relaxed me. My shoulders fell and I leaned back in the chair.

"Do I hear a bit of sarcasm in that statement?" he questioned.

"Oh, no. I'm just tired. Let's talk about something else." I gulped my wine.

"Okay. So, do you have any sisters or brothers? Family?" he said, as he crossed one leg over the other.

I shuttered. I didn't want to discuss family either. But, I thought it rude not to provide some answer. So, I responded in a blunt, direct tone, "No, I am an only child and my parents are divorced."

"Really, my parents are divorced too, but my mother's remarried."

"Oh," my interest grew. Meeting Derek was an unplanned event, and he was an unlikely candidate to launch into this discussion with, but without much further thought, I started my monologue.

"My father just got engaged. My mother is devastated. I don't think she thought they'd ever get back together, but she never expected him to remarry. She never had those intentions. She has always loved him, you know, and I think always will. They just couldn't live together anymore."

"I know what you mean. My father was a bit surprised, but he handled it pretty well. He's now dating someone."

With a guarded tone, I asked, "How did—" But, stopped abruptly. I didn't want to get too personal.

"What?" he encouraged, peering over the rim of his cocktail glass. "Go, ahead, ask me."

"Um, how, did you handle it? I mean, when your mother announced she was getting married?"

"At first, I was angry. I thought she was abandoning us. I had decided that she didn't love us anymore and wanted a new life. But, that wasn't true at all. She wanted to be happy. Dad ran a strict household. He didn't have a sensitive or comforting personality. I don't think they were ever friends. I never realized how unhappy my mother was until I got older and how selfish my response to her marriage seemed. I mean, not everything's about me, right? I understand that now. I just want her to be happy. She is a great mom. Strong. Independent. Loving. That's what I want."

"I want a friend," I said. "Your spouse or boyfriend or whatever should be your best friend. You should be able to tell him or her anything, be your one confidant, you know? Trust each other 100% and stand together no matter what." *How on earth did we get on this topic?*

"Yes, I do. It's hard sometimes, though, to find that one person who can be everything. I think we all have a one-time chance. It sounds silly, but I believe in fate."

"It's not silly." *This guy is not for real.*

I wasn't sure what to think. My brain said, "He is a client, remain professional." The rest of me wanted to crawl over the table and wrap myself around him. *One drink!*

Three hours later, the bar had cleared, but we were still talking. I kept my promise of one glass of wine. But, I stayed much longer than I had intended. I did not want to leave. I longed to tell him everything, anything. When I glanced at my watch, it was midnight. A stack of unread profiles awaited me.

"Derek, I've got to get going. A boatload of work is waiting for me in my room. And, I am sure I've talked your ear off…"

"No, I've really enjoyed talking. I hope we can get together again while we're here."

I wanted to say yes right away, but I didn't want to appear desperate or too anxious.

"We'll see," I said.

I collected my things and went to my room.

CHAPTER 7

I plopped on the bed and selected a file to review. But, instead of reviewing the Duncan and Cohn file, I opened the Voeltgin file. I read every line, knowing that this was going to be a problem. *I cannot have a crush on a client. That goes against everything I've been preaching. What would the people at work think? Or, worse, say? No. No. No one can know, not even Sara.*

I finally fell asleep with the file balancing on my chest.

***

This time, my groom had a face. I stared at his nose and mouth, searching for something I recognized. His face possessed a soft gentle smile, with curved cheeks and a firm chin. His gray cloudy eyes peered at me, sad and dreaming of somewhere else. I could not blame him. Who would have their wedding in a graveyard?

We danced in the middle of the on-looking crowd. Every eye at the reception focused on us. I smiled and gazed at my new husband. The music drifted off and became a dull hum. Along with my phantom husband, I greeted guests and chatted with cousins and coworkers.

"Natalie, let me fix your dress," a voice yelped, coming closer. A pudgy little lady started tugging at me.

"Please, I can do it," I said, stopping the chubby fingers from adjusting the massive bow balancing on my buttocks.

"Sorry," the woman said disapprovingly. I straightened the ornamental bow and then turned toward the lady. Ms. Messer's face met mine. My lungs stopped their constant flow of air, and my eyes grew dry as they stared at her.

"Natalie, mom was only trying to help," my new husband said.

My stomach jolted, and for a moment, I thought whatever I ate might jump to my chest and heave all over the groom's tuxedo.

"No need to be upset, Natalie. I'll take care of you," Ms. Messer said, with a wicked smile. I stared at the manipulative mother-in-law and screamed, "I don't want this!" I reached for my dress until the train was clasped in my grip, my lungs filled with air, propelling me out from under the tent and into a sprint. I ran and ran. I ran until I stood surrounded by faded grave markers.

But this time, I stopped, with breath caught in my chest. Markers stretched across the field, enclosed within a wrought iron fence, its gate squeaking gently back and forth. It was the children's section of the cemetery. I pushed the gate open and stepped inside.

The years 1982-1984 etched the marble of the first marker that met my feet. The next read 1994-1998. I walked from stone to stone, reading the inscriptions. Eight years old. Six months old. Four years old. My heart swelled, and tears rippled from my eyes. Poor innocent souls, pilfered from their mother's arms.

Along a narrow path, I reached a different section of the cemetery. A huge old oak tree stretched across the pebbled walkway, its branches barely touching the grass. Five children were buried in this small sanctuary. I read each tombstone, but when I arrived at the last marker, a loud bang echoed through the trees and the ground started to rumble and crack. Under my feet, the earth opened and swallowed the graves. I walked on air as each soul was sucked into the earth's core. My body became the next victim. Yanked into the ground. And, then, silence.

***

When I woke up, I touched my face, my shoulders, my legs, searching for my body. Looking around the room, I tried to figure out where I was. *Underground, buried alive? What happened to the other children?*

It was another dream. I was in bed at the hotel, saving Mr. Beatler's ass, again.

This dream felt harsher, more violent, more real. I whipped the covers off and pulled my knees to my chest. I rocked silently trying to recapture each moment. A new panic fell over me and now more than ever, I feared telling anyone about my bizarre romps in the cemetery.

What is wrong with me?

CHAPTER 8

Marcie waited at the entrance of the hotel as she had promised. After scrutinizing what to wear, I selected a deep claret suit with a delicate line of buttons running down the front. A miniature flower decorated the center of each button. The same flower pattern weaved the hem of the skirt.

I overdressed.

The bellhop opened the car door and I slid in. He lingered much longer than necessary, creeping me out. *No exposed cleavage here, buddy.* He jumped back as I shut the door.

"Good morning, Natalie." Marcie wore a black pants suit and a yellow button down cotton shirt. A ladybug pin balanced on her lapel. Her red hair sat piled on top of her head. "Hope you had a good night," she continued.

I struggled to suppress the grin threatening to spread across my face. "Yes. Quiet. Thanks."

The sun beat down. People congregated on every street corner. Lights turned red, then green. The city bustled with an underlying sensation, like the center of the universe waiting to erupt. Marcie zigzagged through the streets, and I grew dizzy watching the buildings pass like pages flipped in an art book.

"So, like I said, Duncan and Cohn come across like used

car salesmen. Duncan is really annoying, ya know?"

"Uh huh." My stomach lurched as we flew into a parking space. My hands shook opening the car door and my pesky lump resurfaced. My mouth dried as if I had not brushed my teeth in days. My tongue shriveled and burned. *I hate myself. Why am I scared? Mr. Beatler has confidence in me. God, do I need to find that confidence. 'It?' Oh, 'it.' Where are you?*

Marcie and I walked through the revolving doors. A dazzling entrance, with large marble columns encircled a Scandinavian inspired desk. A petite woman, with cropped brown hair and darting eyes studied us. Her stare narrowed as if to say, "How dare you enter my empire, this lobby—it's mine!" She did not greet us or smile. She carried on, glad of our quick exit. *If this is the first impression, no wonder clients are running for the door.*

Marcie led me to the twenty-third floor and started introducing me to the Jameson employees, all of whom seemed much more pleasant than the witch guarding the lobby.

We stopped at the conference room where the meetings would take place. The wallpaper was a soothing cream color. A mahogany table sat square with ten jade and chardonnay colored chairs. *I will spend a lot of time here.*

Other staff arrived and we huddled in the corner of the room and discussed strategy. I explained that a significant concern among the clients was the lack of response and service, specifically with Duncan and Cohn.

"I think we should listen to what they have to say, let them vent and present some options and solutions," I told the staff. "Duncan and Cohn were students together through undergraduate school but went to separate law schools. They remained friends and after graduating decided to open a firm together. They've been very successful. We need to leverage their relationship." The group did not seem convinced, but it was too late to argue when Mr. Michael Duncan and Mr. Adam Cohn entered the conference room.

Mr. Duncan, a large stout man, stood tall. Mr. Cohn's skinny frame towered over everyone. I swallowed a laugh.

They mirrored Loral and Hardy arriving on the set. Instead of busting out, I took a deep breath, and approached them, hand extended, greeting them like a hostess at a grand event.

"Good morning, gentlemen. I am Natalie Swan. It's a pleasure to meet you."

As usual, my whole persona changed. *How does that work? A client enters a room and I become an actress, transforming into the role needed. People say they are more confident when intoxicated or high. I'm more confident during a confrontational meeting with clients. How do I harness that feeling in my personal life?*

"Yes, Ms. Swan," Mr. Duncan began, "I hope that we can fix this mess today. We've got cases to attend to and back-to-back meetings this morning."

"Yes, sir. I completely understand. Your time is valuable and we will do everything we can to discuss the matter and present some solutions to you without taking too much of your time. Would you like some coffee or anything?"

"I—," Mr. Cohn began.

"No thank you," Mr. Duncan finished.

"Fine, let's get started. First, let me introduce the Jameson staff. This is Marcie Jones, Phil Barnes, Stewart Mann and Kate Wright.

"Well, gentlemen, we are here today because your service has not been satisfactory. If I were in your shoes, I'm not sure if I would have agreed to this meeting."

The other Jameson employees would be stunned by this tactic. Each staff members' eyes widened, confirming their uncertainty.

"Well, Ms. Swan," Mr. Duncan began, as he glanced over to Mr. Cohn, "I did consider dropping you completely, but my colleague here, Adam, talked me into meeting with you."

Okay. Cohn has the heart. Duncan is the brains.

"Well, sir. Customer service is the most important thing a business can offer. When I am paying, I want the best. If I am not happy, I expect someone to fix it. To respond timely, with a friendly professional attitude."

I seized the seat at the other end of the table.

"Jameson has not delivered quality service to you, and I apologize on behalf of us all. Let me assure you that the proper steps have been taken to resolve the situation. Today, I'd like to hear from you. Your needs are our top priority. We'd like to address your specific concerns and expectations and solve any problems you've encountered. Kate will be assigned to you. She has an excellent background in marketing and PR, but she also has been a paralegal, so she's familiar with your business. Her time will be completely dedicated to your account to ensure you receive exactly what you need."

Mr. Duncan and Mr. Cohn peered at each other. "Um, well," Mr. Duncan started, "our biggest problem was that we couldn't get anyone to return our calls. I mean, we just renewed a significant contract with Jameson, and we were told that someone would be getting with us. But no one ever did. So, now, you are telling me that this Kate will be doing the same thing. How can we trust that we will get the service you promise?"

Kate surveyed the faces surrounding the table. I wished she had not looked so scared. Her concerned eyes fixed on me. I could tell she was waiting for brilliance to spew from my lips. I wasn't sure if what I was thinking would work, but I had to try.

I got up, walked around the room and stood between Mr. Duncan and Mr. Cohn.

"Gentlemen, how long have you known each other?" I asked. A memory pulled my focus, playing with a little boy in the backyard. *No, that was a dream.*

"Since college," Mr. Cohn answered.

"To damn long," Mr. Duncan chuckled.

The laughter interrupted my thoughts and I continued cautiously, "So, um, maybe twenty years?"

"Longer. Is this supposed to make us feel better?" Mr. Duncan smirked.

"I do have a point. So, you've known each other for over twenty years. Do you trust each other?" I walked to the frosted glass wall adjacent to the hall. Silhouettes passed by.

The shuffling of papers and the repetitiveness of a copy machine murmured.

"Yes, except when playing chess," Mr. Duncan said. "He's quiet, but sneaky."

"Did you trust each other the same way you do now when you first met?"

"Are you kidding? When we first met, he acted like an idiot. He would do the craziest things in college. But, worse, I'd do them with him," Mr. Cohn said.

"Well, gentlemen. My point is that trust comes with time. I can't build trust with you today or tomorrow. But, I can say that if you give us the opportunity, we will earn your trust, just like you earned each other's trust, over time."

Similar to an old married couple, Mr. Duncan and Mr. Cohn exchanged looks again. They realized I was right.

"Well, Ms. Swan. Okay. We'll give Jameson another six months and then assess," Mr. Duncan agreed.

"Fabulous. I'm glad to hear it. We won't let you down. Before you leave, Kate will schedule a time to meet with you and your staff to discuss everything in detail and to begin developing a marketing strategy."

Mr. Duncan, Mr. Cohn and Kate left the room. The remaining employees stared at me like displaced sheep waiting for the herder's direction.

"What? We got them. What's wrong?" I asked, collecting my materials and files.

"Nothing. I think we're in shock. Mr. Duncan's reputation is infamous, a real hard ass, and he listened to you," Phil said, pushing up his black rimmed glasses that balanced on his crooked nose.

"Yeah, the whole trust thing seemed to work," Stewart added.

"We were lucky. They could have viewed it as desperate and cheesy. Fortunately, it worked. The others may not be so easy," I replied.

"Well, Barry wouldn't have thought to try it," Phil huffed.

"I guess he was too busy trying…" Stewart stopped.

"Never mind."

I wanted to learn more about the Barry scandal, but decided to ignore Stewart's comment and refocus the conversation.

"What do we need to work on now?" I asked.

"Um, I don't know. I think that's all you have today," Phil answered.

"Well, it's only 11:00 o'clock. There must be something I can help with."

"Natalie, isn't this supposed to be somewhat of a vacation for you?" Marcie asked.

"Yes, I guess, but I was just going to do the sights on the weekend. I assumed I'd be in the office working, with you."

Surely, they did not expect me to journey out into the unknown.

"That's not necessary. I'd go have some fun. You're welcome to my car," Marcie said, as she pushed her chair under the table.

I can't imagine spending the day alone in this unfamiliar city.

I excused myself from the group and went to an empty office, pulled out my cell phone and called Mr. Beatler.

"Hi, John. It's Natalie."

"Nat, hey. How's it going?" he tossed out brusquely.

I started to speak, but stopped. Straining, I heard banging in the background, "What's that noise?"

"Oh, ah, nothing. They're working on the AC again. It's hot as coals in here."

"The AC, huh? Well," I continued, "Duncan and Cohn has agreed to stay with us for another six months. I think that will give us the time to prove to them they made the right decision."

"I knew you could do it. Well, have you seen anything, met anybody?"

That seemed strange. *Have I met anybody?* I had met the Jameson employees and the clients. And, of course, Derek. I certainly was not going to tell Mr. Beatler about that encounter.

"Not really. Just the employees here and Mr. Duncan and Mr. Cohn."

"Any other meetings scheduled today?"

"No. That's one reason I called—" He interrupted me.

"Well, you should go out," he barked.

"Don't you want me to work in the office and help them here?" I asked in a hopeful manner.

"No, no. You've already made a huge improvement in where we stand. And, next week is going to be busy. Take the afternoon and weekend and have some fun. Call me next week, okay?"

"Yeah, okay. Thanks." I hit 'End' and tucked my cell phone in my purse. I groaned, dreading the prospect of being a hostage, confined to my hotel room changing channels.

I returned to the conference room. Marcie zoomed around tidying up, putting everyone's chairs back under the table, picking up scattered papers and collecting coffee mugs.

"So, how 'bout it? Want the car?" Marcie asked, as she wiped spilled Sweet'N Low. "Phil, he always spills something," she mumbled.

"It doesn't seem right taking your car. I mean, I don't have a clue where I'm going. I could likely end up in Nevada and you'd be out of a ride home. I'll take a cab."

"Are you sure? I don't mind," Marcie said, turning off the lights.

"No, that's fine, really," I replied, following Marcie to the door.

"Okay, well, I'll drive you back to the hotel so you can change and decide what you want to do. Hey, have you been to Alcatraz yet?" I shook my head. "Oh, well everyone has to go there. It really puts things in perspective, you know?"

I didn't know, but smiled at Marcie politely as we left the conference room.

"I wish I could send my husband there for a few weeks," Marcie continued. "It'd be nice not to wrestle for the remote and Wii." Marcie smiled, enthusiastic with the possibility of having control.

Marcie dropped me off at the hotel and said she would call me Sunday evening to discuss the schedule for next week.

I pushed through the revolving door and snuck into the

building, peeked around the corners and tip-toed over to the elevators. I selected the button and the doors opened. The elevator was empty. With relief, I reached my room undetected. The last thing I needed was to run into Derek.

The curtains were pulled wide open. Sunlight flooded the room. I kicked off my shoes, tossed my purse on the chair, sat my papers on the desk and turned on the TV.

The hotel channel popped on the screen, blaring. I quickly turned down the volume. The advertisement displayed all the sights in San Francisco. I partially listened as I meandered over to the edge of the bed and sat.

"Alcatraz is on every visitor's sights-to-see list," the blonde hostess announced, smiling wide. She spoke so joyfully. *I don't remember reading that Alcatraz's was a "fun" place.* Aerial shots of the secluded island flickered across the screen.

I grunted and shut the TV off. I pulled the pillow out from underneath the comforter and plopped my head on it. *I will just close my eyes for a second and then figure out what to do.*

***

Old iron gates lined the conference room walls. It was dark and a creak murmured from the ceiling. I recognized the people sitting at the long rectangular table—Marcie, Kate, everyone that attended the Duncan and Cohn meeting. Instead of their engaged and inquisitive expressions, soulless stares dulled their faces.

"Marcie. Are you alright?" I asked.

She did not respond. I walked over to her and poked her shoulder. No response. I poked a little harder and her rigid body leaned to the left and like a game of dominoes, Marcie's body hit Kate's and Kate's hit Phil's, and so on. Until they all lay on the floor. Plastic faces and bodies, piled up like used mannequins.

I backed away until the door handle pushed against my hip. Before I could reach the door, it opened.

"Natalie," a voice whispered behind me. "Don't be afraid."

***

My eyes sprung open. I did not move. As if someone was lying on the bed next to me, I stiffened.

Why is this happening to me? I had to get out.

Peeking toward the other side of the bed, seeing no evidence of a guest, I pushed myself up.

I eased over to the full-length mirror, placed my hands on my hips and gave myself a nod. "I'm going to Alcatraz. What the hell. It has to be better than being cooped-up in here, alone, and lost in my ridiculous mind."

I changed into a teal cotton shirt, blue jeans and tennis shoes. I slipped back out to the front of the hotel, where the bellhop whistled me a taxi.

CHAPTER 9

The taxi channeled through the city's hilly terrain and winding streets, dodging oncoming cars. Captivated, I stared at the spiked hills and cramped avenues. Even though Marcie's driving alarmed me, her ability to navigate these roads impressed me.

Miami seemed so far away and different. San Francisco's intricate Victorian homes sat nestled like holiday cottages, competing with the modern cityscape. In Chinatown, endless shops lined the streets, and the smell of fried egg rolls and wontons lingered in the air.

Over each hill, a new world appeared.

As we approached the harbor, my nose filled with the aroma of freshly caught shrimp, baked fish and steamed crab. My stomach growled as I stepped out of the taxi, leaving me in the middle of Fisherman's Wharf. People crowded in corners, peeked in shop windows and waited in lines at endless restaurants.

I headed toward the pier, bought my ticket and took the ferry across the bay to Alcatraz. From a distance, the Golden Gate Bridge rose up like a backdrop of a Hollywood movie, glistening in the sunlight.

The isolated spot of land grew daunting and intimidating as

we approached. The waves crashed and thundered on the sharp rocks. I thought of my last trip to the jetties with Scott, the water spraying on us, and then suddenly, the coast guard shining lights on our naked entangled bodies. *I have a lot of embarrassing moments.* I snickered to myself as the crew tied the ferry to the dock.

Once on the rock, its decades of trauma transported me to a different era. The air turned thick, even with the wind beating the remote island. The ghosts of the past watched us walking through the entrance. Inside, the walls suffocated me. An eeriness chilled my bones. I almost heard the whispers of Al Capone, Machine Gun Kelly and the Birdman.

Through my earphones, I listened to the historical facts and stories. Solitary confinement. The D-Block. *Scary.* I had never been claustrophobic, but the lack of light and sound, and the institutional smell, panicked me. *This is prison. My closet has more space. Why would anyone want to come to this end?*

I resumed my expedition down the creepy halls. The other cells were just as solemn—a small bed, basin and toilet sitting behind an immense steel door. I stood inside one of the cells and peered through the tightly aligned bars. Regret threw a punch at my gut, forcing me against the wall.

"Natalie."

What the hell! My shaking hands pushed the massive door aside, much more easily than I had thought possible. I marched toward the end of the hall, where a guard stood, watching.

"Miss. Are you okay?" he asked.

"Um. Yes. I think so. Just a little claustrophobic. I guess." The wall served as my support.

"That happens. Rest. Have some water."

"Thank you," I said. I entered the mess hall, shaking my head. *What is going on with me? What does all this mean?*

My breathing started to return to normal, and I began analyzing the dreary place, pondering the prospect of sitting day after day, year after year, eating the same food. Ms. Messer's self-imprisonment came to mind. *We all create a prison for ourselves. Somehow or another.*

I scanned the room, moving my eyes from one end to the other, investigating each crack in the wall. Like a rainy day that never ended, grayness seeped from the crevices.

In the middle of my thoughts, a familiar figure entered the hall. I couldn't see his face, but I knew from the way he carried his body and how his hair glided as he moved, it was Derek. *How could he possibly be here? How can I escape from here without him noticing me?*

I turned away and shifted along the wall until I reached the entrance of the room. I watched him as I eased out. I strutted straight for the exit and snuck to the south bank. *I'll take a couple of quick photos and slip out as if I had never been here.*

Water slapped against the jagged rocks at the edge of the island. Birds buzzed above the cliffs searching for food and a place to build a nest. The sun penetrated my skin. Small droplets of sweat sprouted on my forehead. The cityscape captivated me. I squinted my eyes as the immense light radiated and reflected off the buildings. The city seemed alive even at this distance. How cruel to be locked away, so secluded from the world, yet able to hear the sounds of the city.

A frosty haze glowed behind the Golden Gate Bridge. I snapped a couple of shots and whipped around, determined to vacate the island.

Derek stood in front of me, the sunlight shining through the strands of his hair, his eyes glowing underneath. I would have dropped my camera if it hadn't been hanging from my neck.

The corners of his mouth rose. He scanned me, top to bottom. I tried to hide my shock and the fire roaring through me as he came closer. The white and navy stripped shirt contrasted with his black hair and cobalt eyes. His stance had a casual, yet savvy look, like he had stepped off a yacht.

"Fancy running into you here," he noted, as he cupped my shoulder, turning me to face the skyline. "How did your meeting go today?"

"It went well. Duncan and Cohn have decided to stay with Jameson." I sneaked a peak from the corner of my eye to gauge his reaction.

"That's excellent. Great start. So, Jameson lets a beauty like you go around this town unescorted?" he teased. "They should be ashamed. I think you need some company."

His warm breath brushed against my skin, and involuntarily, my neck raised and lengthened, drawing nearer to him.

"I've been doing fine actually," I remarked, responding to his smugness. "I was just going to take a look out here and then head back to the port." I inched my way closer to the island's edge.

"Do you plan on eating? I mean, since we have to go back to the city anyway, we could order some food. You'll never find seafood as awesome as at Fisherman's Wharf," he said, as if he had cooked it himself.

"Well, in Florida, we've got some pretty good seafood too, you know?" I flirted.

"Yeah, but it's different. It's not San Francisco. Come on." He bent down, pivoted me toward him and looked me in the eyes. "Let me take you to dinner."

"No, no. We'll go Dutch." *Shit. What did I just say?* I had no intention of going to dinner with him. I spurted it out without thinking.

"Well, as long as I have you as company, okay," he resigned.

I can't allow this to happen. It's dangerous.

The boat ride to shore was smooth, yet queasiness still gripped my stomach. Derek kept glancing at me, as if he thought I might hurl at any moment. By the time we reached the pier, I longed for the land under my feet. Moments later, my stomach settled. The mysterious island, now far away, confused and disturbed me.

"Natalie, I'm starving," Derek broadcast, as he grabbed my elbow and helped me down the ramp and over the curb. "And, I need a drink."

Some traditional seagoing cuisine sounded good when my tummy started to rumble. We walked around Fisherman's Wharf, searching for the perfect dinner spot and watching performers play instruments and mimes mocking the tourists. We stumbled on a quaint seafood grill.

I ate stuffed flounder. Derek inhaled his broiled Mahi-Mahi. We talked non-stop like two long lost friends catching up on old times. Our eyes darted back and forth, missing each other's stare. I wiggled my toes in my shoes. The nude-colored knee-highs stuck to my sweaty soles. Every time I swallowed, my chest constricted. I felt like a stammering schoolgirl, while he seemed to speak so eloquently. When our eyes met, the world was swept away. We were the only two people left.

I accepted Derek's invitation to drive me back to the hotel. I even let him walk me to my room, where we stood outside the door. I fidgeted with my earrings, tapped my feet and blinked like dust had been blown in my face. *Can I be any more awkward?*

"Uh, thank you. This was, ah, nice. I mean, the food was tasty." I fumbled in my purse for the room key.

"Yeah, it was. So, um, what are you going to do this weekend? We're both going to be here, right? So, I thought we could do something, together. What do you think?"

He is a client. It is not appropriate. My mouth seemed to have a mind of its own as I found myself leaning slightly toward his lips. At last, my room key surfaced from the depths of my purse and I slipped it slyly into the slot before I fulfilled my temptation. As I eased the door closed, I said shyly, "I'd like that."

"Perfect. Let's meet downstairs for breakfast at 8:30," he replied, leaning into the doorway. The thought of tasting his lips overwhelmed my senses and my voice, barely audible, mumbled, "Okay. Good night." I shut the door, leaving him alone in the empty hallway, with only the silent stares of a painted Doberman to keep him company.

Once out of sight, I balanced myself against the mirrored

closet. An elated smile transformed my face. I was flying in the air like a kite, floating for a moment, then quickly soaring to greater heights, a slight tug and climbing again. I had never experienced such a high.

I fell onto the bed afraid to fall asleep. Afraid to discover where the dark hole that swallowed me in my dreams would lead. I stayed awake for as long as I could. Thinking about Derek helped. The last time I remember looking at the clock, it was nearly 2:00 a.m.

***

Like being transported at Alcatraz, I found myself standing under the enormous white tent in the middle of the dance floor. Sweet honeysuckle filled the air and anxious chatter stirred through the crowd. While watching couples dance, a hand touched my shoulder. I feared that the faceless man stood behind me, or maybe Ms. Messer and her tag-along son. But, when I shifted my body to face the unknown person, Derek stood before me. The muscles in my face relaxed, as it formed an accepting smile. *This is the one.* As soon as I thought it, the figure of Derek began to dissolve, growing fuzzy and out of focus. I blinked trying to make him out clearer, but the harder I tried, the blurrier he became.

I stepped back, bumped into another person, whipped around and saw the snowy outline of my father and mother. I surveyed the crowd, all of which now resembled a collage of black and white dots. The figures closed in on me until they were a solid sheet of snow. I turned dizzy and fell, but my fall did not stop at the floor. I dropped into what seemed like a bottomless pit. Finally, it grew silent, and I felt a hard surface underneath me. Grass tickled my ears. I opened my eyes and pulled myself up.

A huge weeping willow hung its tentacles above my head and its long branches quenched their thirst in a creek. My white dress was stained with green and black scuffmarks. I smoothed out the gown and walked toward the flowing water. Across the trickling brook stood a young boy. He only looked about four, but the expression on his face told a different story. His eyes exposed an old soul, as if he was much wiser than his appearance.

"Excuse me. Do I know you?" I shouted. The boy had a familiar face. He did not respond. He wore green trousers and a washed-out blue shirt. His shoes were dirty, like a little boy's shoes should be.

We stared at each other in silence until he broke the tension.

"I want you to go back," he said, running into the woods. "This is a mistake."

"Wait," I called after him, but it was too late.

A cool breeze fluttered through the air stirring up the fallen leaves and carrying them gently on the water. A chill rushed over me.

***

The alarm buzzed on the side table and I awoke groggy, like a hangover hit me out of nowhere. Cloudy and disoriented, I moved my wobbly head. A pain shot between my eyebrows. I shoved my head under the pillow and pulled the blanket up to my chin.

At the moment when all the air had been used, seconds away from pulling the pillow and covers off, I realized where I had seen the little boy. He had stopped me in the street the night Scott broke up with me.

CHAPTER 10

So much rattled my brain. I sipped my cream laden coffee, wondering why I had accepted Derek's invitation. I almost knocked over my cup when he approached, but caught it before it spilled onto my lap.

"Are you drinking a coffee or a milkshake?" Derek taunted.

"I like cream," I replied, more playfully than I meant.

"Yes, yes. I do, too," he said. He paused. "What's wrong?"

"What? What do you mean?"

I hoped he had noticed how my yellow sundress draped over my shoulders. I never thought of my skin as sexy, but for some reason I wanted to show off my delicate, smooth and long neck. I assumed Derek sensed more than my desire for him. I imagined my expression revealed the unknown world that I longed to discover. *The little boy, my guide.*

"You seem, well, different. Preoccupied."

"Work," I lied.

"Ah, I understand. That can kill everything. Let's get rid of those thoughts right now."

I nodded. He recapped our previous evening. With each of his movements, it seemed as if a gentle ocean breeze rose up and hovered under my nose. I wanted to nuzzle my face in the curve of his neck.

His stare penetrated through me. His face softened, as if he reminisced about someone he had known and cared about for many years.

My imagination kicked in. I convinced myself he felt the same as I did.

We drove leisurely toward the bay and the Golden Gate Bridge. The humidity floated in the air, dense and stifling. I pushed the dreams way back into the corners of my mind, giving Derek all of my attention.

"So, you enjoy the computer field? I mean, I assume you do since you started your own company," I rolled my eyes, realizing how clumsy I sounded.

"Well, actually, the company is my brother's. He was the technology wiz. I like the business-side, making things happen. He asked me to be his Vice-President of Strategic Development, whatever that is. But, then, well—" He tapered off. His eyes turned blank and empty, as if he relieved a horrible dream.

"What?" I asked, watching him like a bird inspecting its prey. Even in this state, Derek remained strong and handsome. I wanted to touch his jaw and run my fingers through his hair. But, his tone had changed. Something bothered him.

"He," Derek paused, "passed away. Um, cancer. He already knew when he asked me to come on, apparently grooming me to take over the company. What was I supposed to do, let him down? No way. So, I took over. Jake's shoes are hard to fill. My brother was a smarter and better person than me."

His eyes twinkled in the sun, although it might have been the glimmer of restrained tears.

"I'm so sorry. I am sure he is proud of you," I responded, thinking that none of this information was in the file. "When did you take over?" I hoped my question did not sound insensitive.

"About three years ago. We've been with Jameson for

two."

"So what type of problems have you had with Jameson?" I asked, changing the subject.

"Well, at first things were fine. Barry handled our account. We attended the same college. He was a good guy. We contracted with Jameson because of my relationship with him. We're based in New York. Endless companies solicited our business, but I trusted Barry and he helped me out a lot with Calculus, you know?" I forced myself to listen, but became distracted watching the movement of his mouth. *Listen to him, this is important. Listen!*

"Anyway," he continued, "about six months ago, I stopped hearing from him. He didn't return any calls. Basically, the guy fell off the earth. I made an appointment to see him. He didn't show up. Later that night, he called me. He was completely wasted. He kept asking me to come meet him. He got downright ugly, demanding I get my, as he said, ass down there now. Well, I don't mind a drink or two, but he was falling down drunk. I don't do business that way. I told him no and asked that we meet the next morning at the office, after he had cooled down a bit. He was rude, vulgar. He sounded like he had called from a bar or club."

"His behavior was totally unprofessional," I said. *What about mine? I keep forgetting he is a client. I must remain professional.*

I shouldered some guilt, getting information on the side to use against him later.

I turned toward the window of the car and watched the buildings pass. The smell of the bay grew closer. The wheels in my head spun fast and hard.

"What's wrong, Nat?" he asked, placing his hand on top of mine.

"What?" I paused. "Wait. You called me Nat," I remarked.

"Well, sure, is that okay?"

"Yes, it's just, only a couple people call me Nat. It sounds, funny, coming from someone different."

"I'm sorry." The car slowed, as he tackled another curve.

"No, it's okay. It's good." I turned my hand over and clasped his. "I guess I'm just concerned about what you'll think of me."

"What are you talking about?"

"You've already had enough unprofessional Jameson employees to contend with. I don't want you to think poorly of me. I mean, flirting with clients is not my usual behavior."

"Flirting?" he smiled, raising his brow. "Are you flirting with me?"

I did not answer. I wanted to fling the car door open and leap out.

"Thank God," he continued. "I was hoping you were."

"Derek. I don't understand what's going on here." I pulled my hand away and reached for my purse.

"Can't two people who are attracted to each other spend a pleasant weekend in a town, where they don't know a soul?"

"I guess."

"Look, I understand. You have integrity. It's a rare and wonderful trait. I'm impressed. But, Nat, I like you. I think you are attractive and smart. I don't care if you work for Jameson. I want to know more about you. Get to know you. I hope you feel the same. So, let's forget about this client relationship for this weekend and have a nice time. Believe me. Relax. Have fun."

Why not have some fun.

One last turn, and then it came into view—the Golden Gate Bridge. It rose up from the water, cutting the thick heat with its strong steel towers.

We crossed the bridge and parked. I was so excited I forgot to unbuckle my seatbelt. After manhandling the buckle, I got out of the car and dashed to the edge of the bridge. I sighed at the breathtaking views, and breathed the soft air swimming across the historic site. Derek followed behind. Like a child, I peered over the rippling bay, enthusiastic and innocent.

We leaned against the rail. Derek's body pressed firmly against my side. Heat ignited between us. He placed his arm around my shoulder.

"It's beautiful," I gasped.

"You are an angel," he said. I felt more like the devil, but his comment softened my inner stress.

After our secret glimpse across the bay, we returned to the car and continued on our journey. We arrived at Muir Woods. As Derek parked the car, I poked my head around eagerly like a prairie dog watching for intruders. He rushed to the other side of the car and opened the door. I gawked at my surroundings as we made our way into the vast forest.

As we walked further into the maze of redwoods, the mammoth trees blocked the sun's light, darkening the paths that winded in and out of the encroaching trees. Their magnitude stunned me, as they soared through the air like skyscrapers.

"They are magnificent," I exclaimed, stopping in the middle of four gargantuan redwoods. I danced, swayed and threw leaves up in the air. I stared toward the sky, where a narrow opening provided a sliver of blue. Cracking leaves crunched as if under the feet of a cautious stalker, stopping my romp.

"What is it?" Derek asked, approaching me in short focused strides. I remained silent and strained my ears to hear the sound again. Derek placed his hands gently on my shoulders and rubbed them therapeutically.

"Maybe it was just a bird, or a squirrel," he suggested. "Don't be so paranoid. I'm confident that no Jameson employees are lurking in Muir Woods waiting to capture us together."

"I know," I replied, turning toward him. Our faces were only inches apart. My legs weakened. *Kiss me!*

The sound of crackling timber broke the tension. Scared at what may lie behind the six-foot trunks, I grabbed Derek's hand. We glanced at each other, sparks flowing through me and drums pounding in my chest. Derek squeezed my hand hard and pulled me to him. His other hand slithered up my arm to my neck, cradling my head in his hand. He bent his head toward me. My breath stuck in my throat. With a third shift in the leaves, we separated. Derek scanned the overwhelming forest.

"Look, there," he pointed at one of the gigantic trees. "It's that bird. See him?"

Heat channeled between us as I squinted. A bird hopped from place to place, digging its beak into the ground.

This intimate moment vanished, but it remained in my mind as we spent the next couple of hours frolicking in our own private amusement park. I felt like *Alice* as she scurried along the endless path exploring and discovering the mysteries hiding in each corner. As the sun started to fade, we emerged from the forest.

A high-pitched chirp greeted us. I had left my purse and cell phone in the car. I frantically grabbed my purse and started searching madly for the phone. *Four voicemail messages.* My heart clutched with the thought. I had not called my mother since I arrived in San Francisco. Derek had consumed all my focus. A wrinkle tightened across my forehead.

"My mother. I told her I would call when I got here, and I have been so, ah—" I stopped to think for the right words, "preoccupied, I haven't been timely in calling her. I'm certain she is overwhelmed with worry. Do you mind if I go ahead and call her back?"

"No, not at all."

A sickening guilt ate at my stomach. This would be a topic of conversation for the next decade. Two rings in, and my palms started to sweat. I remembered a time when I was seven years old, and I accidentally colored the new carpet with crayons. I could picture the look of disappointment on my mother's face, as she scrubbed the red and yellow marks.

"Well," my mother answered, her voice shaking. "I thought you were laying on the side of the road somewhere, in a gutter. Dead. Your father was ready to coordinate a search party. Head north, cover the whole damn state."

"Mom. Don't say anything. I already know. I'm horrible. Things here just happened so fast. Before I knew it was Saturday. I'm sorry." I tried to be discrete and smile occasionally in Derek's direction, but he could hear every word.

"You always call me. I was really worried." Her voice crackled.

"I know. I'm sorry." I peered out of the window, blankly. My heart sank out of my body, seeped through the car doors, fell on the ground, run over by the car's turning wheels. Road kill.

"Mommy," I whispered, "why don't I call you when I get back to my hotel."

"Well, at this rate, I'm not sure if I want to talk to you. I am so upset," her dramatic sniffles added to my self-torture. The last thing my mother needed was more worry, and here I was creating more stress.

"Don't say things like that. I just got a little absorbed in all this." Derek looked straight ahead as we drove through the city.

"Nat, you know how I am. I'm nervous and a worrywart. I always assume the worst. I love you so much. I could not stand living if anything happened to you."

"I know. Let me call you later and I'll tell you all I've done so far."

"You can't talk now?" she pressed.

"Not really. I am with a, um, a client, at the moment. We are talking about some," I paused, "business matters."

"It's a man, isn't it? Is he cute?" she asked, much more perky than necessary.

"I'll talk to you tonight, okay?" I replied, trying to give her a hint.

"Okay," my mother said deflated. She'd be ready to fire off a million questions at me about this 'client.' When it came to curiosity, my mother killed the cat.

"I am sorry for not calling," I repeated. "It's not like me. But, I'm fine and I'll call you later tonight." After stuffing the phone back in my purse, I refocused my attention on Derek.

"I'm so sorry. She worries. I suppose it's got something to do with me being an only child. Anyway, I always call. I don't know what's gotten into me. I've never forgotten before." I fumbled in my pocket until I found my lip gloss.

"I have distracted you," Derek offered.

I straightened my back, dropping the lipstick between the car seats.

"I mean," he continued, "dragging you all around town, out to the woods. Oh, and, you might not want to tell your mother you went out to a forest with a man you barely know."

"Well, I think I came on my own accord. No dragging. I wanted to come."

I dug around searching for the gloss, my clumsiness surfacing again. I stretched my fingers far between the seat and the middle console. I balanced the small tube between my fingers until it was free. I shoved it back in my pocket, abandoning its use until later.

"Well, I hope you want to go to dinner too. I am starved." Derek turned the corner and headed to the Fisherman's Wharf. "But, let's try something different tonight."

I didn't even try to make excuses. I wanted to go more than anything.

What if he is the one?

CHAPTER 11

We decided on an almost empty, intimate restaurant on the edge of the Wharf. One couple sat in the back, quietly sharing bites of cheesecake. On the other side, another couple ate their dinners in silence. They glanced back and forth, never meeting each other's eyes. They ate. Nothing more. They reminded me of my parents.

An odd sensation fell over me observing these two extremes. I wanted to be the first couple—oblivious to the rest of the world because they were lost in each other. I could not stand any more arguing or hate.

Derek ordered a bottle of Cline Old Vine Zinfandel. His eyes sparkled in the candlelight. Like a princess swept away in a fantasy, my fairytale transported me to another world. I tried to block out the imminent Monday morning.

Derek filled my glass with the ruby wine. "Cheers, Natalie," Derek toasted, raising his glass. We clinked and took a sip. As if he read my mind, he reached across the table, caressed my hand and intertwined his fingers with mine.

The food arrived and I stared down at a giant-sized portion, the Mount Everest of pasta. I swirled my fork in the center of the large spoon, wrapping the linguini tightly, sneaking a peek of Derek.

"So, technology, huh? Sounds scary to me. My computer is pretty lonely."

"I was actually concerned about it, working in the technology world," Derek explained, as he cut his filet.

"Things work out for a reason. You're doing an amazing job."

"I pay people well for spreading that rumor. Secretly, between you and me? Most of time, I just wing it. I haven't a clue on most things the IT guys talk about."

I never thought of a guy just 'winging it.' Maybe I don't have to feel so inadequate all the time. Maybe everyone feels that way.

"Hmm. You don't strike me as a man that lets others on to his, ah, vulnerabilities."

"How polite. I am a good actor."

"So am I." I puckered my lips as a noodle disappeared in my mouth. *I hope he doesn't think I'm acting now.*

"But really," I continued, "things do work out."

I lifted my glass, tipping my nose beyond the rim to sniff the Zinfandel's black cherry and white pepper aroma.

"I mean, I have no idea why we are here, yet we are. Why?" I asked, not expecting a dissertation on the subject.

"Well, we're here because I forced you to have dinner with me, again. I'm a lucky man." I shook my head and smiled.

I'm on a roller coaster. A euphoric nausea climbed from deep in my gut, up my torso, to my diaphragm, settling in my chest. My arms tingled. My legs stiffened. The world zeroed in on me, blackness inching along my peripheral. I was falling in love.

"I'm sorry. I keep cutting you off. What were you going to say?"

My revelation stunned me. I was falling in love. *What am I going to do?*

"Natalie?" Derek repeated, "Where are you? Hello?" he said sing-songy.

Snapping out of my dream-state, I blurted, "Oh, I'm sorry. I was off in my own world." A strange and foreign heat exploded inside me, while a chilled tickled my skin.

"What were you going to say?" he asked.

"Um, oh, oh yeah. I was going to say. Well, I want to serve a purpose, make a difference, you know. Sometimes I think, wow I've done a lot. You look at my résumé, for example, and think 'impressive.' But what does that mean, really?" I sipped the wine and blotted the corners of my lips with the napkin.

"A piece of paper with a whole bunch of elaborations of how fabulous you are says nothing about who you are," I forced myself to continue, working hard to disguise my feelings. "Yet we create these neat little packages of ourselves and hold it up as a prize. Things are much more complicated than that."

I sat my glass down and propped up my head with my hand, my elbow barely touching the edge of the table. Tilting my head, I watched Derek reach for his glass. He was in control. He could take on any challenge, mental or physical, and win. I assumed he had already figured out how I felt about him. We were playing a friendly game of chess, but he had just shouted checkmate. Minutes before, I knew the game was over.

"You never know what you are gonna get," he suggested, as he shrugged his shoulders. "Take your résumé example. Like you said, someone can appear like a superstar on paper. They can even interview well but after you hire them, you find out they are a lazy sack of—well, you get the picture. Life is a mystery. You don't know what you're gonna get or where you're gonna end up." He cut into his steak.

"You know. I guess I'm crazy," I straightened in the chair and placed my right hand over my left on the table.

"Why?" he asked, as he replenished my glass.

"Well, in the same second, I am grateful and disappointed, for what I have and don't have. I don't mean material things. I mean, what I have done, accomplished. One minute I want to do everything and be everything. The next, I wonder what's the point."

"I think the point is that you do as much as you can for as

long as you can and touch as many people as you can. You can't do and be everything." He studied his meat, identifying the best bite and murmured as he chewed, "This is really good."

"I can't believe I'm telling you all this. You must think I'm nuts." I dropped my hands on my lap and compulsively picked at my nails.

"On the contrary, it's one of the most intelligent conversations I've had on a date."

"Date?" I questioned, as I placed my napkin next to the plate.

"Well, yeah, sort of. Want to try again—tomorrow?" Derek slid his arm across the table. I just stared at his open palm.

"Derek. I feel uncomfortable about this. I've always said I would not become involved with a client." I glanced over my shoulder, sensing a presence behind me.

"Well, putting it like that doesn't sound like a lot of fun."

"You know what I mean? Going out with a client. It's unprofessional. I am sure Mr. Beatler would not approve."

I reached down to pick up my purse, indicating it was time to go, but Derek started talking in a stronger, direct tone.

"A couple of things. First, Mr. Beatler is not here. Second, we are here. And finally, let's just play it by ear. Believe me, it's okay. And, I'm not ready to leave. This steak is too good."

Why the hell am I so paranoid?

"Fine," I conceded. "I need to know you won't, ah... Never-mind. Let's just enjoy the food."

"Nat, you worry like your mom. You can't let everything bother you and bear everyone's burden. Promise me that you'll work on it. Life is way to short to stress this much."

"You're right. I've had a lot of things happen, that make me, um, worry, I guess." *Right now, I worried that he didn't feel the same.*

Later, at the hotel, Derek walked me to my room. I wanted him to lift me in his arms and carry me to the nearest bed. *Breathe, Natalie.*

"What would you like to do tomorrow?" he asked firmly.

"Well," I said, as slowly as possible, "I would love to visit the ocean."

"Done. See you at breakfast at 8:30?" he confirmed. I nodded, opened the door and squeezed through the opening. I peeked out of the narrowing crack, until the door met the frame and locked.

I leaned against the door, soaking in my feelings. I could have let him work his way into my room. *But, no, not yet. This one is different.*

CHAPTER 12

I stared in the mirror as I brushed my teeth, toothpaste gathering in the corners of my mouth. Like a newly transformed butterfly, a rejuvenated spirit soared through me. I tried to convince myself the whole evening had been a dream. But, it had happened. I'd met a man. A man that made me feel alive. Who made me believe there was something beyond the four walls comprising my mundane life. An infatuation of being in love gripped my insides. I wanted more, but wasn't sure whether I could, or should, have a taste.

As promised, I called my mother.

"Yes, mom, he was a man. No, mom, he is a client. Yes, I know I need to meet people, mom. I am working on that. I realize how old I am. Yes. Okay. I love you, too. I understand. I'm sorry, okay? Bye."

I lifted my legs onto the bed and slid them under the covers. My thoughts turned to the night ahead. The sick part of me longed to go to sleep so I could learn more about my alternate reality. I had seen the little boy before. Him stopping me in the street saved my life. I wanted to follow the white rabbit. The other part of me wished, that for one night, peaceful rest would let me dream about Derek instead.

***

Hard rocks of a stone path cut my bare feet as I raced along. Everything was gray—the sky, the earth and the trees—no color. Only my white dress glowed in the dim surroundings.

In front of me stood a dilapidated iron gate. A force, this time from within, caused me to unlatch it and step into the grounds. A splash of color caught my attention. A fresh bouquet of lilies and irises sat on top of a grave. I walked directly toward it, bent down face-to-face with the old stone, squinting, struggling to read the name. *Someone had been here, recently.*

After years of decay, only the last three letters were visible—W A N.

Silence deadened the air. Even my heart ceased its relentless thumping. I jumped away from the grave. The purple and white flowers transformed, decomposing into black brittle wisps floating in the wind. Whispers murmured from the trees, their branches rotting and falling to the burnt grass.

Three figures stood in the distance—a woman and two men. One man held the woman, tears running down her face. I tried to run toward them but the earth took hold of me, my feet cemented in decomposing earth. I stretched my arms, nearly pulling them from their sockets.

"Help!" I pleaded. No one responded. I tugged my legs but the earth's grip strengthened the more I tried to escape.

My parents turned in my direction, their heads hanging. My mother fell to the ground, my father bending over comforting her.

"Mommy! Daddy! I'm here. Help!"

A minister turned away from them, and walked straight toward me. I crooked my head back seeing the gravestone. Like glow-in-the-dark lights, W A N shined a brilliant fluorescent lime.

"Oh my God!" I screamed, putting two and two together. The grave—W A N. Swan. Swan!

The grave is mine.

***

I gasped for air, falling out of the bed and landing with a thump on the floor. My elbow hit the side table. Grabbing the edge of the mattress, I pulled myself up. For about ten minutes, I sat rocking, holding my arm and wondering what the dream meant. *Was my life in danger? Where was the little boy?*

I did not sleep the rest of the night. I thought about calling Derek, but instead I walked the halls looking at all the dog paintings. I made my way back around 4 a.m. I lay on the bed, but stayed awake. Soon, the Sunday sun skirted the outer edge of the horizon. Heat crept up my face, until the light was directly parallel with my eyes. I grabbed a pillow from the other side of the bed and smashed it into my face—darkness once more. An hour later, the alarm filled the room with a harsh buzzing.

I peeled the sheets from myself. No amount of makeup could cover the stress my face showed. *How will I hide this from Derek?* Time flew by as I studied the evening, picking apart the dream, wondering why someone would paint dogs in suits, and thinking about the energy I needed to make it through today.

Now late to meet Derek, I ran out the door fastening the top button of my shirt.

"I was wondering if you'd changed your mind. Wow, I like how you walk," Derek said, as I approached the table. My body shifted under the antique white cotton skirt. My pink colored sandal straps wrapped my ankles.

"Hey, are you okay? You look like you didn't sleep," he continued.

"Yeah, well. I didn't, much," I replied, strands of hair whipped across my face. I tried to think of something to say and finally, tossed out, "You know, these pillows, too soft. I should have shipped my pillow to the hotel. Anyway, I did not change my mind, just a little behind."

"Okay. Well, you tell me if you want to come back or something." Derek took my hand and smiled. His touch and tenderness lifted the stress, a little.

We drove toward the ocean. My huge sunglasses cut the

sun's glare and hid my red eyes and dark circles. My pink scarf floated through the air. Our hair tossed wildly. I leaned my head back and gazed up into the pearly sky. *This is why someone rents a convertible.* We were like two stars driving to a movie premiere.

We neared the coast, the ocean's smell and sound erasing all my worries. The salt air, crashing waves and squawking seagulls signaled that the water sat within our reach. I swung the car door open, tossed off my shoes and ran straight for the beach. Derek followed.

I reached the water's edge and stopped shy of an oncoming wave, and stared into the infinite blue. The sand warmed my soles. The next wave found its way to shore. Chilly unforgiving water flowed over my feet. I stood my ground, noticing the large rock formations sitting right off the coast, waves misting high above their cliffs.

"It is the most beautiful thing I have ever seen," I turned toward Derek, who, like a mesmerized child, stood staring at me. His face stayed strong, but the muscles in his neck tightened as if he had lost his breath. I touched his cheek with the back of my hand. He followed it with his own. Our hands wove together. Our bodies grew closer. Derek's lips parted, and he released a deep sigh. The heat of the earth seemed to rise up from the ground, creating a warm shield around us. Slowly, naturally, and as gently as possible, Derek pressed his mouth against mine. He slid his arms around my waist and pulled me closer. The rhythm of the waves became our song. The crispness of the water soothed the fire radiating under my skin. The beach was full of onlookers. Yet, in that moment, we were alone, sharing a secret kiss on the edge of the world.

When our lips finally parted, our feet were buried deep in the sand. My legs were limp, mutated into flimsy noodles. If he had let me go, I would have tipped over.

Time stood still, as we stood arm-in-arm, taking in the endless ocean. Once my balance returned, I seized his hand and we walked, kicking sprays of water toward each other. *Freedom.*

The beach flooded with more families and tourists, so we started the trek up the shore to the car, which seemed like a small speck miles away. We meandered back, watching couples and families settle on the beach, umbrellas up and coolers open and then I had a strange feeling—déjà vu. I stopped abruptly and turned around. A young boy and girl frolicked in the water, splashing each other. For a second, I swore a little boy in green trousers walked passed, waving at me.

"Natalie? Are you okay?" Derek asked.

"Um, yeah. Sad to leave, I guess." When I glanced back, the boy was gone. *Get a grip, Natalie.*

Throughout the day, we were like high school sweethearts, yet, at the same time, old lovers, comfortable and cozy.

After dinner, we returned to the hotel and went straight to Derek's room.

Windows wrapped the walls and a mini-bar sat under the counter, filled with tempting spirits. A quaint sitting area overlooked the balcony and the atrium beyond. The separate bedroom was exquisitely decorated and the bathroom included a shower and whirlpool bath. My entire apartment would have fit inside Derek's hotel room.

Derek leaned against the bar, mixing a martini. "Would you like something?" he asked. I continued to inspect the space. "No, I better not. I have an important meeting with a client in the morning." In the reflection of the glass, a sly smile appeared on my face.

"I think that the client would understand if you had an after-dinner drink," he crossed the room smoothly holding his cocktail. He brushed his body behind me. The sensation rushed over me until warmth penetrated deep into my center. I moved to the couch, steadying myself.

A kiss on the neck or a wandering hand, and I would be helpless. How would I act the next day seeing him at the meeting? Would I run and hide and bury my head in the sand? At the same time, I want to wrap myself around him, to touch him and be touched.

Before I processed what was happening, Derek's hand

stroked my cheek. I floated a few feet off the ground. From above, I watched myself. I had never experienced this before. Excitement and fear mixed inside me. As soon as his lips touched mine, I relaxed and became lost in our world. My heart beat like a cougar on the run. Disheveled, I pushed him away and said, "Derek, I'm sorry. I, um, I think I need to go."

"Are you okay? Is this okay?" he uttered, transforming from lustful to loving.

"Yes. I'm fine. I'm still uncomfortable. I keep thinking about how you will look at me tomorrow and whether I will get through the meeting."

"I wish I did not intimidate you so much."

"I'm not intimidated," I snapped, facing him. "I just don't believe my behavior has been appropriate. I need to leave," I turned away, collected my things and paraded to the foyer. Like a scolded puppy, he ran after me. He reached the door before me and placed his hand on the doorknob, preventing my exit.

"Natalie, I'm sorry. I don't want you to feel awkward. I really like you and I think our day together has been one of the best ever. Tell me what I can do."

"Tomorrow. Don't mention that we know each other. They wouldn't understand. I'm not sure I understand," I said, as I reached up and brushed a dangling hair from his brow. I opened the door and left.

I returned to my room and sat on the bed for a long time thinking about the day's events. I worried about the meeting and my reputation. In some odd way I was afraid of losing Derek, this man I just met and barely knew.

Marcie had left a voicemail reminding me that she'd pick me up in the morning. After deleting the message, I dialed my mother. The answering machine picked up.

"Hi. It's me. Are you there? It's late. Hello?" *Mom never goes out this late.* Disappointed, I continued, "Okay, well, call me on my cell. I love you." I wanted to hear her voice.

I tossed the phone onto the other side of bed and laid my puzzled head on the uncomfortable pillow. I had not changed clothes or brushed my teeth. In a few minutes, I drifted off to sleep.

CHAPTER 13

I moved like a sack of potatoes being dragged across sand, annoyed at what woke me. But, then, I realized, it was Monday and the high-pitched squeal was the alarm buzzing like a boiling kettle. I looked down at myself and remembered I had fallen asleep without changing. *Here I go again.* I closed my eyes tightly, clenched my teeth and propped up my head with my hand. *Why I'm I always behind the curve?*

After a moment of pondering my ineptitude, I jumped out of bed and sprinted from my suitcase to the bathroom, from my purse to the closet. At one point, I was hopping on one leg yanking pantyhose on my dangling foot. Despite the chaos, I managed to get ready in lickety-split time. I strolled out the front of the hotel as Marcie drove up.

We arrived at the office, zooming past the scary greeter. She was applying red lipstick, peering in a handheld mirror, smacking her lips together. Evil radiated from her dead white skin. Anxiously, I smashed the elevator button with my hand desperate to escape her presence.

Oh my God. I slept through the night.

I leaned on the wall for support, my reflection staring back at me from the glossy steel doors. I had forgotten what I had dreamed of, or if I had dreamed at all. No cemetery. No little boy. Gone. I wasn't sure whether to be relieved or sad.

Derek and his staff were already sitting at the conference table when we walked in, a few minutes after the scheduled appointment. The conversation in the room stopped.

It's official. I've been sent to the principal's office.

All of the Voeltgin staff, including Derek, sized up the situation, including me.

"Good morning," I said, as I moved across the room toward Derek. "I apologize for the delay. I guess I am not used to the Pacific Coast time yet. Mr. Voeltgin," I continued, as I reached out my hand to shake his, "It's a pleasure." Derek rose from his chair, as I approached and generously shook my hand. *Will the others wonder how I knew it was him?*

"Mr. Voeltgin, before we begin, would everyone introduce themselves?" The Voeltgin staff began. Eric Samms, the Vice-President of Marketing; Bill Murphy, the General Operations Manager; Adam Manson, the Comptroller; and Derek were in attendance. The same Jameson team sat studiously along both sides of the elongated table.

During the introductions, I moved to the small credenza in the back corner and poured a cup of coffee. *How could I be so foolish to fall for a client?* My hands trembled as I splashed a sizable helping of cream, barely hitting the cup. I had not been that nervous since I competed in the semi-final middle school spelling contest.

Why don't I remember having any dreams? Could they really be gone? I wanted to find out where the little boy would lead me. I had come to expect him. Plus, the last time, I was presented with an alarming vision—that my life may be in jeopardy.

I sat at the opposite end of the table, Derek directly across from me. I lost ammunition allowing him to see my vulnerable side. Denying I'd had an amazing weekend would be a lie. I found him irresistible, but guilt churned in my gut. *Will I perform my best? Shit! Come on, Natalie. Stay focused!* My leg shook obsessively as I picked my nails under the table. I looked straight ahead making no eye contact with anyone.

"Um, Natalie," Phil summoned, sounding alarmed. "Do

you want to start us off?" he asked.

"Uh, of course," I finally said, opening the file and flipping the pages. "So, Mr. Voeltgin."

"Call me, Derek," he flirted, his gaze never leaving me.

"Okay, Derek," I continued, cautiously. My shoulders dipped forward, and my head hung. With every ounce of my being, I forced, "Jameson is extremely concerned about your business, and we want to know how we can help." Silence, then pain. I had picked the skin on my thumb so bad, it started to bleed.

The other Jameson employees moved their anxious eyes from one to another subtly. I wasn't my ass-kicking self they had witnessed last week.

"What problems have you encountered?" I asked. I pressed my thumb against my palm, trying to stop the blood from dripping on my suit. Someone was talking but my listening skills had disappeared.

Get it together. This was the meeting you were most concerned about. You can't fail. Derek will be completely unimpressed. Remember! You have the 'it' factor.

Mr. Samms was the one rambling. "We do business honestly and expect the same from those we work with. And, I don't—"

An idea surfaced. *I can win this battle. Use Barry.*

"It sounds to me," I interrupted, "that there has been an integrity issue."

Mr. Samms stopped talking and glared at me. "Well, yes, in a nutshell."

A burst of confidence shot through my veins. "Voeltgin is an excellent company with a nationwide reputation. Jameson also has a strong reputation. That's why, when we became aware of Mr. Thorton's behavior and performance issues, we took action. Jameson is a value-based organization. Voeltgin is as well. If you look at our company's values, they are shockingly similar." Remembering from the Voeltgin file, I continued. "Our values are Service, Quality, Excellence and Integrity. Voeltgin's values are Service, Quality, Teamwork and Integrity. Integrity," I repeated. "You probably selected Jameson because we have similar values and philosophy. There is not another company that will parallel so closely. Mr. Thorton created a situation where the integrity of our company was called into question. The reason you should stay with us is because Mr. Thorton is no longer here and a message has been sent that our company expects the best at all times, and we won't tolerate unprofessional, unethical business practices."

Oh God, what am I saying? Unethical. What about my behavior? Gallivanting through the countryside with a client. Fantasizing about meeting with him under the sheets instead of in the conference room. My tongue would have dragged on the floor watching him if not for my bottom lip holding it in place. Thoughts of kissing him and unbuttoning those little white buttons never left my thoughts. And, I had the nerve to talk about ethics. Certainly Derek wanted to laugh, questioning *my* integrity.

Before I said another thing, Derek spoke.

"You're right. We did pick Jameson because of its reputation. And, we've generally been pleased with the service."

Mr. Samms interrupted, "But it seemed to us that when Jameson found out about Thorton, action wasn't taken fast enough. Months went by, meanwhile our account suffered."

"Mr. Samms, I understand what you are saying, but to our defense," I said, "we'd never had a situation like this. It was unique to our company. We had to digest it, investigate it. Now we are armed and have the tools to respond." I hoped I was on the right track. I wasn't real sure what happened with Barry and Jessica.

"I have a deal for you," I walked around the room, stopping to lean on the table between Derek and Mr. Samms. "Jameson has been studying your company and has identified some innovative strategies specifically for you. Give us three months, work with us, and I guarantee you will realize an increase in service, and in profits."

"What if your guarantee fails?" Mr. Samms questioned, but Derek cut him off.

"We'll take that deal," Derek declared, rising from his seat and turning to me. He reached out his hand. My eyes trailed down his arm. I hesitated, but then in a professional stiff manner, grasped his hand and shook it.

"Thank you, Mr. Voeltgin."

The guests collected their items and started to leave. Derek twisted around covertly, like an undercover cop and announced, "Ms. Swan, one request. I'd like you to work on our account exclusively." He paused. My face turned cold. My eyes darted around the room. "I'll call you when I return to New York," he continued, "so we can discuss our relationship further."

"Uh, wait, Mr. Voeltgin," I stalled. "I will need to confirm that with Mr. Beatler, my boss. I have a number of projects assigned to me. I am not as familiar with your industry as some of our other associates."

Derek took a couple of steps toward me, swallowed his last sip of coffee, bent down and quietly said, "I don't really care if you understand my industry. I want you."

His brows lifted, widening his eyes as he glided to the door, turned his head and winked at me.

He manipulated me. His calculating, confident and sexy demeanor were driving me insane. These feelings were outside my normal realm. I was losing total control. For the first time, my emotions clouded my ability to function.

Instead of asking Marcie for a ride, I called a cab to take me back to the hotel. I ran past the lobby Nazi and flung the doors open. Like a sprinter, I approached the curb within seconds. Next to the brick stairs, Derek leaned against the wall.

"Oh, Natalie," he shouted, clapping his hands. "Impressive. You did a great job in there. I think you definitely won over the boss. So, what do you want to do today?"

"What? Are you crazy? I'm on the verge of losing my mind, and my job."

"A little overdramatic. Don't you think?" he teased.

"I don't think it is appropriate for me to see you on a social basis. Especially now that you have requested me to assist you. I already feel guilty about last night."

I stepped into the street proudly, but wasn't sure were to go. Derek followed loosely, tailing me.

"Last night?" he pressed, as he reached me. "Look, we kissed. I want to kiss you now. I guess I don't understand what's wrong with that. I've extended my stay just so we can be together. Can't we have some more time? No one has to know."

He tilted his head back and seemed to study me, wrinkling his brow, and said, "I notice things. I can read you, what you're thinking. This, you and me, is nothing like Barry's issue." He stroked my cheek, brushing it with the back of his hand. I couldn't resist.

"Well, then, let's hurry up and get the hell out of here before someone spots us in front of my employer's building," I blurted, surprising myself.

We shared the cab on the way back to the hotel.

CHAPTER 14

All the joys of the world connected when Derek and I were together. My senses were restored. My confidence and spirit had reemerged. I slept soundly each night, not recalling a single dream. Once in a while, I wondered where the little boy had gone, why he left me, but then Derek would say something, and I'd lose the thought.

On Wednesday, we spent the evening in Derek's suite. Tomorrow he would leave. I dreaded the moment. I tried to push that fear deep into the back of my mind and enjoy what was in front of me.

A collection of Bach and Mozart played softly through hidden speakers. Twinkling lights from the atrium lit the shadowy room. Half empty wine glasses sat on the coffee table.

We cuddled on the couch. He caressed my hair, his mouth barely touching my forehead. A magic spell was cast upon us, as we lay isolated from the world. Our bodies were entangled like vines in the woods, wild and free.

Derek's fingers snuck under and up the back of my blouse and climbed to the clasp of my bra. He unhooked it effortlessly and glided his hand over my breast. Every thought, every concern, washed away with his touch. My back arched slightly, my hair flowing down the side of the sofa.

Hours passed. He kissed my skin from the curve of my neck, over my breasts, down the sides of my stomach, all the way to the tips of my toes. I remained mostly clothed.

When the sun swept the room, my eyes opened, Derek's body still cradling me.

Today he will leave.

He packed. I tried to distract him, wanting to prolong our time together. *Maybe he'll miss his flight.* An hour later, we were in the cab, driving toward the airport.

Masses of passengers lined the security checkpoint. Nerves vibrated inside the walls of my skin, as he turned toward me, ready to enter the line. I wanted to tell him not to leave. But he had to.

"I am so happy we met," he whispered. "I won't forget this week. Everything was perfect." He kissed my cheek, as if to say goodbye to a childhood friend. Tears formed in the corners of my eyes. I firmed up my face and forced them back.

My mind swam in a circle of rough waters. Confusion overcame me as my reflection starred back from his eyes. How had I become a foolish schoolgirl? In one second, I thought it was best if we never met again. In the next, I didn't want to ever let him go. Electricity surged between us. He felt it too. I did not want to lose that spark.

Derek collected his items and as he swung the laptop case over his shoulder I asked, "So, when will I see you again?" My tone was lighthearted, but inside I seriously wanted to know.

"You're working on my account, remember? Soon. Very soon."

I smiled weakly. "Oh, of course. I don't know what I was thinking. But, even so," I looked down at my brown leather pumps, "It probably won't be often."

As he started to walk away, he turned back and winked. "I wouldn't say that."

I stayed until he was out of sight.

I already missed him, or at least the thought of him, before

I left the airport.

My life had transformed, from dull days to a living dream, and I did not want it to end. Yet, guilt lay in the pit of my stomach—guilt for wanting him so desperately, being afraid to tell him and scared of the repercussions, both professionally and personally. My heart could not endure another disappointment.

I returned to the hotel. I plopped my purse on the desk and started searching for my cell phone. I had a missed call from my mom.

"Hi, honey. I am so sorry I missed your call. I was up in the attic, cleaning. I know, really? On a Sunday night. I got in the mood and figured, why not. Anyway, I am looking forward to seeing you. Call me when you get home Friday. I love you."

In the attic? What's up there? Is it worth cleaning the attic? I deleted the message and noticed that the light on the hotel phone was blinking. I tossed my phone onto the bed and listened to the message.

"Hi, there," Derek said. "I know, I've already called you and I haven't even left the ground yet. I thought I'd leave you a message at the hotel so you would get it when you got back. Hopefully, a little surprise. I will miss you. I wanted to let you know. Thank you for a fabulous week. You are amazing. I'll call. Oh, and don't worry so much."

I replayed the message four times. My heart thumped like a drum pounding the rhythm of an African dance. My mind carried a new sensation—a chaotic peace—excitement, with an odd sense of balance. I put the phone back on the receiver, but did not erase the message. Not yet. It was a little piece of him that I had, at least for a little while.

On Thursday, we met with the last client. I did not have any problems persuading them. Over the week, only one client decided against staying with Jameson, Nedman & Farms. They were a small account. Even with this, I was proud of what I had accomplished. Nedman & Farms was a minimal casualty.

I stressed over whether we could live up to all the

commitments and promises I had made during the meetings, but there were no other alternatives. I was grateful to be a part of the process, to build new relationships and to create hope among my co-workers. They inspired me. I still had no understanding of the issues associated with Barry, but it did not affect my tasks and I decided that the details weren't relevant. Even with so many positives to celebrate, disappointment lingered.

Before leaving the office, I held a short meeting with the staff to discuss the week's events.

"Natalie," Marcie started. "We want to thank you. For cleaning up this mess. You are awesome, and we all wish you could stay."

"On the contrary. You're the ones that made this work," I stressed. "Thank you." *If they only realized how they helped fix me a little too.*

"Ask Mr. Beatler for a transfer."

"I'll think on it," I chuckled, visualizing the shock on his face if I'd asked.

I collected my purse and folders, said my goodbyes and headed to the hotel. I packed my clothes, my heart growing heavy realizing that Derek sat in his New York City office, on the opposite coast. I wondered what he might be doing—reading a proposal, listening to a dreadful presentation, checking his email. Maybe even thinking about me. *I hope.*

He had not called since leaving on Wednesday. I sat up for as long as I could each night, daydreaming about him, and listened to his voicemail multiple times. But, it too, had been deleted.

Friday arrived and I stood anxiously at the terminal waiting to board the plane. I would miss my temporary home, but I also longed for my apartment and to see my mother and Sara.

In Atlanta, I tried to find something for my mother. I still planned on driving to her house in West Palm Beach the next day and wanted to bring her a gift. *Shopping for her is always a challenge. She doesn't wear jewelry and has too many household items. Clothes are completely out. Books are boring, and she doesn't watch movies.* I could not find a single thing. I decided to buy her a plant at the nursery on the way to her house. *Not flowers. Because they die. A plant. That will be good.*

My little car sat waiting for me covered in pollen. A tired woman stared back from the rearview mirror. My hair stood up like a mini version of Edward Scissorhands. My makeup had disappeared and dark canyons had replaced my eyes.

Juggling my two suitcases, laptop and purse, with the mail clinched between my teeth, I struggled to open my apartment door. I held it with one foot, eventually dropping everything on the floor. Out of the corner of my eye, I spotted it—the answering machine blinking. I clicked play and the first message began.

"Natalie? Natalie, are you there?" my mother's voice squeaked through the speaker. "Are you screening your calls? I thought you were getting home at nine and it's almost midnight. I am worried. Call me as soon as you get this."

My flight left San Francisco at 9 a.m. I was sure I told her right, but all of a sudden, my stomach lurched like I had eaten a rotten egg. *What if mom called the police?*

Reluctantly, I played the second message.

"Natalie, it's your dad. Your crazy mother called me, shouting. I know that's not unusual, but she said you told her you'd be home by 9 p.m. I tried to remind her when we were arguing last night that she had told me earlier that your flight left at 9 a.m. I also explained that, with the layovers, you'd probably get back late. Anyway, she doesn't believe a word I say. I don't even know why she called me. But, anyway, would you please call her when you get in. Oh, and call me, too. We need to talk. I love you."

Well, at least he understood the times. It angered and disgusted me thinking about that awful woman marrying daddy.

I went to the kitchen, poured some flat Diet Coke and sat down by the phone. The Coke tasted like dirty water, but I drank it just the same. I took a couple of deep breaths preparing for the third degree and dialed my mother's number. She answered in tears.

"Where have you been?" she insisted.

"I told you that my flight left at 9 in the morning, not that I was getting home at 9 at night. I had a three hour layover in Houston and a two hour layover in Atlanta. And, the Atlanta flight was delayed. I should have called you during the day to give you an update."

"Yes, that would have been considerate. I've been worried sick. Figured someone kidnapped you or something or you were stranded in that God forsaken state, now that your father and his woman will be occupying the place. I don't like this flying thing and you going off by yourself."

"I know. I'm home and I am safe. Are we still on for tomorrow?" I tried desperately to stay calm and positive. *I am so tired.* If I wasn't too careful, I could slip into a "tone," as my mother called it. So, I diligently strived to act chipper.

"I don't want you to drive up here. You just got back from traveling. You need to rest."

"I've been resting all day. The airport is not the most exciting place. I want to visit, catch up and spend some time with you."

"Well, if you really want to, but don't feel like you have to."

Here we go again. "I will call you when I leave. I probably should go. Daddy wants me to call him too."

"Oh, so now he cares? Okay, fine. Go ahead and call him."

"I still love him, you know?"

"Of course you do. I'm just—no, go and call him. I'll see you tomorrow. I love you."

I hung up, rolled my eyes and shook my head in disbelief. I've always had a difficult time balancing the love I shared for each of my parents. It would become harder after my father remarried. I wanted them both to be happy. Even after all these years, I wished the walls they had built around themselves would crumble, and they would love each other as they once did.

Before calling my father, I kicked off my shoes that were cutting into my feet. I plopped on the couch and the phone rang. I dropped it between the cushions, naturally. I figured my mother was calling back to remind me to drive careful in the morning or something. The caller ID said, "No Data." *Peculiar.* I answered the phone and walked over to the living room window.

"Uh, hello." No one responded. I heard breathing. "Hello," I repeated. "Is someone there?" Then, an abrupt click. Whoever had called, hung up. I slithered back onto the couch.

For the first time since I moved into my home, I felt uncomfortable, as if someone were watching me. I sprang from the couch, hurdled across the room and locked the door. I pushed a chair under the doorknob and walked around making sure all the windows were secure and the blinds closed. My heart weighed heavy as I considered that someone knew I was alone.

I grabbed the phone and dialed my father. He answered groggily, "Natalie, is that you?"

"Yes, daddy. I'm home. I would have called you sooner but…"

"You've been on the phone with your mother. Not surprised."

"She worries. I should have called her, both of you, during the day to give you an update." As I spoke, my words broke and my voice sounded shaky.

"Nat, are you okay? You sound different."

"I'm fine. Just tired."

"Well, I really want to talk with you about some things. Especially, Sabra."

"Ah, well, I want to talk too, but can we later? I'm exhausted."

"Sure, sweetie. Now you be safe and call me this weekend. I love you."

I wanted to tell him about the mysterious phone call. But, I didn't want him to worry. It was probably a wrong number, or something. Even so, as I crawled into bed I placed some scissors on the side table and tucked the phone between the pillows.

The next day, mom and I shopped and ate at a small café. Occasionally, she reminded me of the late night return from San Francisco and the torture I had caused her. She only referred to Scott once. I did not dare tell her about the mysterious phone call. Mother would call out the Army.

I struggled to make her laugh, to take her mind off things. I did not mention my father at all. Didn't bring up Derek, either. Not yet. If it worked out, maybe. For now, I wanted it to be my little secret.

CHAPTER 15

Sunday arrived, marking my imminent return to reality. A street lamp flickered outside my window as the night fell. Shadows shifted across the walls of my apartment until all the light vanished. I curled up in my bed, clients' files tossed on the floor. I had planned to finish my report on the week's events, but I was worn out. I could not keep my eyes open any longer. I still carried an uneasiness in the apartment since the odd call and kept the chair tucked securely under the front doorknob.

I closed my eyelids and listened to the silence, pondering why my relationship with Scott had lasted so long. *What a waste.* In the short time I had spent with Derek, I had experienced more passion and desire than in all four years with Scott. And, Derek had only kissed me. *So far.* The more I thought about Derek, the more I wanted him.

***

Steam rose up from the tub. I peeled the terry cloth rope off both shoulders and let it drop on the cold tile floor. I laid back, the warm and relaxing water barely touching my chin. The cool air hardened my exposed nipples. Candles illuminated the room. I started to close my eyes, but Derek appeared in the doorway totally naked. His eyes never left mine as he walked to the tub and stepped in. He reached for my hands and lifted me up, water dripping from my shoulders, breasts and down my legs. One of his hands pulled me closer, while the other slipped down between my legs and caressed my inner thighs. His tongue traveled down my chest, stopping to kiss my breasts. He lifted my legs and wrapped them around his waist. I felt his warm skin and his strong desire for me. He stepped out of the bath, carrying me, and turned toward the bedroom.

***

The alarm again. My eyes opened. *Why now?* Even though I had been dreaming, I found my hand had automatically crept its way under my panties. This was a much better dream than being lost in a cemetery, imprisoned in a pool or seeking a strange little boy.

In front of the bathroom mirror, I yawned, while haphazardly brushing my teeth. Not caring about anything much at all until my toothbrush fell from my grasp into the sink. "Shit!" I yelled. "It's not Saturday! Fuck, it's Monday!" I scrambled to find my watch, which sat conveniently on the side table next to my bed. It was 9:00 a.m. I was already late for work.

I darted to the living room and searched in my purse for my cell phone. In my frenzy, I dropped the bag, the contents spilling out. The phone lay sprawled out surrounded by all my personal items as if the iPhone had been violated in some way. *Maybe I should get a new purse. This one seems to have a self-spilling mechanism.*

I hit the speed dial for the office. As the phone rang, I clambered on the carpet clutching the items that had crashed onto the floor, clasping them to my chest.

Sara answered, "Good morning, Jameson Research and Marketing. Natalie Swan's Office."

"Sara, it's me. Running a bit late. I guess my body hasn't adjusted to the old time yet. Still on West Coast time," I chuckled half-heartedly. "Anyway, I am on my way."

"Um, Natalie. Have you checked your email? Mr. Beatler wants you to provide a status on last week."

"What time?" I shrieked.

"9:30."

"Oh, crap." I worked to balance the phone tight between my shoulder and ear, dropping everything else. "I'm not going to make it. Is there any way to postpone?" I asked desperately.

"I don't know. Mr. Philips is here from the main office."

"Damn. Okay. I will do everything I can to get there. Try to stall them."

I hung up. I pulled on some black stretchy pants and an olive-colored button down shirt. I combed my hair, deciding to put makeup on as I drove to the office. I grabbed my keys and threw the contents of my purse back in. I ran out, slamming the door.

I navigated through the city like my car was the only one on the road. Steering grew difficult as I applied eye shadow, but my last peek in the rearview mirror proved that I looked presentable enough. *I can make it. Only a few minutes away.*

I contemplated what I would say and then it dawned on me. I had forgotten the files. They sat lying on the floor next to my bed. I almost slammed the brakes in astonishment. It was too late to go back. I would have to wing-it. I grabbed my cell phone again and called Sara.

"Sara, it's Nat. I am about five minutes away. But, I forgot all my notes. Do you still have a copy of the package Marcie sent with the company profiles and schedule? Oh, and the names of the people we met with?"

"Yeah. Yeah. I've got it. Hey look, Mr. Beatler and Mr. Philips are still in a meeting. You might have a few more minutes."

I pulled into the parking lot and ran toward the building.

"Hold that door!" I screamed, as the elevator doors began to close. Ms. Messer poked her head round and stopped the door with her foot.

"Thanks. And, good morning," I said, pushing the third

floor button. I couldn't help but shift my eyes in her direction. She stood straight with her hands folded in front of her. I had never noticed how short and plump her frame was, like a female Danny DeVito. This was the closest to her I'd ever been. The metallic doors closed.

Ms. Messer got off at the third floor too. I had never seen her on this floor. *She must be dropping something off.* I didn't have time to think about it.

When I arrived at Sara's desk, copies of the client profiles were ready. I snatched them and trotted down the hall, as I flipped the pages. I paid little attention to where I walked and ran smack into Mr. Philips, who stood chatting with Ms. Bennett, the Human Resources Director, and Mr. Beatler.

Sheets flew into the air. The hard floor bruised my bottom. I sat in the middle of a waterfall of papers. Pathetically, I looked at Mr. Beatler and Mr. Philips.

"I'm here," I said.

"What the devil?" Mr. Beatler exclaimed. "Natalie, what, where are you going?" He turned to Mr. Philips. "What can I say, Jim, you know we're busy when we've got folks jogging the halls." Mr. Beatler glared at me as if I had run over his kitten.

I crawled around picking up the papers. With all the sheets crumpled in my arms, I reached out to shake Mr. Philips' hand. "It is a pleasure to finally meet you, sir. I'm sorry for my exuberance. Back from a productive week, though. I have some good news to share with you, um," I uttered, struggling to find the words, "after I collect, um, these files." My sentences sounded like a chipmunk with its mouth full of nuts.

"Yes. I'd like to hear about what happened. I think that, perhaps, you should take a few minutes, though, and gather your thoughts and materials," he cleared his throat, "and we'll meet around 10, eh?"

"Yes, sir. Sounds like a plan, sir," I said, papers falling from my grip.

Suzie Mott, the office gossip, made her way down the hallway. She stopped and smirked in my direction. *I can't stand this bitch*. Just like mail-boy Darren, people didn't like Suzie. And, she didn't like most people. Darren shared the mailroom and ego with her. Suzie had a knack of saying the wrong thing at the wrong time, like the rumor she spread about my fake affair. She was the niece of one of the board members, so there wasn't much to do about her behavior, performance, or, for that matter, her attire. Today, a mini denim skirt, a low cut purple tank with fake crystals and four-inch orange-strapped heels.

Suzie marched up to Mr. Philips, with a broad smile as if she knew something he didn't, but then turned to me, crossed her arms and said as she raised her eyebrows, "Did you know you have one blue shoe and one black shoe on?"

"Thanks, Suzie. You're so observant," I stated, dropping the papers. I performed an about-face and walked away.

"Some people just don't have any fashion sense," Suzie remarked sarcastically, batting her eyes at Mr. Philips.

I didn't care what Suzie said or thought. *If she thought*. But, the day wasn't going well. I had such an amazing week and accomplished so much. I had saved eleven accounts. I didn't want my clumsiness and lack of preparedness to lessen the excitement of my trip and good work.

"So, what happened?" Sara asked, as I approached her desk.

"Mr. Philips thinks I'm a jackass."

"What? That's not possible. He thinks you're amazing." I meandered into my office like a beat down dog. Sara tailed behind me. "Tell me what he said."

"He didn't say anything. I ran down the hall and smacked right into him. My papers went flying, and I landed on my ass. Then that bi—, um, Suzie, had to come along. Yuck. Why am I such a goober? Anyway, we are supposed to meet at ten."

"Well," Sara said firmly, "get off your ass and get ready. Show him what you're about and that he can't live without you. You've got to get that, um, what the hell does Mr. Beatler call it?"

"Don't even go there!"

"Okay, fine. Some energy, some spark. Come on. Get up. You haven't lost yet." Sara took a hold of my shoulders and shook me a little.

"Did I mention I have a headache," I said, shrugging off Sara's hold. "I know. I know. I'll get it together. I hate feeling stupid."

"You are not stupid. You are one of the smartest, most talented, people I know. I wish I was like you."

I mused over Sara's statement for a minute. Had I really given off that kind of impression? How can it be that Sara wanted to be more like me, when I wanted to be more like her?

Sara proceeded to collect the profile sheets for me and helped organize them, while I made some notes on the events of the week. Sara even had a pair of black flats in her car. They were snug but at least they matched. About five minutes before the meeting, I pulled out a dull, pink lipstick and the spotty mirror from my top drawer, and applied the color. I licked my lips and nodded, affirming my ability. I headed toward Mr. Beatler's office with a renewed attitude.

I knocked lightly on the door as it crept open. Mr. Beatler and Mr. Philips were lounging in the guest chairs in mid-laugh.

"Excuse me. Are you ready for me?" I asked, poking my head around the door.

"Oh, yes. Come in," Mr. Beatler said, as he got up from his chair, offering me the seat. Mr. Beatler returned to his brown leathery chair behind his desk, which was worn with the twenty-plus years that Mr. Beatler had worked at Jameson. As Mr. Beatler wiggled in his chair to find the comfiest spot, he said, "Natalie, tell us about last week."

"I have to be honest," I began. "I wasn't sure how this was going to go, meaning whether the clients would understand and give us another shot. The staff members were remarkable and taught me so much."

"Ah, Nat. You're being humble," Mr. Beatler said. "Jim, this girl here, she has it, and I mean 'it.' Nat, the staff all sent me emails about how amazing you were with the clients. You taught them."

"I appreciate that, Mr. Beatler. Eleven clients are sticking with us, only one decided to leave, Nedman & Farms. It's a minimal loss. But, for the others, we have a lot to do in short order. And, we've got to come through, or they will walk." I provided them a brief overview of each of the clients, their concerns and how the matter was resolved.

"Well done, Natalie. Well done," Mr. Philips commented. "Mr. Beatler told me you were one of his best and you've proven that."

"Thank you, Mr. Philips," I replied, as I began to get up. But, before I could leave, Mr. Beatler added, "Nat, I hear your father is remarrying."

Like an earthquake creating deep crevices in the earth, I could feel newly formed wrinkles on my forehead. *How did Mr. Beatler know about dad's engagement? It is astonishing how people find out things.* Through gritted teeth, I answered, "Oh, yes, sir. He is engaged."

"My wife, Marge, knows one of your mother's friends, Marlene. Anyway, they talked over the weekend. Give your father my best."

Without support, my legs would buckle beneath me, returning my sore bottom back to the floor. I needed to retreat before I said something I would regret.

"Yes, Mr. Beatler. Thanks," I said, as I left.

"Interesting girl, John. A little high-strung, perhaps," I heard Mr. Philips say.

"She's just finding her way. She'll do great," Mr. Beatler explained, as if he knew me better than I did. *Maybe he did.*

For the rest of the day, I locked myself in my office. Not even Sara interrupted my solitude. Finally, I emerged about 4:30 with my purse. I'd had enough. I had reached the idiot quota for the day. Sara sat at her desk typing. When I materialized, she scanned me and grinned, "I'm glad to see you've decided to join us. I haven't talked to you all day, not even about your trip."

"It was fine," I answered, as I opened my purse and dug for my keys.

"Well, did you meet anyone interesting?" Sara asked.

Derek flashed in my mind.

"What do you mean?" I asked briskly, trying to play dumb.

"Well, I mean," Sara seemed to hesitate. "I mean, were the San Francisco office people nice? Did you go anywhere, see anything?"

I eased a little. I felt so emotionally drained at this point, the thought of having to justify my time with Derek stifled me. I considered how quickly my father's engagement news spread. It alarmed me. I breathed deep and reminded myself that not every question people asked pertained to Derek.

"Oh? Yeah, they were great. Marcie was really helpful."

"Did you get to see any sights?"

"Yeah. I went to a lot of amazing places. Alcatraz. Muir Woods was one of the most amazing places I have ever seen. The trees are enormous. You feel like an ant in an endless forest."

"Sounds awesome. Did you go with anyone? From the office?" Sara grilled. "I mean, I wouldn't want to do all that by myself."

I agreed. Under normal circumstances, I would never have gone to those places alone. Sara waited for an answer and I quickly said, off the top of my head, "The couple of tours I took were organized by the hotel, so a group went. I figured, why not?" The response seemed to suffice.

I zipped up my purse, keys jingling in my hands, as I said goodnight to Sara.

"Oh, Nat, I almost forgot," she added, before I turned the corner. "There is a staff meeting Thursday. I'm sure Mr. Beatler will expect a briefing for the managers. So, don't forget your notes."

"Right. Thanks."

The wide glass doors closed behind me. Walking toward my car, I noticed the sky had turned a shade of purple, with streaks of red and yellow. The sun was setting in the distance, hanging weightless like a puppet being held up by strings. I wanted to reach out and hold it in my hands.

Tomorrow is a new day.

CHAPTER 16

I hid along the back wall of the conference room, feverishly doodling on my notepad. Infused in my thoughts, completely unaware.

Apparently, Mr. Beatler had called my name multiple times.

"Natalie, Mr. Beatler is talking," Sherry turned and poked my arm.

Embarrassed, I flipped my pages so no one noticed the amateur drawings filling the page.

"Natalie, would you, perhaps, join the rest of us at the table?" Mr. Beatler insisted. I collected my papers and dropped them on the conference table, almost missing it altogether.

Mr. Beatler started discussing the recent employee morale issues and missing supplies. Ten minutes into the meeting, I found myself running in the redwood forest and skipping through the leaves. The adventure played over and over in my head while my body sat limp.

"Natalie!" I heard Mr. Beatler yell, his fist pounding the table. The large wrinkle above his brow deepened. His piercing voice startled me. I accidentally knocked over Mr. Brown's coffee. He was the conservative Finance Director, who already treated me like a melodramatic teenager. *This will not help his impression.*

The cream colored liquid ran across the table and formed a small river of Folgers Dry Roasted that flowed to the edge and ironically dripped onto Mr. Beatler's polished loafers.

"Natalie, what is wrong with you?" Mr. Beatler yelled, his voice echoed beyond the small room. Mr. Brown scowled at me as if I had spilled the last eight ounces of coffee the world had to offer.

"I am so sorry, Mr. Beatler, Mr. Brown," I apologized. The others sprang from their seats and like a disturbed flock of birds, scattered in different directions to help clean up the chaos. Their efforts only angered Mr. Beatler. A pink, reddish color rose up from his shirt collar and slithered up the sides of his neck, reaching the top of his head. Everyone stopped in their tracks and looked at him. I popped down to the floor and wiped up the remnants of the mini-Niagara coffee waterfall.

"Natalie, in my office. Now!" Mr. Beatler bellowed, as loud as a roaring lion. My head poked up from underneath the table, like a cock-a-too springing up from an empty food bowl. I stumbled getting up and left the conference room. Mr. Beatler hiked three paces ahead of me, his large behind barreling back and forth. When we reached his office, the red blistering flames consuming his mighty face subsided to a dimming pink flicker.

He walked around his desk and fell into his chair, out of breath.

"Close the door," he said, between gasps of air. At the end of his sentence, I reached the doorway. I stepped into his office and shut the door.

I hope not all his anger is directed at me. I had found out about the argument he'd had with his wife that morning. I was sure that wasn't helping his mood. Nonetheless, I was the one sitting across from him, waiting for him to unleash his fury.

"Natalie, what the hell is going on? Have you lost your mind? Something is different, and I don't like it. You seem preoccupied. Where is your brain?" With a gasp of air, he rattled on, "You know, I think you're the best and you've saved my ass so many times I've lost count, so I can't believe we're having this conversation. You have got to get it together. Since you got back from San Francisco, you seem detached from everything around you. Is there something you need to tell me about that trip?"

"No, it went well. I thought I did everything you wanted. I mean we still have all but one of the clients."

I knew I had changed since San Francisco. And, he knew it, too.

"I'm not talking about your work," he continued. "I'm talking about your attitude." He leaned forward, eyeing me like a suspect.

"Maybe, um," I scrunched my forehead as I thought hard, "um, the big city got to me?"

Mr. Beatler struggled out of his chair and sauntered around his desk, watching me suspiciously. "What? Are you living in the same place I am? This is Miami—it's a small country, Nat. All I'm saying is that you don't seem focused. I don't know what it is and it may not be any of my business, but I need you and I need you to figure it out. Okay?"

He crossed his arms in front of him, resting them on his belly. He was right. Then, out of the blue, Mr. Beatler blurted, "Does any of this have anything to do with your father?"

If I opened my mouth, sparks would fly out. I did not want to talk about my father's engagement, especially with my boss. So, instead, I avoided the question by muttering, my lips barely moving, "No, no, I'm sorry. I'll definitely get it together." I turned to leave, but he raised his hand stopping me.

"One more thing," he started. "I got a call from Voeltgin yesterday."

As if a crater opened up under my feet, I felt sucked into the depths of humiliation. The fear that I had created within myself, the paranoia I had manifested, would now come tumbling out. *Mr. Beatler found out about Derek!* I'd tried so hard to keep it a secret.

My body froze like a statue. Fanatical thoughts ran through

my mind, like a lab rat in a maze trying desperately to escape. *I'm busted. What will he do knowing I've been seeing and fraternizing with a client?*

Mr. Beatler wiped the sweat from his face and continued, "They said they were impressed with you and wanted you to come up to their headquarters in New York. It will be only a few days. I figured, since you hesitated on the San Francisco trip, you wouldn't want to go. I told them that I would talk with you and let them know."

Relief washed over me. *He wants me to come. Mr. Beatler doesn't realize.* A crooked and devilish smile tugged at the corner of my mouth. *Maybe Derek is sitting at his desk, playing the same fantasies in his head, wishing I were with him.*

"I'll go," I said.

"Are you sure? I know you don't like to travel."

"It isn't too bad. I'd be happy to go. I've never been to New York City."

"Okay. It's set. You should stay a couple extra days or the weekend, experience the city. But, Natalie, I mean it. You need to get it together." He shook his finger at me and turned toward the window that overlooked the street below.

"Yes, sir. I'm sorry." I left his office, my subtle smile transforming into a grin that stretched across my face. My steps morphed into small skips.

I arrived at my office where Sara sat in my guest chair. Her arms were crossed and she seemed a bit put out.

"Well, what is going on with you?" Sara asked.

"Nothing. I need your help. I am going to New York."

"New York?" Sara leapt from the chair and placed her hands on her hips. Her face wrinkled like a prune. *This is out of character. Childish, in fact.*

"Yes," I answered, scanning Sara. "Voeltgin has asked me to come and assist them with their marketing plan."

"Uh-huh." Sara huffed sarcastically. "I'll go ahead and get your reservations together." As Sara left my office, I wondered if Sara knew about Derek. She seemed so calculating during our short interlude. *Nothing to worry about. I'm doing my job.*

On my way home, I stopped at my favorite stores to pick up a couple of new outfits. I couldn't remember having so much fun shopping. Everything seemed to fit, which never happens. My shopping spree left a huge dent in my wallet, but I didn't care. I even slept soundly. *I should write this on the calendar—squeezed into a size eight and slept through the night.*

CHAPTER 17

The flight was long, but this time, I wasn't fazed. I looked forward to seeing Derek at the airport terminal waiting for me. But when I arrived, Derek was nowhere to be found. I stood at baggage claim for what seemed like an hour awkwardly searching for him. Surely, he had not forgotten.

I strutted down the huge hall of JFK toward the "Transportation" sign, my bags rolling behind me. A young man with a sign—Natalie Swan—rushed over to me, dodging a number of eager travelers.

"Uh, hi. Are you Natalie Swan?" he asked.

"Yes, that's me."

"Oh, excellent. Fabulous to meet you," he said shaking my hand. "I'm Matthew Jones. Mr. Voeltgin has been detained and asked that I pick you up. He sends his deepest apologies," Mr. Jones remarked, as he led me to the limousine. "Ms. Swan, this is JJ Stevens. He is our driver, but also, let's say, a jack-of-all-trades."

"Miss. May I?" JJ took my luggage and stowed it in the massive trunk and opened the door for me and Mr. Jones. I had never been in a limousine before and wanted to touch all the buttons and gadgets. For the sake of not appearing like a child in a toy store, I sat firmly with my legs crossed and my hands laying tenderly on my lap. Meanwhile, my heart beat wildly.

Mr. Jones and I talked on the way to the office, but I don't remember what I said. We came to a halt and within seconds, JJ opened the door to escort us to the entrance. Mr. Jones followed, thanking JJ as we reached the front door of the building, which soared so high, I squinted to see the top.

Mr. Jones and I shot through the air in the elevator as if we were taking off for space, but hovered for a moment and stopped. The doors opened and people zoomed past. The office looked ten times busier than Jameson. I couldn't believe the staff didn't collide, they were moving so fast. I stepped out of the elevator cautiously. A palpable energy filled the space. Adrenalin rushed through me. The anticipation was like bubbling water ready to boil over the sides of a steaming pot.

Mr. Jones led me down a hallway and toward a corner office.

"Come in, relax. I'll inform Mr. Voeltgin you are here. If you need anything, coffee or soda, ask Janice, Mr. Voeltgin's executive assistant."

Once he was out of sight, I melted into one of the oversized leather chairs and began investigating Derek's office. Floor-to-ceiling windows took up two walls. His diplomas and awards hung behind his desk. Books and knickknacks occupied three bookshelves. He had a least four laptops sitting on his desk as well as a computer on his credenza. Software manuals were neatly piled in a corner and a couple of boxes sat full of various cords.

What overwhelmed me the most was Derek's scent. I sucked in the sweetness, relaxing into the comfy chair.

I spotted a picture on the side table next to a second brown leather chair. I managed to propel myself up and over, collapsing into the other chair. I picked up the frame, which contained a photo of two children, a boy and a girl, smiling at each other. I thought, perhaps, they were family, a niece and nephew, although I could not recall Derek mentioning either.

Hearing voices approach, I placed the picture back on the

table. This time, I flew out of the seat. Without a moment to spare, the door opened and Derek waltzed in. I had not seen him so dressed. He wore a gray pinstriped suit with an off-white shirt, well starched, and a charcoal tie with a small white diamond pattern laced throughout. His shoes were as shiny as a Christmas ornament. Three other men followed him hanging onto every word he uttered. He turned around to address the men, glancing at me.

"Gentlemen, if you would please excuse me, I've got company," Derek said, in a deep voice, as he herded them to the door. The last one, with words still spilling from his lips, piled out.

Derek faced me, hesitating. The intensity between us radiated for miles. Only the small controlled breaths of air I swallowed could be heard. Without a word, he walked, reaching out his hand toward mine. When our hands connected, he pulled me close. Our noses almost touching. Every muscle in my face disappeared. I had been dreaming about this moment ever since he left me standing at the airport in San Francisco. *Kiss me! Kiss me!*

"I'm so glad you are here," Derek said between shallow breaths.

After peering into his eyes for silent seconds, I finally replied, "Me too. Thank you for making it happen." My mouth reached his in a soft gentle kiss. His hands glided around my waist and rested on my hips. He pulled me even closer. The heat of his body and the strength of his arms seduced me. Within his grasp, I felt defenseless, yet at the same time, safe. Both of us deepened our kiss, and we were lost in a world all of our own.

Sounds from outside the office hummed. The sun shone through the giant windows. Derek teased my lips with his mouth. I surrendered as our kisses became intensely passionate. Sweat ruptured on my forehead and my heart pounded like a runner on the last mile of a marathon. My face grew flush when our lips parted. *Yes, this is what I wanted.*

"I am planning a fabulous evening for us. I won't get off

until about six o'clock. But, JJ will take you to my flat. There is wine and a gift waiting for you," he said, walking me over to the window.

"I probably need to go to my hotel and check in," I explained, uneasy with the idea of being at his apartment alone.

"Hotel?" He grinned. "I want you to stay with me."

Did he just say he wanted me to stay with him? My brain began working overtime trying to process his words. Staying with Derek was tempting, but dangerous.

"Derek, I appreciate that. But I'm not sure if that would be appropriate. I mean, you are still my client. No one at the office knows—" I tapered off and peered out at the intimidating skyline.

"I have two bedrooms. And," he said, teasingly into my ear, "no one has to know."

Reluctantly, I agreed, committing to myself that nothing was going to happen. I was spiraling on a journey that would result in breaking every rule I had created for myself. I feared what might happen if Mr. Beatler or Sara were to find out. I could lose my job or even worse. The office gossips would devour every morsel. *Did you hear about Natalie Swan? She's been seeing that Derek Voeltgin. I wonder what he's been getting out of it? Yeah, now we know why he decided to stay with Jameson.* I swore that I would not allow him to lure me into his sensual lair. With a quick kiss and hug, he sent me off to meet JJ, who waited by the elevator.

I didn't notice a single building on the ride to Derek's apartment. I kept touching my lips with my index finger, the warmth of his mouth lingering.

We arrived and JJ escorted me up to the apartment, carrying my bags. It looked just as I had imagined. Everything was drenched in white—the walls, furniture, linens, everything. It had a contemporary, modern decor. The furniture had hard straight lines with fitted upholstery. The woods were a soft maple. Chrome accents and accessories decorated the walls and tables. It looked sharp, but still like a bachelor pad.

JJ left after giving me a short tour. I walked back into my

room, where a magnificent package awaited me, centered on the fluffy white comforter. A deep burgundy paper wrapped the box with a large gold bow on top. A card sat tucked under the bow. I slipped it out from underneath the satin ribbon and opened the envelope. I pulled out a cream-colored parchment, and read,

Natalie,
    I am so happy you are here. I have been searching for you, and I hope that you have been looking for me too. This is a little something to let you know I've been thinking of you. Enjoy.
Derek

The package was elegant and beautiful. I laid my head on the pillow and stared at it for a long time. Then my hand crawled over and started picking the corner. Before I realized it, the entire package had been ripped open. I lifted the top off the box. Inside was a terry cloth robe, slippers and all the supplies needed for a luxurious bath. My afternoon was set.

CHAPTER 18

I shifted in the bed, the cottony white blanket moving with the curve of my body. Slowly I opened my eyes and looked around curiously. The clock's green glow read six-thirty. *Derek must be home.* I swung my legs out from underneath the covers and yawned, stretching my arms over my head. As I rose from the bed, I slipped the robe off my shoulders. It fell on the floor revealing my naked body. My afternoon was exactly what I needed. First, a hot bath, facial and pedicure. Followed by a long nap.

In the bathroom, I brushed my teeth, dried my hair and applied some rouge and lipstick. I wore my aqua panties and blue and white poke-a-dot bra. From my suitcase, I pulled out a pair of jeans, a turquoise cotton tank and short sleeve yellow blouse, covered in tiny white flowers. When I entered the living room, no one was there.

An iridescent hue lighted the living room. Two golden drinks, dripping with condensation, sat on the bar. I meandered toward the sinful beverages, but did not pick one up even though I wanted to drink the whole glass. *Maybe it would help my nerves.* The window and the glow of the city caught my attention.

A presence filled the space. I smelled him—that lustful

scent infused in my mind. Although I had been staring intently out of the wall of glass, the energy radiating from him seemed to turn my body like a mechanical puppet, until I faced him directly. His head tilted to the left and his strong chin pointed downward. His eyes were clearly focused on me and mine on him. Remnants of my dreamy afternoon disappeared with thoughts of the evening ahead.

Derek's eyes drifted to my exposed shoulders and then slowly to my waist. I wasn't sure where he was looking anymore, but I heard the air ease out of his chest. His eyes closed. *God I wish I knew what he was thinking.* When they opened, he moistened his lips with his tongue. I was certain we were imagining the same thing. My teeth bit my lower lip. The pain—a momentary reminder to remain professional. *I cannot let him consume me.* It was too late.

His attire did not help conquer the passion stewing deep inside me. He had changed into a white cotton shirt. The three top buttons and last button were undone, exposing a fair amount of his skin. His dress slacks had been replaced with a tight faded blue jean. As I regarded his ability to easily switch between professional and playful, Derek sauntered toward me, picking up a drink on the way. He leaned his head back to swallow. I noticed his strong neck and rough chin. My heart beat faster. My pierced lips separated so air could move in and out.

"I made one for you," Derek glanced over toward the drink, sitting alone on the bar. "It's my favorite. Do you like them?"

"What is it?" I asked.

"A Manhattan."

In a leisurely manner, I inquired, "What is in it?"

"Well," he started, appearing a bit proud of his concoction. "I like to use a rye whiskey, sweet vermouth, a couple of dashes of bitters to give it an edge, and, of course, a succulent cherry with the stem," he added.

"Sounds deadly," I led him on.

I walked toward the bar, but he grabbed the glass and

handed it to me, spilling a little on my hand.

"Let me get that for you," he said, bending over and kissing the spot where the drink had landed. His mouth felt warm. "Sorry about that. I guess I'm a bit clumsy around beautiful women."

I was certain it was no accident. Either way, I didn't care. I turned away and quickly smelled the cocktail, drenched in alcohol. My mouth touched the rim of the glass, dipping cautiously so the sweet liquid brushed my lips and warmed my mouth.

"It's good," I remarked.

"Do you like it? Really?" he asked.

"Yes," I confirmed. My eyes darted across the room, and I sipped the wicked drink.

"So, Natalie," Derek said abruptly. "Ever since I left San Francisco, I haven't been able to get you out of my mind."

"You've been on my mind as well," I said.

I carried my Manhattan over to the window facing the skyline and peered intently through the glass. I glanced at my drink, took a sip and whirled around to confront Derek.

"Do you think it is a good idea for me to stay here?" I asked. "I'm just not sure if Mr. Beatler would approve," I continued.

I started to place the martini glass on the bar, when Derek darted toward me in an aggressive manner. My heart felt like it had stopped beating for a moment as he took the drink from my hand and said in a low, earnest tone, "Don't leave."

Shivers ran up my spine and my throat shrank two sizes. *If I stay, he will have the power to devour me.* I was defenseless and I would not be caught in this awkward situation. I struggled to open my mouth and speak. "I think it would be best—"

"No, wait. I really want you to stay. My intentions are completely honorable. We can just talk. I promise," he pleaded.

"I am just wondering whether it's professional for me to be at a client's home, drinking Manhattans and looking out over this amazing view together. I'm not sure, but I think I have stepped over the line, and I am sorry for putting you in this position."

"What position? I wanted you to come. Why can't you understand?" Realizing his harsh tone, he breathed a deep plea, "Look, why don't I make you another drink?"

"Oh, well," I said, gasping for air, "I don't know. A second one would do me in."

"Well, I'll make one for me and you can just have a few sips here and there. Sound like a plan?"

"Ah," I hesitated. "Um, okay."

Derek went to the bar to mix another Manhattan. He poured the ingredients into the shaker. I watched his every move. His exactness and attention to detail were incredible. He returned to my side promptly with a fresh drink and began sipping it. I couldn't help but focus on each muscle moving in his face as he smiled, talked and squinted his eyes. His red velvety lips became wet with every sip. He offered me some, but I refused.

Trying to think of something to do besides stare at him and torture myself, thinking of all that could go wrong, I searched for a new topic. Noticing the piano sitting snugly against the wall, I walked over and admired it.

"It's a lovely piano," I commented, trying to remember the last time I played.

"Do you play?" he asked.

My embarrassment made me hesitate, but then I answered, "Years ago."

"How long?"

"Gosh, um, about ten years or so. How about you?"

"Oh, me? Heavens no," he chuckled

"Then why do you have a piano?" I wondered.

"Well, it was actually my aunt's. Aunt Marion. She played every day for forty years. She was very good and had even performed in some concerts. She met Liberace once. It was the highlight of her life. I can't help laugh thinking about her excitement when she would describe him. 'He is just like a Christmas tree,' she'd say, 'in the center of town that everyone had placed an ornament on.' She would always add that his smile was peaceful and genuine. He loved playing the piano and entertaining people. There was not one other thing he could do.

"Well, anyway," he paused, "she died a couple of years ago. She didn't have any children and no one wanted it, so I thought I would take it, out of respect. It defined her, and she was good to me and cared for me many times. It's like having a part of her with me. I love it, even if I can't play. I know this all sounds a little cheesy, but it's true. And, it makes a good conversation piece."

"I don't think it's cheesy. It's nice that you cared about her and wanted something of hers. You should learn to play. Your aunt would like that."

"I'm sure she'd be thrilled or she'd be slapping my hands. I didn't get her talent-gene and with work and everything, it's hard to find the time."

"It's important," I replied, "to learn about something, something else, besides work, I mean. Playing the piano, or painting or something. It's an escape, a balance. I wish I'd have never quit. I need a mental vacation." The conversation had turned serious. "Anyway, sorry," I muttered, "it's been ages. I wouldn't know where to start." I laughed at myself.

"I'd love to hear you play. Of course, it's probably out of tune." Derek banged a few keys. I cringed.

"Oh, stop. Stop!" I crouched over him. "Maybe you're right!" His touch on my skin was gentler than his blundering on those white and black victims. I reached around his shoulder and spread my hand evenly over the center keys. The C chord rang, in perfect tune.

"It sounds pretty good," I said.

"There is some old music in the bench, if you want to check them out. So, I guess that means you're staying?"

"Can I have a sip of that?"

He handed me his cocktail and I took a long, hard sip. My inhibitions faded. I opened the bench seat and ruffled through the sheet music. They were old and yellow, a bit dusty.

Obviously, he had never looked at them. The songs were classics. I found one that appeared somewhat easy, "Love Story." I studied the notes, closed the bench, sat down and positioned myself. Slowly, I began to play.

"Wow, you're not so bad," he joked.

"I can't believe I can even remember these notes."

"You should play again. Really play. It would come back to you."

"I don't have a piano at home and like you, no time." I continued playing, struggling a bit, but I was getting through it.

"Well, you've impressed me."

I worked through the piece, while he watched. It had been so long since my hands touched piano keys, but it seemed natural, like riding a bike.

I played, wondering what he was thinking. I finished the song but stayed on the bench. Derek sat down next to me. I stared straight at the sheets, the notes blurring on the pages. My eyes were desperate to peek at him, to see his expression.

"It's wonderful that you can do so many things. You should be more confident in yourself."

How could he know whether I was confident or not? And, why does he think he knows me well enough to say it? At the same time, I trusted him, like no other man before. He leaned ever so slightly toward me. His breath tickled my neck. He inched closer to my cheek, and gently pressed his lips to my skin. I slid off the piano bench and stood up quickly.

"Are you hungry?" I asked, trying to change the mood.

"Well, actually, yes." Derek did not stop looking at me as I stumbled.

"Um, I—"

"Oh, you mean for food?" he teased. "You are delightful."

"I'm clumsy and—"

"Amazing."

Oh my. Is this for real? I am a dork. The one that no one wanted to date in high school. I got my first real kiss at nineteen, for God's sake, and this guy makes me want rip my clothes off and fling myself onto the bed. What am I going to do?

"Okay, I know a place you've got to go to when you're in New York City and it's not far away. It might be packed," he mentioned, as we both stood up. He pushed the piano bench back to its original spot, offered me his hand and added, "Ready to go?"

I looked back at the piano, and then at Derek.

I had discovered something abandoned inside me.

CHAPTER 19

During the ride to the restaurant, I forced myself not to look his way. But, as if addicted to a drug, I found my eyes wandering in his direction.

"I want to tell you something. But, I don't want you to be angry," he started.

I wanted to close the window between us and JJ, rip off my shirt, straddle his body and kiss him like my life depended on it. His serious tone, however, interrupted my sexual fantasy.

"I was just thinking about what you were saying earlier. About needing an escape," he continued. "Why? Why do you need an escape?" He shifted toward me. Derek didn't realize what a difficult question he had asked. Under my sweet expression lay a complex woman, who did not understand her own dimensions well enough to explain them to him.

I did not respond right away. My brain tried to transition from naked Derek to thoughtful meaningful Derek. I stared out of the window, contemplating my answer. I couldn't tell him that on most days I felt insignificant, like an ant, a flea or a speck of dirt on God's glorious globe. *Maybe I am just a woman, with ordinary dreams, goals and feelings. As special as a nightstand.* The seconds flew by and thoughts jumped in and out of my head. He asked again, "Nat, why do you need it? What is an escape to you?"

I screwed up my face and put on a fake smile. Part of me wanted to share my feelings, the other part wanted to recoil like a snake and slither to its secret hole in the dirt.

"I think," I started, "everyone needs a balance. Can't only go to work, you know?"

"Right. I agree. But, when you said it, you sounded different." Derek placed his hand over mine and moved closer.

"It's just, sometimes I wish I was doing something else. I mean, I've got a great job. Jameson has treated me well, but I haven't been challenged in a while. Everyone has those moments. I am sure it will pass."

"I understand. Work can suck sometimes. What can you do?" He seemed to consider what he said. "I guess you could seek out another job? Ever thinking of moving to New York?"

"Um, not really. It's far away. And, cold."

"New York isn't far away from anything. First of all, you can take twelve flights down and once you're out on the street everything you ever wanted is at your fingertips—food, shopping, plays, bars, museums. It's the greatest place on earth. And, it's only cold for part of the year. The snow covers the streets and everyone is bundled up from head to toe. Perfect for cuddling."

"Yes. It might be all that, but it's far away from my parents," I paused. "I guess though, with my father moving to California, he'll be on the other side of the continent anyway."

"So, bring your mother. She'll love it."

"I can't move here. I don't have a job. Anyway, that's not the only—"

"I have an opening. In the marketing department." His face turned a wicked white. Whether he was telling the truth or not, he acted determined to convince me.

"What? No, no. Are you trying to destroy my career?" My hands moved away from my lap and crossed in front of my chest. His hand fell dramatically on the black leather seat.

"Yes," he said sarcastically. "I am trying to ruin the career you don't want. No, really. You would make a real difference. We need some new, fresh ideas. Keep it in mind."

Maybe I will. Although my job frustrated me, there were a dozen things on my mind. I wanted to know why the dreams had vanished. I didn't want to be tortured in my sleep each night, but for some mysterious reason, I longed to follow the path, to discover the answer. *What does it all mean?* The dreams provided an escape, and now they were gone too.

Derek took me to Roxy in Time Square. People were crammed in every corner. We were lucky to get the last table. As the food arrived, I gawked at the portions. My roast beef sandwich appeared before me, four inches thick of pure meat. Miniature slices of bread held the masterpiece together. No way could I eat all that food, but it tasted so delicious I stuffed myself with every morsel. Then we topped it off with an Apple Strudel Cheesecake. Cinnamon drenched apples nestled on a rich creamy mountain. *Heaven. Murder to my belly, but heaven.*

After dinner, we walked the streets—Broadway, 42nd Street, Madison and 5th Avenue. Lights illuminated the city and people jammed the sidewalks and toppled out onto the streets. Derek grabbed my hand so we would not be separated. We made our way back to his apartment at almost one o'clock in the morning and then talked on the couch for another hour.

My eyes grew heavy. I couldn't keep them open any longer. I started to lean my head on Derek's shoulder as he continued to talk about routers and firewalls. I threw in a couple "Uh huhs" here and there. I assumed he carried me to the guest room, because I smelled crisp laundered sheets.

"I had a fabulous time," I yawned.

"Me too," he leaned over and kissed my cheek. "Tomorrow we will have a full day. So get some rest."

"Good night, Derek." I smiled, as he left my side.

***

I found myself running in a thick forest, slashing my arms

as I hurried through the spiky brush. I mirrored a pasty white wedding cake, decorated in blood red ornaments. My skin was pale, drained of color. Scarlet lipstick smeared across my mouth and cheek.

Finally, I came upon the endless green landscape, hills flowing as far as I could see. I searched the horizon for the little boy, but instead Derek appeared behind me and called my name. Like a robot, I turned toward him, puzzled as to why he approached from the treacherous forest without a scratch.

"Natalie, so, you finally figured it out," Derek said. I did not respond. I studied the mysterious figure planted before me, like a block of marble not yet chiseled by a master. He continued, "Don't you see, this is not the dream. This is reality. What you think is your life, us, that's the dream," he looked around, back toward the forest and beyond the greenery. "You need to realize it now, there's no escaping this place."

"I don't believe you," I screamed at him. "You're lying! This is a dream. Where is the little boy? Where is he? You don't belong here. This is about him and me, not you."

"There is no little boy, Natalie. He's not here. He's gone. Forever!"

"Why are you being so cruel? You are not the Derek that I have grown to love."

"Well, you may love me in your dreams and may believe I love you, but here in this world, I don't give a damn about you or anything else." He turned away as though hiding his face from my investigating eyes. As he started to reenter the forest, his body seemed to dissolve, becoming one with the dreary darkness.

I fell to the ground, sobbing and tearing the blades of grass, which did not budge from the earth's hold. Then, the sound of the narrow slivers of green shifted, as if a soft wind floated across the top of the lawn. I pushed myself up, twirled around, noticing each person who had formed a circle around me—Sara, Derek, Scott, mom, dad, Mr. Beatler, Ms. Messer and the little boy.

"Why are you here? No one wants you here," Sara said.

Before I could respond, the earth began to pull apart. I dropped, falling and falling, my screams echoing. Faces tipped into the opening, watching me descend into the endless pit.

***

I woke to Derek shaking me.

"Natalie! Natalie! Wake up!" he yelled. "It was a bad dream. That's all. Wake up!"

"Derek," I said weakly. "Is this a dream?"

"No, no. You had a dream. A bad one. Are you okay?"

In his arms, I felt helpless. Sweat ran down my neck.

"You're okay, now. I'm here."

After a long silence, Derek gently laid me back down, my head rested comfortably on the pillow. "Try to sleep."

CHAPTER 20

I rolled my head back and forth on the pillow, scrunching and rubbing my face. I yawned. When I opened my eyes, nothing looked familiar. *Where am I?* I pulled the covers off and walked over to the window. *New York City. Derek's apartment. Life couldn't get any better.*

The clock read 9:00 a.m. *Derek is probably waiting for me to wake up.* I searched my suitcase for the perfect outfit—a pink Ann Taylor button down shirt, the most comfortable slacks—Chico's Travelers—and a white and pink striped jacket. After I fixed my hair, applied some light makeup and put jewelry on, I emerged from the bedroom ready to behold my sexy acquaintance. But, the living room was empty.

"Derek," I stuttered. "Derek?" I searched the rest of the apartment. Finally, I surrendered and plopped into the chair. *If only I had a white flag.*

Moments later, Derek appeared at the door, balancing two lattes and a huge brown paper bag.

"You're up. How are you?" Derek asked. I darted out of the chair and hurried over to him as if I had not seen him in months. He placed the items on the bar and wrapped his arms around me. "You're okay, then."

"I didn't know where you had gone. I, well, felt odd, I

guess. Anyway, what do you have there?" I walked over to peek inside the bag.

"Just a little breakfast," Derek answered. "Bagels and cream cheese. And, then, I have the day planned."

"Don't you have to go to work? I mean, don't *we* have to go to work? The marketing plan?"

"Oh, well, yes. But we can do that later. First, the important things—the Empire State Building, the Statue of Liberty, dinner at Sardi's and a show."

"Wow. That all sounds exciting." I turned toward Derek and smiled. "Thank you, Derek."

"I like the way you say my name."

"Derek," I repeated. Stress flooded his face. "Derek, are you okay? What's wrong?" I approached him, reaching out my hand.

"Um, it's nothing. Just tired," he shrugged.

"We don't have to go anywhere. I'm happy just being here with you."

"No, no. That's not it. I want to go. I've planned the whole day."

"Okay. You seem—different," I hesitated.

"Last night. Do you remember?"

"Remember? Oh, no, I didn't do something stupid and now you think I'm a jerk or whacked out or crazy? Was it my bad piano playing or my ridiculous paranoia?"

"No, the dream. You had a dream. Well, a nightmare. It scared the hell out of me. I woke up with you screaming across the apartment, and ran over to your room. You seemed to be better when I finally left, but still…I, well…"

"Oh, no," my heart tightened. I remembered. A wave of embarrassment rushed over me. "I'm sorry. I, I don't know why I'm having them."

"Them? You've had more? How many? How often?" Worry shook his voice.

"Derek, it's okay. I mean, I appreciate your concern, but I've had them on and off since I was a child. I thought that they had stopped, but a few weeks ago, they started up again.

When we met, they seemed to disappear, but—"

"You said my name. In the dream. You screamed it. You sounded angry. Do you remember why?"

I stared out of the window, trying to remember. Each dream seemed to morph into one another. I recalled a circle of people and falling into an abyss.

"You didn't want me. You told me that the dream wasn't a dream and what I thought was real, wasn't. You didn't know me or care about me. Then, everyone close to me let me fall." I slumped into the couch and began to cry.

"Natalie that was the dream. This is reality."

"That's not all. The dreams center on a little boy. I keep following him," I explained. "We end up in a cemetery or an endless field, where you can't find your way out. Dead or lost."

"You're neither. I just wanted to make sure I hadn't done anything to give you nightmares."

"Oh, God, no. You're the only thing keeping me going."

We held onto each other like Humphrey Bogart and Lauren Bacall, as if nothing else mattered. Our soft breaths floated up and hovered, creating a cocoon around us. The temperature began to rise in our secret bubble. Passion soared between us, rushing through my veins, growing stronger every second. As if it was the last thing he would ever say, Derek whispered, "I love you, Natalie."

The three words erupted in my ears. His body trembled. For the first time, I was in control. I knew exactly what I wanted.

"I love you, too," I said.

Fighting my temptation to whisk him away to his bed, I seized his hand and off we went for a day of adventure.

When we returned—bellies full and hearts pounding—we stumbled into the apartment, laughing, clutching each other. The drinks from Sardi's were still lingering in my head. We had seen an amazing show—*Phantom*. The romance, seductive overtones and mystery had swept me away into another dimension, where work and friends and parents didn't exist.

Just me and the man I loved.

Once my spaghetti arms and legs hit the soft couch, my eyes began to sag and tire. Derek rambled on about some project. I yawned uncontrollably and then found myself snuggled in my bed. Alone and disappointed. The timing wasn't right, especially since I was half asleep and tipsy.

On Sunday, I began working on the marketing plan. The stress of not researching the matter before the trip and not using my time wisely, began to worry me. I had let go. But now, I grew concerned that I would regret my indulgences. Tuesday morning would arrive before I could blink, and I had to have something to show Mr. Beatler.

I sat at the edge of the couch, my laptop balancing on my knees, and began to type. All the Voeltgin files were sprawled out on the coffee table like a paper tablecloth. I thought, looked at the ceiling, thought, and then typed. Flipped through files, read notes, and typed again.

Derek walked in, still wearing his pajamas and slippers. His bare chest distracted me. Small dark stubbles had begun to appear on his unshaven face. He was a picture out of GQ.

"Good morning," Derek said, encircling me with his arms. "What on earth are you working on? It is so early. I think we should get some breakfast and take a nap."

"Nap? Breakfast? Are you crazy? Someone has to do this marketing plan. The reason I am here? It's not all for fun and games you know?" I paused for a moment, realizing how direct I sounded and then continued, "Now, don't get me wrong, I've had an amazing time, but I need a few hours to get this started and still need to meet with your staff tomorrow."

"Okay, okay. You are being entirely too serious. How 'bout a mimosa?"

"What? No!" Once I got in my groove, no one could get me out until I had accomplished my mission.

"Don't work. I want you to be with me. There is still so much for us to do." Derek went to the kitchen and returned with two mimosas.

"Derek, I want to be with you too. But, I have to show Mr.

Beatler something when I get back. I can't come home empty handed. If I can work for a while, I can get this done pretty fast and then we'll have time to do some things. Okay?"

His face drooped, and his smiled transformed into a disappointed frown. "Okay, I will be in my room. I'll shower, get dressed, check my emails and come back out. Maybe by then, you'll be done."

I nodded, secretly thinking that there was no way I would be finished that quickly. Derek began to walk to his room, but stopped and asked, "Your dreams better last night? I didn't have to run over at 3 a.m." I smiled, nodded and turned my attention to the computer screen to resume typing.

Within a couple minutes, my cell phone started ringing. I sighed and rolled my eyes. *I don't want to talk to anyone. I just want to get this work done.*

I moved the pile of files that were on my lap to the corner of the coffee table and scurried over to the side chair, where my purse sat nestled among the cushions and pillows. Surprisingly, the phone lay at the top. I answered it. "Hi, daddy."

"Hi, Nat."

"What's up?"

"Well," he started," I had mentioned to you when we talked last that I really wanted to chat with you about some things."

"Oh, okay. Well, I am in New York City right now, for business. But I will be coming back on Tuesday. Maybe we can find some time after that."

"New York City? I didn't know you were going there. You sure are doing a lot more traveling for your job."

"It was kinda a last minute thing. A follow-up with a client that I met with in San Francisco."

"Well, I am proud of you. You're doing great. How about if you're old dad takes you out to dinner this Friday?"

"Are you going to be in town?" I asked.

"As a matter of fact, yes. Sabra has a sister and cousin in Ft. Lauderdale."

"Oh." My voice shrank. "Will she be coming?"

"Ah, no. I thought it would just be the two of us for dinner. Unless, of course, you'd like to meet her," he needled.

"No, no. You and I will be fine. Look, I'm in the middle of a lot of work that I need to finish by tomorrow. Why don't I call you when I'm back home?" I suggested.

We said our goodbyes, and I sank back into the couch like a chastised child.

Derek came out of the bedroom. "Did I hear talking out here? Hey, are you okay? What's wrong?" Derek sat next to me.

"That was my father. He wants to take me to dinner on Friday."

"And, that's a bad thing? It sounds nice."

"He only wants to talk to me about Sabra. He's coming to Ft. Lauderdale with her, to visit her family. I guess—it's just hard. I can't believe that he is going to marry someone else. I understand that my parents haven't gotten along for a long time. When I was at home, there would be days when they didn't speak. People complain about their parents fighting, screaming. You know what's worse? Silence. Little secrets that you don't understand. They try to brainwash you with *Bugs Bunny* and *The Three Bears,* but kids aren't stupid." I paused and sighed. "And finally all the emotions build up until you explode. You don't know what anyone's thinking. You wonder if everyone's crazy, or if it's all your fault. I have to try to accept this. I have to. He is my father and I love him. I guess I feel abandoned in some way."

My eyes were heavy like weights. I tried not to show Derek how upset I was about Sabra, but finally, as he watched me with his caring eyes, tears began to slide down my cheeks. Derek held me and reached over and plucked a tissue from its box. I blew my nose and leaned my head on Derek's shoulder. I glanced at him with big wet eyes and then smothered his lips with kisses.

He laid me back against the pillow, my legs placed on either side of him. He nestled on top of me. This was the closest we had been. All of my concerns seemed to disappear, as our kisses became deeper and our bodies intertwined. Before I knew it, an hour had passed. I could no longer feel my lips.

I saw the clock on the mantle out of the corner of my eye, and I almost choked. I pushed him away gently.

"Derek, I've got to work. Please. Then, we can—" I trailed off. But he knew exactly what I meant.

After a few more hours of work, I shut off the computer, put the files away, and turned to Derek, who sat patiently reading *Wired Magazine* on the couch.

"I'm ready for a drink," I blurted out. I was still upset about dad, and my brain had been drained of every creative idea, all of which had been included within the pages of the marketing plan. I needed to relax.

Even with my self-induced stress, it seemed like I had lived in New York City all my life and had been with Derek for years, still living like newlyweds, spending a quiet weekend, soaking in every moment of being together.

The afternoon passed faster than I had hoped. We spent the evening at the King Cole Bar at the St. Regis Hotel. Derek ordered us the crab cakes and the lobster tempura. The tiny corner we were snuggled in, provided a fabulous view of the Maxfield Parrish mural. Two stunning Vesper martinis arrived, and we sipped our cocktails and munched on the scrumptious appetizers. Instead of taking a cab right back home, we wandered the streets of New York City, hand-in-hand.

At the apartment, I reviewed my notes, preparing for tomorrow's meetings. My eagerness to put my ideas to the test resonated as morning approached. Derek didn't even try to keep me up. He understood that I was too focused to think of anything else.

Monday was a whirlwind, from the moment I entered the office to the second Derek's leathery chair engulfed me at the end of the day. I had met with the sales staff, the training manager, toured the facility and visited with each unit supervisor. I had so many notes about the company, I wasn't sure where to start. All the while, thoughts of my departure crept into my mind. *How would I say goodbye to Derek? Again.*

How will I function each day not seeing his face, missing his touch?

Tuesday arrived and I handled it better than expected. This time, I had a feeling that I would see him, soon. We sat at Starbucks drinking coffee. A rumbling echoed, and I wondered if it was thunder or my heart.

"I'll hear from you soon?" I asked.

"Totally. I love you, remember."

"Yes, I do." I looked back at him once I got through security.

The thunder may have been pounding my chest, but it also boomed from the sky. Moments before I boarded the plane, the attendant announced that a storm was moving into the area and if the passengers boarded quickly, the plane could take off before the storm arrived. Passengers collected their items and lined up to board the plane.

The plane pulled out onto the taxiway as the sheet of darkness grew nearer. The rain rushed past, cut only by the enormous wing. I sat in my seat trying to control my breathing so I would appear calm. All around the plane, chaos flowed like an angry river. The storm brewed, jostling the plane. The rain had turned into a massive wall of water, hiding the airport from view. The wind swept around the body of the plane as though it was flying, but it sat planted on the runway waiting for the thunderous storm to pass. I wished the pilot would have returned the plane to the gate. Not even my magazine helped occupy my mind.

Finally, the captain announced that they would not take off until the strong winds and rain passed, but that it would be at least an hour. I stared out of the circular window, the rain streaming down the other side. *An hour I could have spent with Derek.*

A bolt of lightning rose up from the earth, illuminating the gray mass above.

I laid my head back on the chair, closed my eyes and thought of Derek. Every seat on the plane was full yet I had never felt so lonely. I wondered if Derek still waited at the airport.

The plane continued to rock, the lone aircraft waiting out the downpour. It seemed as though the crew and their passengers were being tossed around in high seas like a ship fighting the roughest waters. My stomach rolled with the wind outside.

Thinking of Derek soothed the lining of my quivering stomach. As I fought to rest, the swaying of the plane's shell rocked me like a baby. I drifted off to sleep.

***

I found myself wrapped in white sheets, stretched out like a princess. The warmth of the sun beat down on me, comforting my core, which pounded. My heartbeat pulsed between my legs. A soft breeze rippled the edges of the sheets. The shimmer off the white sands cast a glow upon the shadowy figure that sat on the bed's edge. It was Derek. The sun glistened on his sweaty body and his chest grew wide as he inhaled the fresh air, flowing in from the salty gulf.

Derek rose from the bed, stretched his thick arms above his head and turned slightly toward me. My eyes focused and I examined his body. Breath caught in my throat. His physique was perfect. We fit each other well.

"Natalie," he began to speak, "are you okay?" He leaned over my swaddled body, the sheets hiding my engorged breasts and trembling thighs.

"Um, yes. You?" I asked, trying desperately to avoid looking at his arousal, which longed for another moment together.

Before I could say another word, the sheets had been peeled away, exposing my nakedness, inviting him into my warm, wet sanctuary. He carried me to the water and laid me down. Sand tickled my toes as sprays of water shot in the air and over our tangled bodies. Every moment seemed better than the one before, rising higher and faster.

***

As quickly as it had come, the rain stopped and the angry

skies retreated. The engines roared and the plane flew into the sky, heading for home. I found myself snuggled in the cramped seat, oblivious to the passengers around. *How I wish I had made love to Derek hours before.*

Despite my despair, I was happy to arrive at my apartment. No matter if the walls were bare and the carpet gray, it was still home. With my tidbits of life.

Every time Derek found his way into my thoughts, I felt like a bird flying from one cliff to another, looking down on the sparkling sea.

I had worked as much as possible on the marketing plan and decided that I could finish it at work and show something to Mr. Beatler by Friday. *Friday. What will I say to dad? How can I accept this new woman in his life? What will I tell mom?* One side of my brain had already determined that Sabra was the wicked witch of the west, while the other part, the logical side said, "You haven't met her yet, don't be so judgmental."

I continued to struggle with this conflict throughout the week, until the meeting with my father arrived.

CHAPTER 21

A walk along the boardwalk helped me think. *Be positive. Don't get frustrated.*

My father loved the Rusty Pelican. Each time he visited, his only request was to order their scallops. So, when I arrived, I was not surprised to find him already seated, drinking an O'Doul's.

"Daddy!" I hurried over to the table, widening my arms.

"Oh, Natalie. It is so good to see you." He kissed my cheek. I had missed his warm bear-like hugs. "Wow, every time we get together, you look more beautiful." As he paused, he studied me. "This time, though, you seem to be glowing."

I knew why. I had someone in my life that was in love with me.

"Thanks, daddy. You look great, too."

My father towered over me, at least six foot two. He always looked down on those he loved. I did not get his tall gene, but my nose matched his when we stood side by side. I became more like him every day and that was probably why we regularly disagreed.

Before our food arrived, I told him about my trips to San Francisco and New York, minus the Derek parts. I stuck to work related topics.

"I knew you had a good head on your shoulders, Nat. You are moving up. I am proud of you. So—" I predicted what was coming. "Natalie, I understand this whole Sabra thing is difficult. I wanted to talk to you because I know this is hard. And, your mother doesn't make it any easier."

The name alone made my stomach turn. *Couldn't he have waited until after I finished eating? Be positive. Don't judge. Stay calm. Be positive.*

Dad waved the waitress over and nodded toward his empty bottle.

"Why should she?" I challenged, as I took a sip of Merlot. "Make it easier, that is."

"What? What do you mean? We've been divorced for a long time, Nat. I think my life now, anyway, is mine." The waitress barely sat the fresh bottle down, yet dad already had a grip around the cold glass.

"She's upset and feels betrayed. She's so fragile. The news shocked her."

"Betrayed? Fragile? Huh, that's amazing," he smirked, swigging his O'Doul's. "Look, Natalie. You're mother's issues could fill a warehouse. We both know that. I'm not saying she's not a good person, and, yes, at one time, I loved her. But times change, people change. It's time to move on. I love Sabra and I'm going to marry her. She makes me happy and, believe it or not, I haven't been in a long time." He paused, wiping his mouth with the back of his hand. "And, I want you to accept this and support me. You are the most important thing in my life."

"Tell me something about her. How old is she anyway?"

He blurted, "Thirty-four, I think."

"Thirty-four? Thirty-four years old?" I repeated, as though I misunderstood. *Surely, he meant 54.* No, I heard him correctly. I imagined someone knocking me off the merry-go-around.

I had told myself to control my anger, but this news crossed my threshold. Without another breath, I launched, "What are you thinking, daddy? I can't believe this. I don't know what to say. If you want to go off and be a playboy, fine. Have it your way. I can't be happy. I'll try to accept it. But, I just think about mom sitting at home each night, alone. Thinking of you while you're out gallivanting around with a kindergartener. It's shameful."

"That's not fair Natalie. You don't understand everything that happened between your mother and me. You don't know what I was put through."

"Well, you don't know what both of you have put me through. The secrets, the silence, the nightmares."

"Nightmares? What are you talking about?"

Pretending not to hear his question, I kept hammering. "She loved you, and still loves you. So do I. I thought family stuck together through everything, anything. I guess I'm stupid. No matter how old I am, I want my mommy and daddy to be together." I drained the glass. "In some small way, I think all of this is my fault."

"It is not your fault. I am not marrying Sabra because of some childish fetish. I love her and care for her. I need someone, Natalie. It can be lonely out there."

"Mother would take you back in a heartbeat."

"That is not going to happen. I don't want to argue. You're mad and upset. I understand. I didn't expect you to jump for joy. I figured that you and your mother had torn Sabra from limb to limb without even meeting her."

"That's not true—" I pushed my chair back, with the intent of getting up.

"Listen to me. You are my little girl, and I love you more than anything else in this world. Marrying Sabra is not going to change that. Don't be afraid of losing me."

"What? I lost you years ago," I snapped, throwing my napkin on the table and reaching for my purse.

"Don't say that."

"It's true. This is the most we've talked in my adult life."

"That's not true," he maintained.

It wasn't true, but words flowed out of my mouth like a dam breaking.

"Just tell me you'll try. That's all," he continued.

"You want me to lie. To run around all happy." I acted as though I was talking to Sabra, being sickeningly nice. "Oh, Sabra, it is so nice to meet you. I'm so thrilled that you've come into my father's life, broken my mother's heart and tormented us both."

"This has nothing to do with Sabra and you know it. You're still annoyed with me for the way I treated Scott."

"What? I don't give a damn about Scott. I'm not with him anymore."

"Then who are you with cause these trips around the globe must be more than just some paperwork. What exactly do they expect from you in this job of yours?"

I was stunned. As I got up, the chair screeched along the floor, my eyes never leaving him. "That was uncalled for. I need to go."

"Natalie, stop. I'm sorry," he said, as he started after me.

"Dad, you need to get a grip. You go off and have your mid-life crisis. I've got to go live my life. The way I want to. You're just an old, sad man grasping for any straw of youth. Get over it." The hard clapping of my heels as I bolted out the door turned every head in the restaurant.

When I returned to my apartment, I flopped helpless onto the bed, crying like an infant. I had regretted what I said the moment the words left me. But more lay behind what expelled from my lips than my feelings toward Sabra. My own guilt and torment festered within me.

Building up my relationship with Derek caused my paranoia to run wild. Everything made me think of him. I daydreamed constantly, wishing to run away and never return. To start a new life where no one recognized us. The thought of never seeing Derek again felt like winning the lottery and then someone saying, "Oh sorry, it was a mistake."

My fierce words hurt my father. I truly loved him and wanted him to be happy. I just couldn't block out those childhood images of the fighting, my mother sobbing, the late nights and the silence. Part of my anger had been building for years. Maybe now I could move on, forget about the past and focus on the future. Stop the vicious cycle.

I slipped into my cotton T-shirt and pulled the sheets over me. My temples throbbed. A burning flared behind my eyes. As I snuggled in my cozy bed, I pictured the disappointment in my father's face. *How will I make this up to him?* Then, my eyes fluttered and closed.

***

Mournful guests filled the white tent. They walked slowly, like zombies unleashed. They wore black, and their eyes were deep pockets of darkness. My white gown glowed like a fluorescent light in the sea of blackness. I surveyed the group, trying to seek out someone I recognized. Finally, I noticed my mother dancing on the portable floor. I streamed through the crowd, a white comet floating toward her. When I arrived in the middle of the dance floor, I stood face to face with her. She also wore black. Instead of her soft worn face, her eye sockets were bruised and fallen. I turned to my mother's partner expecting it to be my father, but to my surprise it was Mr. Beatler.

"Where is daddy?" I asked, as though none of the oddities of the moment affected me. "Where is he? I've got to talk to him now," I demanded.

No one answered.

An angry rumble shook the earth and the ground turned to quicksand, my body disappearing. Before my gaping mouth was sucked below the surface, I called out, "Daddy!" in a desperate scream. Beneath the ground, my legs dangled. The stifling air caused my pores to seep sticky sweat. I kicked my feet, swinging them to and fro. After my head disappeared through the sand, it emerged below, underneath the earth. I was falling. With a hard bounce, dust flew up around my landing spot.

Grime and dirt covered my face. My mangled hair stuck to my cheeks and neck. I carefully lifted myself up, dusting off my arms and legs.

A new land materialized before me.

Rust colored mist rolled over the red mountains in the distance and gray rocky terrain surrounded me. It was hotter than the most humid day back home. I started to walk, the rough surface cutting through my delicate white wedding shoes.

"Ahhhhh!" I screamed. Massive prickly roots broke the surface of the ground, grabbing me, stripping off my dress. I stood in the open, among the claw-like rocks, in my white slip, bra and panties.

"Oh my God. I have to get out of here."

I scanned the dirt ceiling, hoping to inspect the hole through which I dropped into this new world. But it had disappeared. Dry heat hovered above my head. I couldn't breath. A red-sanded path grew from my feet spreading, curving toward an orange moon, the only softness this place possessed. My feet burned, and my shoes stuck to the sweltering soil. I started to run and almost fell, but stopped just in time. My calves cramped. My toes gripped, struggling to balance me against a rocky cliff. A tiny graveyard sat nestled between the mountains.

I climbed the dangerous summit down to the hidden valley, drenched in a steamy haze. *Why am I always brought to a cemetery? What is happening to me?*

I arrived at the gate. All the graves had been opened. Unearthed crypts and demolished tombstones were tossed aside like rubble.

My eyes moved from one dilapidated corner to the next, finally falling on the little boy, who sat on the edge of an empty grave, his feet hanging inside the root infested tomb.

"He didn't mean it," the boy squeaked out, barely moving his lips.

"What, what are you talking about?" I pushed open the gate. The iron burned my fingertips. "What is your name?"

The boy broke a root off the side of the grave's dry wall and began writing in the dirt next to him. Without looking at me, he insisted, "I should not have brought you here. Please go back."

I moved slowly through the gate. The earth shuddered below my feet. "I don't know how. I want to be here."

"Why?"

"To find you." I stepped further into the cemetery. The tombs lay uncovered and empty. No one else was there, except the little boy, yet I sensed I was the center of someone's attention. "What is this place?"

"Can't you guess?"

From beyond, a rustling in the charred trees forced me to whip around. "What's that? Is someone there?" I asked, investigating every burned branch, searching for the source of the sound.

Out from the red branches and floating dust, arms emerged from the murky mist. I ran through the maze of tombs, jumping over the open graves, struggling to find my way out of the cemetery. When I thought the gate would close on my grip, I tripped over a protruding tree root and fell to the ground. As I looked up, rubbing the dirt from my face, a black granite stone lay within arm's reach. In large letters W A N were barely visible. The first letter had been rubbed away completely. I stretched my hand to the letters, and gently touched the space of the missing letter. "Daddy," I whispered. "Oh, no, Daddy."

***

"It's daddy, not me!" I screamed, as I woke in a pool of cool sweat. My eyes were deep and heavy, as if they had sunk into my skull. I threw the covers off my steaming body and sat at the edge of the bed, wondering how I would repair the damage with my father, before it was too late.

CHAPTER 22

The next morning, I crept into my office and plopped down into my guest chair, my head leaning like a bobble-head. The park below was empty, but a flock of pigeons sat on the picnic bench, cleaning their feathers.

Sara entered carrying a huge stack of files and piled them on my desk.

"What is the matter with you? For the last few of weeks you have been out of it. You know, if Mr. Beatler comes in and finds you hunched over like a broken rag doll, he will be livid. I think he is going insane himself."

"Why?" I asked.

"Well," Sara peeked outside my office door. "The rumor is he's having an affair and a lot of marital problems."

"Oh, God, I don't believe that for a minute." I swallowed a laugh.

Sara stared at me as if I were the most naive creature on the planet and puffed a rough "Ha!" toward my direction. "I can believe it," she huffed.

"Sara, have you looked at John? He's a great guy and all, smart, the best boss, but nothing, and I mean nothing, would make me want to sleep with him."

"Well, that's you. Some people don't hold the same high

expectations. I wouldn't be surprised if he's got himself a little something wanting to move up the company giving him some…" Sara winked at me and smiled.

"Well, I refuse to accept it. He is married, an honorable man. I can't think of him doing something so despicable and disrespectful."

"Hey, I'm just the gossip messenger. Now you've heard the latest. What I really want to know, is what you are keeping in that brain of yours. You've been somewhere else."

"I had a huge fight with my father." Of course I had more issues going on than that, but this one I could share. "He wanted to talk about Sabra, the woman he is marrying. I had some pretty harsh things to say, especially when he told me she was, like, thirty-four or something."

"Really? Hm, I bet that didn't sit well with you."

"No. I know he hasn't been happy. Mom hasn't been either, but getting married? It all seems so sudden, and out of character, plus Sabra's younger than me. Probably pretty and skinny too."

"Bitch."

"Yeah, maybe. Anyway, I feel like crap," I continued, "and I need to make it up to him."

"Well, yes. But, you can't cover up how you feel. You're hurt. That's okay."

"I don't want him to think I hate him."

"Nat, he knows you love him. You should plan some Natalie-time. Take the weekend or something and relax. After you've had time to think things through, call him, when you're calm. He'll be in a better place too."

"Maybe." Finally acknowledging the load that Sara left, I asked, "What are all those files you so boldly placed on my desk, as if I am supposed to do something with them?"

"Not much, just old files that need going through at some point. Oh," pulling an envelope out of her pocket, "you got this in the mail yesterday. You had already left when it came."

I recognized the handwriting immediately. Sara kept talking, but I ignored her. My fingers fondled the corners of the envelope, knowing that a note from my soon-to-be lover lay inside.

"Well, I've got to go down and talk to Betty," Sara said, smirking.

"Betty? You never talk to her. As a matter of fact, I remember you saying that you thought she was the biggest bitch and would not be caught dead associating with her."

"Oh, I still think that. But, she knows Barry's cousin's sister. So, I'm sure I can get the scoop on what happened in San Francisco since you didn't do any digging. I'll keep you posted." Sara left the office, with an evil grin stretched across her face.

Relieved that Sara was gone, I gently removed the note and unfolded the letter. My heart escaped my chest, and the pounding that I had experienced in my dream on the plane spread across my hips and deep within me. I glanced at the signature and then read the note. An invitation to a secret rendezvous in St. Augustine with Derek. The timing was perfect and fit into Sara's suggestion of taking the weekend to relax and think things through.

I relived my conversation with my father during the drive up I-95. I reached for my phone multiple times to call him, but I was not sure what to say. I wrote a dozen texts in my head, but could not find the right words.

St. Augustine, 15 miles. When the sign passed by, the thought of seeing Derek helped push the pain and concern for my father further back in my mind. *I'll call him Sunday. For now, enjoy Derek.*

I drove down King Street toward old St. Augustine, searching for Granada, a small road running alongside of the Lightner Museum. The intricate buildings and the fascinating architecture of the Flagler College dominated this quaint village. Specialty shops and restaurants filled the narrow cobblestone streets.

I reached Cedar Street. The bed and breakfast Derek had booked for me was in sight. I pulled into the narrow driveway and parked in one of the three spaces. The Victorian structure rose up like a doll house in a young girl's dream painted in a deep pink and antique white trim.

I walked up the steps to the front door. Rocking chairs sat on the porch, and I heard water trickling nearby. A sign hung over the doorbell that read, "Welcome to the Dixie Cottage. Our house is your home."

A woman opened the door seconds later, before my finger touched the button. Her inky hair was pulled back and red reading glasses hung from her neck. Her snow-white skin seemed to illuminate the otherwise dark doorway. Not a single line graced her face. She reminded me of my third grade teacher, Ms. Mableton, whose beady eyes would stare the class down over the top of her readers.

"Welcome to the Dixie. I am Ms. Valor," she said in a strong Southern accent.

"Hello, it's a pleasure. I'm Natalie Swan."

"Ms. Swan, please come in. I have been expecting you. All your arrangements are in order. Oh, and Mr. Voeltgin left you a message."

Ms. Valor and I stepped into the foyer. She walked to her desk, which sat sandwiched in a cubbyhole under the staircase, to retrieve the note from Derek. I stopped only a foot inside, distracted by the furnishings and antiques adorning the living and dining rooms. My eyes scanned the mahogany carved railing leading to the second floor. Elaborate brass chandeliers bejeweled the ceiling and oriental rugs flooded the hardwood floors.

Ms. Valor handed me the card. I opened it, my hands shaking, as I read,

> Natalie,
> > Meet me at the Columbia on St. George Street.
> > 6 p.m.
> > > > I love you, Derek

While Ms. Valor searched the room keys, I sniffed the edges of the paper, remnants of Derek lacing the card. "Ah, yes, here is your key," Ms. Valor announced, as she turned toward me. I placed the note in the inner pocket of my purse.

"Let me give you a tour of the house. This is the parlor. In that small refrigerator are complimentary sodas, beer, wine and water. Please help yourself. In the morning, tea and coffee will be served in here starting at 8 sharp. Breakfast will be from 9 to 10 in the dining room."

We walked through the parlor into the dining room then out a small door leading to the back of the house. Water bellowed out of the top of a grand fountain, which decorated the center of the courtyard. Benches and concrete tables were hidden among the lavish landscaping. The sweet smell of honeysuckle saturated the air. Hibiscus trees surrounding the garden brushed the wood fence. A secret fantasy world popped up in between two classic Victorian homes.

"Please feel free to come out and enjoy the garden and courtyard. At night it is lit, a perfect place to relax, enjoy a glass of wine or have a chat," Ms. Valor said, as if she had sat out there many times. We returned to the house and made our way upstairs to my suite. Three rooms were housed at the top of the stairs. We entered the first door off the landing.

The suite consisted of four small rooms—the foyer, bedroom, sunroom and bathroom. Dark pink painted the walls and a floral comforter covered the bed. Lace fell to the hardwood floor on each side of the canopy. Inside the bathroom, a classic white pedestal sink rose up from the tile, terry cloth robes hung from a brass hook and a Jacuzzi tub sat under the window. *Pygmalion*, *Taming of the Shrew*, *The Sun Also Rises* and *Cat on a Hot Tin Roof* lined the bookshelf. In the sunroom, the sound of the garden's trickling fountain eased through the windows. On either side of the window, chenille flowed to the floor. Light peeked through the storm shutters.

I was in love. *Staying in this room forever with Derek would be the perfect fantasy.* My home, my life, seemed so far way and different, yet I was more comfortable here than home, work. Anywhere.

Ms. Valor turned toward the door and said, "If you need

anything, just let me know. Also, if you come back after 9 at night, the code for the door is 1975."

"I guess I won't have trouble remembering that. I was born in 1975."

"Oh, you are a baby," Ms. Valor chuckled.

"Ms. Valor? Could you tell me where the Columbia is, please?"

"Yes, of course. It's close. You can walk. Just go back down Cedar, turn left on Granada, then right on King. It's about a block or two to St. George Street, turn left there and then keep walking. It will be on your left. There are lots of shops and boutiques along the way you might find interesting."

"Thank you," I added, as Mrs. Valor turned to leave. She closed the door gently. Her steps grew silent. Like a magnet, my body was pulled around. I investigated the room again and without another thought, I leapt onto the bed like a schoolgirl at her first slumber party. A snug and welcoming cloud encased me. After struggling to get up, I opened my suitcase and pulled out a garnet colored dress. In the bathroom, while starting the shower, I spotted a note tucked behind the faucet of the sink.

Natalie,

Before meeting me at the Columbia, go to Metalartz Gift Gallery on Hypolita Street. It is next to the restaurant.

Derek

This is quite mysterious. No one has ever gone to so much trouble.

After my shower, I wrapped myself in the terry cloth robe and laid back down on the bed. That soft luscious mattress intended to hold me hostage. *I am a willing captive.* But, adventure called me.

I headed into the bathroom, applied some makeup, fixed my hair and got dressed. Before leaving, I sneaked a peek of my perfect room. *The prince is taking me to an enchanted forest, with tiny clowns and dancing snowflakes.* I shut the door and skipped down the stairs.

Ms. Valor talked with a couple that had just checked in. We returned smiles. I opened the front door, stepped out on to the porch and took a deep breath before starting on my way.

CHAPTER 23

Ms. Valor was right. It wasn't far. I reached St. George Street in about 10 minutes. Stores lined the street. Melissa's Intimate Apparel stole my attention. A pink nightgown hung in the window.

It would be presumptuous to purchase such a garment. Or, I could just buy it for me, for the hell of it.

I had never owned or bothered to buy anything so lovely or intimate. I usually wore a T-shirt to bed.

The next thing I remembered was walking straight toward the pink nightie hanging along the wall and lifting it off the rack. I touched its soft and smooth fabric. It was sensuous, yet classy. I cringed at the price and hung it up like the hanger had caught fire.

"Are you looking for anything particular?" the salesperson asked. *Only a body to fit into this, but I doubt you can buy that here.*

"Ah, no. Thanks. Just looking."

As I pretended to peruse the rest of the store, that strawberry laced nightgown would not leave my mind. I wanted it. *So, how do I justify paying $98 for a nightgown I will probably never wear? Hmm. I have never bought any real nightclothes. This one could make up for all those I've never had.*

A few minutes later, the nightgown lay in a white linen tote, which was free if you spent $50 or more. Swinging the bag and walking on air, I proceeded down St. George Street. I felt lifted, high above the cobblestone path, my face glowing in the sunlight. I seemed taller, more energized and empowered.

I arrived at the corner of St. George Street and Hypolita Street. The Columbia Restaurant lay directly in my path, with its Spanish architecture and ivy crawling up the sides of the building. The cream stucco finish peeked through the hibiscus plants. Ornate Spanish-style tiles spread across the wide veranda up the walls. A brick colored fountain, worn yet elegant, drizzled water down its sides. But that was for later. First, came my visit to Metalartz Gift Gallery.

The door was propped open with a ceramic turtle. Exotic jewelry and stones filled the cases. Shimmering blown glass and beads covered the tables. Brightly colored mobiles dangled from the ceiling and embellished artwork hung on the walls. So many unique things were crammed inside the miniature store. Mesmerized by the color and beauty of the objects, I peered into the store's menagerie. Moments later, I noticed a young lady hidden behind the cluttered counter.

"Excuse me," I started, but a small package lying behind the captured my attention. A cream colored note taped to the box read, "For Natalie Swan."

"Miss?" I'm Natalie Swan. I believe that," I pointed, "is for me."

She handed me the box. Inside rested a teardrop of gold and green amber. I lifted the delicate chain, the pendant swinging. In the light, the necklace glowed like the sun beaming down on a hot beach. I placed it around my neck, found the nearest mirror and admired the jewel against my skin. It was stunning and matched my outfit perfectly, as if Derek had peeked inside my suitcase.

I left the store grinning from ear to ear, wind rushing through my hair and my dress flowing like waves coming onto shore. I slowed my pace as I reached the restaurant.

Derek stood in the Columbia's intimate courtyard like a leading man on a movie set. In his cream linen pants, soft blue and green shirt and flawless hair, he embodied all that was dashing and sophisticated. He walked down the steps, reached for my hand, kissing it, his lips barely touching my skin.

"Hi," he started. "You found the place okay. I would have normally picked you up, but I thought this might be a little more fun. The scavenger hunt and all."

"Oh, yes, Derek, thank you so much for the necklace. It is gorgeous. It's the most beautiful thing I have."

"That's not true."

"What?" I blurted out, without thinking. Then I realized what he meant. "Oh," I said, blushing. "Thank you."

"I hope you like Spanish food. I love this place."

The hostess guided us to a small table, tucked away in the corner. Inside, travertine lined the floors and tile murals hung on the walls, depicting ornate vases and intricate flowers.

A huge pitcher whirled through the crowd of chatting guests, heading straight for us. A waiter mixed a concoction of wine and fruit tableside and then poured two glasses of the Sangria.

After the food arrived, I leaned across the table to get a closer view of Derek's paella. He piled a sampling on his fork and carried it to my mouth. My eyes widened as my taste buds absorbed each flavor.

As the Sangria started to take effect, the night grew darker and more mysterious.

Derek talked about his recent travels to Chicago and Boston.

"It is so cool that you get to go to all those places," I said.

"I guess. It can be kinda lonely. Living out of a suitcase."

"But it is an adventure. I have always wanted to visit Australia. Where do you want go, that you haven't been?" I asked.

"Australia is definitely high on the list. But, I am holding out for one place."

"Where?" I wanted to know.

"Sicily."

"Wow. That would be an amazing trip. Why haven't you

gone?"

"Well, this is a little embarrassing," he stumbled, "but I guess I thought I'd go on my honeymoon, when I got married."

We were both quiet for a few seconds, but then I blubbered, "That's usually what happens before a honeymoon." *Okay, I'm stupid.* Fortunately, Derek saved the awkwardness by asking, "Have you ever considered where you'd like to go on your honeymoon?"

"Well, I've lived in Florida my whole life and I have never taken a cruise. So, I thought that's what I would do, but Sicily would be great, too," I laughed.

"Actually, I haven't been on a cruise either. Sounds fun. Maybe a cruise to Sicily."

We finished our last sips of Sangria and waited for the server to return with the check. Derek reached his hand across the table and caressed my arm. My hairs seemed to rise up toward his touch.

We were interrupted by the waiter. Derek walked around and pulled the chair out for me. We moseyed down St. George Street to the bed and breakfast. The deserted streets possessed a restless peace. The shops had closed, but a couple of bars and cafés remained open.

As we walked to Cedar Street, Derek told me the history of St. Augustine, the pirates and the ghost tales. I listened to him like he was a professor and tomorrow I'd be given a pop quiz.

At the steps of the Dixie Cottage, Derek said, "I had a wonderful night, again. I am so glad we got this chance to get together. After your visit to New York, I couldn't stand the thought of not seeing you, soon."

"Me too. The cottage is incredible, the food, this stunning necklace. I don't know what to say. It's, well, it's been a perfect day. Thank you."

Derek lifted my head with his hand and bent down to kiss me. His smooth lips pressed against mine, reminding me of his tender touch.

"Excuse us," a gentleman said, as he and what I assumed

was his wife climbed the porch steps.

I backed away from Derek, still holding his hands.

The gentleman punched in the code to the cottage and the couple snuck inside. The damage was done. The sparks had been smothered. Standing at the front door reminded me of waiting parents and late night lectures.

"Perhaps, I better get up to my room." I stated, taking a step onto the landing. "Thank you again for a fantastic evening."

"Ah, okay," he mumbled. "I will come by tomorrow morning about 10. I've got a few more things planned for us."

He left me with a soft kiss. I opened the door and went into the cottage. After the climb up the stairs to my room, I fell onto the bed in absolute bliss, thinking about each aspect of the evening. The bag containing my little secret, my new nightie, was inches away. I fondled the corners of the bag and then pulled it closer. Pink tissue paper and a white ribbon wrapped the garment. I lifted the wrapped fabric up, peeled the tissue away and held it to my skin. *Why not?* I took off all my clothes, tossed them on the side of the tub and slinked into the nightgown. When I looked in the mirror, I wanted to cry. I barely recognized the reflection.

I admired myself in the full-length mirror. The silky fabric clung to the contours of my body, my nipples noticeable through its delicate cloth.

A knock interrupted my private moment. I panicked. *Who on earth could it be? Probably Ms. Valor wanting to make sure I have everything I need.*

I grabbed one of the terry cloth robes, pulled it on and secured it firmly with the tie. I unlatched the lock, opened the door and peeped through the narrow crack.

CHAPTER 24

"Derek! What are you doing here?" I squealed, as I tightened the robe's belt. *If he only knew what was hidden beneath this robe. How humiliating.*

The robe forced the satin to adhere to my skin. A wave rushed across my hips as I sucked in a deep breath. Derek made his way through the door, brushing me slightly with his arm.

"I was just walking and thought, well, I really didn't want to wait till tomorrow to see you again. I mean, don't get me wrong. I am certainly not trying to be pushy or anything, so if you want me to go, I'll understand. I, um, I've been thinking about that day in New York, on the couch, you underneath me. Ever since you left, I wish I had made love to you. I can't stand it. I want to be with you."

"You do?" I questioned.

He bent down authoritatively and kissed me. His hands pulled me close, our bodies fitting together like a sculptural masterpiece.

My love for him grew stronger each second. This love, this excitement, replaced all other feelings housed in my soul. I wanted him to kiss me until the end of the earth. To hold me like his life depended on it. *Mine does.* I wanted him say, "I love you." I was engrossed in our world, in a trance. I was unhinged. I had forgotten all I had learned and was a child lost in the woods.

We moved from the petite entry into the bedroom. He started to untie the belt around my robe, but I stopped him.

"I'm sorry. I'm moving too fast," he signed.

"No, that's not it."

"Then, what's wrong?" he asked.

There were so many things to be embarrassed about I wasn't sure where to start.

"Well, I think you'll laugh if you see what I have on underneath," I mouthed, my cheeks reddening.

"I was hoping you had nothing on underneath that robe," he razzed, flipping the ends of the belt.

"Well, there is something, and I'm totally freaking out."

"Well, now I really want to know. I promise I won't laugh."

With a wicked grin, he untied the sash, worked his fingers through the opening, crawled them up to my shoulders and gently slid the robe off.

Derek's smile vanished. He stared, not saying a word, which made me more uncomfortable. I reached for the robe.

"Stop."

"I look like an idiot."

"No. You are stunning and sexy. I just want to take you in for a minute." He continued, "I am so, um, happy to be here with you."

"Huh?" I asked. "You like it?"

"It, you are breathtaking. I. Want. You."

He brushed the back of his hand down the middle of my chest. Static generated between his touch and the smooth velvety fabric. He lifted the edge of the nightie and slithered his fingers underneath the paper-thin cloth. His warm breath hovered over my shoulders sending icy jolts down my back to the tips of my toes.

He left dozens of kisses on my neck and face as he teased my breasts. I trembled when his hands worked their way down to my hips and legs. Trying to hide my shaking fingers, I unbuttoned his shirt and slipped it off. His chest rose and fell in heavy but controlled breaths. He kissed me again and lifted me off the floor, placing me gently onto the bed.

Am I doing the right thing? I can't handle another disappointment.

I lost all reason. Any ammunition I may have thought I had vanished. Derek had won.

I wasn't sure where he had tossed the nightie. Lying beneath him, exposed, I felt scared and elated.

Derek kissed my neck, my mouth, and my breasts. Our bodies, inseparable. He cupped my buttocks, pulling me closer. I wrapped my thighs tight around him, never wanting to let go.

Together, we were like a conductor and his symphony, making the music of masters come alive. Each moment grew more intense. A mixture of confusion, happiness, passion, fear and hunger mingled inside me. I never had experienced this type of intimacy in my life.

I jolted when Derek backed away, wondering what was wrong. Then he knelt between my legs. His hands exploring every part of my body. Then his mouth did the same. He moved toward me, becoming enveloped within me. I could feel his heart pounding.

After we made love the third time, Derek curved behind me, our bodies sealed. A tear rolled down my cheek, curved under my chin and seeped into the soft sheets. I lay awake for hours thinking that my life was different than only a month ago. I felt loved, beautiful, rejuvenated, and safe. I was a new woman. Derek never left my side. The night passed, and I drifted off to sleep in the early hours. When the sun rose over the ancient city, a new life was beginning. My life.

CHAPTER 25

At breakfast, Ms. Valor's right brow rose slightly. I assumed she was surprised to have another guest. Ms. Valor appeared somewhat annoyed with the circumstances, but she could not refuse breakfast to my companion, especially when he was paying the bill.

A large oval table sat in the middle of the room, where two couples were seated and eating Belgian waffles with strawberries. While they laughed, Derek and I watched each other, both blushing like children who were accidentally caught touching. Derek poured me some coffee and we found a table for two at the far corner.

"Do you like to sail?" Derek asked, stirring cream in his coffee.

"Well, I never have, so I don't know. But, I love the water."

I didn't care whether we sailed, lay in the grass, stared at the sky or at a brick wall. I wanted to be with him, no matter what we did or where we went.

Derek had rented a sailboat for the morning. The cloudless sky blended with the blue water below. Derek skillfully maneuvered the craft. I didn't help at all. I peered across the coastline, the wind whipping my hair and the sun warming my face.

From a distance, the Castillo de San Marcos seemed to instill that same eeriness as Alcatraz did when approaching it from the ferry.

"Nat, look!" Derek pointed. Two dolphins swam along side us. Like a game of hide-and-seek, I watched and waited for them to reappear until finally they were out of sight.

We sailed along the bay making our way under the Bridge of Lions and back to the marina. In the afternoon, we wandered down St. George Street to the Spanish Quarter, popping in and out of shops. Stopping for a few glasses of wine here and there. I enjoyed every aspect of the day, sinfully satisfied. Yet guilt still gnawed at my gut. The secret world that plagued my nights troubled me. I was worried about the little boy and my father. *Did my dreams tell the future? Was daddy in danger or sick? Why do I have such a strong connection with the boy?* Every time my mind started to drift to those dark places, Derek would grab my hand or give me a kiss. It was as if he could read my mind.

When we returned to the bed and breakfast, it was late. The sun had set, the moon serving as the sky's only candle. I led Derek to the back of the Inn, where the fountain hummed and the water trickled out from the top. We snuggled on a small bench.

Derek's arm reached around me and fell lazily on my breast. Without resistance, I turned toward him, my eyes unable to focus, our faces so close. His other hand rounded my knee while his mouth commandeered my lips. Moving up my thigh, he reached the zipper of my pants. He slid down on the ground between my legs, tugged the zipper open and pulled my pants and panties off. The cold cement tightened my bottom.

His warm hands rubbed my knees. Inch-by-inch his fingers crept inward. His arms swept my inner thighs, simultaneously opening my legs. As he approached, heat rose within me and sweat erupted on my forehead. His tongue cooled the warmth of my flesh. All my inhibitions seemed to float away as he explored my most tender parts. I quaffed my moans but screams were fighting to escape. The water fountain trickled in rhythm with my fiery breath. I grabbed the back of his head and pulled him closer. *This can never end. Life can't get any better.*

Dizzy and disoriented, I found my clothes and dressed. Derek sat on the edge of the fountain.

"Nat," he started serious, "I'd like to, I mean...these secrets...I want to tell someone about you. This is getting hard to keep inside. I want the world to know how much I love you."

I had no idea what would come out if I spoke—gobbledygook or runny grits. I took a deep breath and said, "I think that would be nice. To let the world know how much you love me."

The next morning, we left. I sang along with Air Supply and ABBA all the way down I-95.

He loved me and I loved him. Nothing would take that away.

CHAPTER 26

I grinned like a lottery winner strolling down the hallway, engrossed in the thoughts of my weekend with Derek. On autopilot, I walked straight into my office, without a good morning or hello to anyone. I still pounded inside from him.

I passed Sara who shot out of her seat, running after me. I stood over my desk, easing my laptop and materials out their case.

"Uh, hello. Good morning," Sara remarked, with her hands placed on her hips. She studied me as if I was a foreign object.

"Hello, there, Sara. How are you doing?" My voice rose as I ended my sentence like an elementary school teacher.

"I guess the question is how are you doing? You seem a bit preoccupied. What happened this weekend?"

"Nothing," I lied.

"So, do you like him?" she asked.

"What?"

I realized my attitude was better than usual, but how on earth would Sara know it was because of a man.

"Come on, Derek? Do you like him? What's going on? I've been dying to find out, but, God, you are so secretive. Tell me!"

A powerful surge burst through my heart. My stomach turned as if I gulped a swig of sour milk. *Could the lotto ticket lie?* My head became hollow and the fear sucked the blood from my body. I narrowed my eyes like a hunting animal, ready to kill its next prey. Wrinkles formed around my pursing lips. My arms stretched out searching for the chair like a blind woman. My legs grew weak. I reached the chair in time and sat down before collapsing. My mind raced, as if a pinball machine banged in my brain. Thoughts jumped from point-to-point, pinging loudly as they bounced off the edges of my skull.

How did Sara know about Derek? I've been so cautious. I played back the conversations I had with co-workers the weeks before, trying to think if I had given something away. Nothing came to mind.

"How do you know about Derek?" I asked, without moving my head, shooting my eyes toward Sara. A knife plunged into my heart as I realized, Sara had known the whole time. *Is she spying on me?*

Anger boiled from the center of my body and radiated in all directions. The sensual thumping in my womb disappeared, replaced by a hammering in my forehead. It was like we were sitting on the sun. Waves of fire pulsating and crackling on the surface. Like an insect poked with a thorny stick, Sara recoiled and bolted toward the door.

"Oh, no you don't. You are NOT getting out of this. This conversation is NOT over! How do you know about Derek?" A demon possessed my soul, stealing all rationale from my mind. The tension in the room mushroomed. *Like a cat on a hot tin roof.* My body seemed to freeze in time, growing hotter than pavement under the sun's power. I was certain Sara's stomach would rise up in her chest and choke her.

"I, I..." Sara began. "I know about Derek," she said.

I stared, boring through her like a drill.

"Derek is a friend of my family." Sara's pace picked up. "Look, you were lonely and wanted to meet someone. Scott was a disaster. You and Derek would never have met, unless you were forced to. That's why I persuaded John, I mean Mr.

Beatler, to send you to San Francisco. So Derek and you could—" Sara stopped.

The room filled with a gray murky air. The edges of the office inched inward. *Solitary Confinement. Alcatraz.*

Oh.

My.

God.

Sara had set me up. Silence rose up around me like a shield. Anger and resentment overflowed.

"Did Derek know?"

Sara's eyes darted away. I wanted her to suffer the awkward uneasy realization that I understood and that she had fucked up. *Dance for me.* My desire to keep my life, especially my love life, secret had been violated. Betrayed by my best friend.

Sara walked to the window and glared down into the courtyard. She seemed to be searching for something to say, but nothing would make sense to me. Sara had crossed the line.

"Do you want to be like Ms. Messer, or do you someday hope to have a life?" she demanded.

"Where the hell did that come from?"

"She sits down in the park every day, alone. Eating her little sandwich and carrots. The only friends she has are those with big fluffy tails. Even they're not really because they only give a damn about her leftovers. Is that what you want? Shit, Natalie! You needed a push. Something to break down the walls you've built. You needed someone to make a move! To help you tear down the barrier."

"Sara, what I do or don't do with my life is my choice. No one has the right to interfere or play God." A virus started eating at my insides, as I heard Sara justify her cause.

Yet, I had said the same thing to myself. *I am afraid of becoming Ms. Messer. But, I will never let Sara know she is right.*

"Do you love him?" Sara demanded.

"Did Derek know?" I repeated, as my lower jaw seemed to shift uncomfortably. The tension in the room was like quicksand, difficult to maneuver in, sinking deeper and deeper. Sara stared me straight in the eyes and, with hardly a whisper, said, "Yes."

It was out there. My face felt ashen as I stood, using my desk for support. Sara turned and paraded to the door. With her hand on the door frame, she turned to me and added, "I only thought it would give you some happiness. To meet someone so special and that really cares about you. God knows you needed someone to make it happen. It wasn't going to be you."

She left.

Hard and painful tears streaked through my makeup down my neck. I tried to walk, but my knees buckled and I fell to the floor. I sat for a long time, reliving my conversation with Sara. The thought of Derek made me nauseous and disgusted. I was a fool, a silly girl who gave her heart away. *Again. Was he somewhere laughing at me, rejoicing in his triumph?*

This betrayal was the worst insult I had ever experienced.

After a while, a heavy and tired ache settled between my eyes. I pulled out a mirror from my purse and was repulsed at my reflection. I threw the mirror across the room, hearing it crash and splinter.

It is time to go. I needed to get the hell out of there and be alone to think this out.

I fell into my car, started the engine and peeled out of the parking lot. I shouldn't have been driving. My thoughts were warped.

On the way home, my car seemed to steer itself straight into the Walgreens parking lot. Next thing I knew, and thirty-five dollars later, I was carrying a bag filled with a ton of stuff I didn't need—two lipsticks that were almost the same color, a bag of 100 tea light candles for $4.99, a deck of cards with pictures of clowns, a *Star Magazine*, a pen with a feather sticking out the end and a lime-colored notebook pad.

If Derek kept a secret this big, what else had he not told me? Or, worse, what did he say that wasn't true? Was the love we made genuine? Giving myself to this web of deceit paralyzed me. *Scandalized.*

A victim. I just want to be home now.

"Natalie?"

What the fuck? Holy hell! I slammed on the brakes in the middle of an intersection. Horns honked but I didn't move.

"Natalie. Keep going."

I am not sure what made me do it. I eased off the brake and pushed on the accelerator. The car's speed increased, leaving a half dozen vehicles scattered in my rearview mirror.

Whipped and on the edge of madness, I dropped my purse and keys on the floor and walked straight to the bed. My body, my heart, my mind—none of it belonged to me. On top of the covers, I laid on my back, looking at the ceiling, like a statue, hard and motionless. I never thought I could feel so manipulated, so betrayed. I was lonely and afraid. Scott had hurt me and I allowed myself to open up again to another man. *Did everyone know? Am I the center of a soap opera that all the world was watching but me?* I felt like a speck of dust, a piece of sand washed away into the waters. As I starred at the ceiling, my eyes grew dry and unfocused. I shut them, the blackness offering a fleeting escape.

***

My dress was ripped. Long slashes cut the delicate fabric as if tearing a sheet of tissue paper. No one was in sight for as far as I could see. The green grass that surrounded me morphed into burnt prickling blades jutting from the earth. Beyond the horizon, dark clouds formed, and the wind swiftly carried them closer. Lightning danced in the sky as thunderous yells echoed. My heart jumped as electric slivers of light whipped at the ground. Repeated slashes of chrome and iridescent knives from the sky attacked me. I ran, sweat drenching my gown.

The further I went, the more tired my body became. Every muscle in me ached as I struggled up a hillside. I reached the top where fields of tombstones covered the earth. White markers blocked my path for miles. Shocked, I stepped backward, lost my balance and fell down the side of the mountain, landing right in front of the mysterious gate. It was raining hard now, and I tried to wipe away the flowing stream of water from my eyes so I could focus. Through the blur of rain and sweat and exhaustion, a shadowy figure stood beyond the gate. He was wearing a black suit and hat. He looked at me and then turned away. He disappeared under the ground, as though slipping down a slide at the playground.

I reached for a thorny branch, pricking my hand. Blood dripped on the barren ground. I stood firm, looking at the gate. I swallowed hard, closed my eyes and listened. The gate twisted, its screech piercing my ears. I walked to it and placed my hands on the latch. *Make it stop!* But the sound did not stop. It grew louder, stronger, more fierce.

The noise transitioned into screaming. A person bellowed from under the ground. I retched, on the verge of vomiting.

***

The screaming became my own as I woke from the nightmare. Even though air flowed in-and-out of my mouth, filling my lungs, I suffocated within my own skin.

I don't want to be me! What am I going to do? If it weren't for the paycheck and bills, I'd never return to work.

I lay there, contemplating what to do. Finally, around 8 a.m., I peeled myself from the sheets, put on a blank face, drove to the office and arrived, disheveled and drained.

I spoke to no one. No one spoke to me.

I sat in the guest chair by my window for a couple of hours, until finally slinking over to my desk. I noticed a file lying on my computer keyboard, with a sticky note from Diane, one of the personnel liaisons.

Natalie,
    Just a reminder. It is time to do Sara's annual review. I know you are usually on it, but with your traveling and such, thought I would let you know.
                                        Thanks. Diane

I gagged thinking about Sara. I certainly had no desire to

work on her evaluation, or talk to her for that matter. All I could think about was, "Liar! Liar! Liar!" That would probably not make for a good review.

The longer I stared at the file, the more enraged I became. The pressure inside me intensified like a boulder inching off a cliff. I tossed the folder on the top of the others and switched on my computer.

A tapping echoed from my closed door, and I turned to it with contempt, hoping it was not Sara. Trying to resume my normally pleasant and professional demeanor, I told the person to come in, but apparently I'd accidentally locked the door earlier. I realized my folly and jumped up from my chair and yelled, "One minute. I'm coming."

In my hurry to unlock the door, I hit the edge of the desk, the corner jutting into me. My thigh throbbed. I tried to balance and clung to my desk, struggling to get a better grip. Suddenly, the files sitting on the corner started to slide off. I stretched my arm to catch them, but they plummeted to the floor.

"Natalie?" the voice yelled from the other side of the door. "Are you all right?"

"Yes," I exclaimed. "I just ran into my desk and dropped some files."

I hobbled toward the door, like a crab that lost a claw. I unlocked the door and swung it open. Mr. Beatler stood firm, with a sour grin.

"What the hell is going on in here?" he shouted, as he stomped into my office.

"Nothing. My files just slid off the desk and scattered everywhere." I inspected the damage, shaking my head. It was a mess. Papers spilled out of the yellow file folders. I reached for the first one, which balanced on top of another pile of documents. It shifted as I grabbed it. *Sara's file.* A number of sheets had fallen out. I bent down, picked them up, straightened them into a neat stack, opened the folder and laid them on top of the other papers.

I started to close the file, but something caught my eye. An old application, maybe from when Sara first applied at Jameson. I needed to take a closer look.

As if a steel pole shot up my back, I stiffened. Like Medusa transforming her victims to stone, my face turned statuesque. A blow to the gut halted my breath. If it were possible, I could have ignited a fire under my gaze. The application and file fell from my hand. I had to leave but had forgotten how to move.

"Natalie," Mr. Beatler started, "I was thinking about what an amazing job you've been doing, especially with the Voeltgin account. And, well, I want to recommend you—Natalie? Are you listening to me?"

"Huh? Um, I'm sorry John. I've got to go." An unknown force pulled me out the room. I felt Mr. Beatler's presence behind me.

"Natalie? Where are you going?" he asked.

"John," I said, my voice shaking. "John, I have some issues I need to deal with. I think I should take the day off."

"Oh. Oh, okay, that's fine," he floundered.

"Just leave the files. Sara," I snarled with a firm bite, "can organize them. Oh, and speaking of, I mean, here's the little witch herself."

Sara appeared at the other end of the hall. When I saw her, I was sure that Hades had invaded my body.

If anyone were watching this standoff, it would have resembled two gun fighters waiting for someone to make the first move. Dust and tumbleweed.

"Well, Sara. Sa-r-a. Hey, John, do you know what Sara's maiden name is?" I scanned the office seeing the minions gather around us. I gloated, egging them on. I wanted everyone to listen. To give them the soap opera they all desperately desired.

"Huh? What the—" Mr. Beatler exclaimed.

No one said a word. Sara glanced at Mr. Beatler as if to ask for help or a way out.

"Isn't there some clause or rule that employees must divulge if they have a conflict of interest with clients? Because Sara, here, used to be—" I slowed my speech and with a sarcastic delivery announced, "Sara Voeltgin." I repeated it firmly, "Voeltgin. As in, Derek Voeltgin. So, is he your brother or something because I don't think he's your father? I mean Voeltgin, not a common name, is it?"

Sara walked in a circle, eyeing the onlookers. Some of them may know, but most would not. Finally, she stopped dead.

"It's not my maiden name. Derek is my ex-husband."

It's hard to explain the few minutes that followed. So much happened in my mind that no single thought emerged out of the chaos.

Derek making love to Sara makes me sick.

Our audience stood shocked, mouths gaping at what they just witnessed.

Behind me, Mr. Beatler asked, "What in the hell is happening around here? No one tells me anything."

This plane was going down, and I needed to jump. *Now!* The emergency exit sign in the corner was my cue. Silently, I strutted to the door and pushed it open. I skipped, two steps at a time, down the stairwell, hearing the alarm blast through the building.

I hid in the park stuck between the buildings for an hour, thinking how naive and foolish I was and how everyone must think so too. *How is it possible that Sara and Derek were married, that they set up this conspiracy so I would meet and fall in love with Derek, and neither of them ever mentioned a thing? How conniving and manipulative. Why wouldn't she just tell me? Didn't she think I would discover the truth eventually? And, Derek, what kind of man goes along with something like this?*

From the picnic table, I peered up at my office, at the huge palladium window and wondered if anyone was looking down on me saying, "Well it's about time, she's turned into the old maid, the weird woman who no one wants to talk to."

What am I supposed to do? Go back up there and look like an idiot? Go home and cry some more? I don't think I can cry any more. Call my mother? She'll just think I've done it again. Find a new job? Maybe. But what in the meantime? All this uncertainty was streaming through my mind, haunting the strands of hope I prayed were lingering deep in my heart.

On my way home, I decided that I would go back tomorrow. If I didn't, I'd never be able to. What kind of failure would I be, avoiding the truth? But, I did not want Derek, not now. I couldn't. I barely allowed myself to think of him. *I wish I could cleanse my body of his smell, of his touch.* It was too late. I wanted to take my love back and lock it in a box, out of harm's way. But, the time for that had also passed.

When I arrived at my apartment, it dawned on me that I had not called my father Sunday like I'd planned. *Shit!* I sat on the couch eyeing the phone and considered calling him then. But, our issues were too big, making this tidbit a blip on the radar screen. If we're going to talk, we needed to fix us, first. I can't pretend all is fine and talk to him about the Natalie-Sara-Derek triangle. No one to talk to. *Maybe Mr. Beatler is right. I need a pet. At least they listen and don't talk back.*

CHAPTER 27

After a horrifying day, which resulted in buckets of shed tears, I had finally drifted off to sleep, to block out the humiliation and heartache.

The phone rang. I slipped off the bed, bouncing my bottom on the hard floor. The phone crooned its high-pitched tone again, gnawing away at my eardrums. I was perturbed.

I rubbed my eyes and methodically lifted myself off the floor. A purple mark from striking the desk earlier embellished my thigh. I ran my fingers over the tender spot as I got up. The phone rang a third time. I tripped over my black pumps that were lazily lying in my path and realized it was 2 in the morning. My annoyance changed into uneasiness as I headed for the living room. *Who would be calling this late?*

A sinister glow hovered within the walls of my apartment, shadows from the street lights crept in through the blinds. It was difficult to maneuver but I made my way to the living room, and searched for the phone between the cushions of the couch, where I had thought I'd last seen it. Finally, as it rang for the fourth time, I held it in my hand, pulling it out from the couch. I sighed and pressed the "Talk" button.

"Hello," I answered, in a sleepy yet anxious voice.

There was no reply, but I heard something resembling

sniffles and heavy sighing. "Hello," I repeated. My heart beat in my hand, vibrating against the receiver. Almost instantly, I seemed wide-awake. A frail whimper echoed from the other end of the line.

"Mom?" I asked, desperately. After an eternal pause, it sounded like she cleared her throat.

"Natalie, I'm sorry to call so late. Um, I had to let you know. Your father," she stumbled, "is in the hospital."

"What?" I cried. I fell on the couch, my legs could not hold me. My whole body shook. "What happened?"

"Well," she started, dimly, "I think it's my fault. We were talking on the phone, arguing at best. I was pressing him about what's her name. Anyway, he started to breathe odd and then he was gone. I kept calling for him, but he didn't answer." Her voice stretched and faded as she reached the ends of her sentences.

"Then, Sabra," my mother said, "got on the phone and was frantic. She sounded like a mouse that had been caught in a trap, a squealing baby. Uh. Anyway, all she told me was that she heard him yelling from the living room and when she came in to see what was going on, he collapsed. She needed to call 911, so we hung up. She called a few hours ago to explain what was happening."

"A few hours ago?" I reiterated, massaging my temples. "Why did you wait so long to call me?" My desire to reach through the phone and strangle my mother caused me to sweat. I was infuriated at why she waited hours to call.

"I needed some time, I guess. I played our conversation in my head, shout-by-shout. I had to remember what we said to each other, the good and the bad, just in case."

"Just in case of what?" I interrupted. "He's going to be all right, right?"

"Well, that's the other reason I didn't call you right away. We didn't know what had happened. I wanted to have some answers before getting you upset."

"Too late. I am upset. So, did you find out anything? What's wrong? Is he going to be okay?" I hurled questions at her like the press core.

"Okay, okay. Stop," my mother insisted. "Yes, like I started to say earlier, Sabra called back. When the ambulance arrived, the paramedics explained that he'd had a heart attack. They resuscitated him and rushed him to the ER. He is in surgery now."

"Oh, my, God!" I sprang to life and started turning lights on in all the rooms. "I have to go. I have to go," I repeated. I stopped in my tracks and asked, "Are you going?"

"I don't know. I'm not sure if he wants me to come. Our fight was ghastly, the worst. I am so embarrassed because she was there and heard. I don't think I can face her, or him."

"He would want you to be with him, with me." I dodged from one part of the apartment to another. "Where did it happen?"

Mom grew quiet and then uttered, "Her place. He's at Kindred Hospital."

"Fine. I guess I'll be heading back to California," I paused. "Alone."

"Don't be mad at me Natalie. I already feel so horrible. I can't bear you being angry with me too."

My list of questions continued to flow like a preacher offering a heated sermon. My mother did not know any of the answers. We both cried, giving each other turns to vent, until exhaustion smothered our grief. I pulled a small suitcase out of the closet and threw clothes into it, not paying attention to what I packed.

"Please come with me. I'll pay for your ticket." My eyes were buried deep in my cheeks, heavy as weights from sobbing.

"That's not the problem, Nat. I just can't. I can't go."

We hung up. I sat at the small round table in the kitchen. *This is all my fault.* I ignored the dream's message that my father was in danger, and on top of everything, I did so with a man that doesn't even care.

CHAPTER 28

I beg Atlas to take the world back. My shoulders are not strong enough. The dreams revealed my father was in danger and I did nothing. I should have warned my father.

I called Delta and made arrangements to leave Miami within the next few hours. Sleep was not an option. I finished packing, focusing only on getting to my father's side. The surgery would be over by the time I arrived in San Diego.

After checking in at the airport, I called Mr. Beatler and Sara and left them both voicemails explaining the situation. Although they had my contact information, I left my mother's number in case they couldn't reach me.

I waited in the deserted terminal. My head ached like I suffered from a hangover. I stared out of the wall of glass, watching an occasional jet takeoff into the dark cloudy sky.

Derek's face appeared in my mind. It seemed much longer, days at least, since I discovered the truth. At this moment, I didn't care if I ever saw Derek again, or Sara. I realized, sitting alone, listening to the thoughts running through my head, that it was time to go, to leave the company, to move on. Start fresh. After my father was better, I would search for a new job, a new city, a new life. Right now, all I wanted was for my father to be okay, to be healthy. I stood in line to board the plane and reflected on my last visit with him. The things I said. I couldn't go on if that was the last precious moment I had with him. I swore to myself, I would make it up to him, no matter what.

The flight stretched across time, from one coast to the other. When I walked off the plane in San Diego, my stomach quaked, anticipating what awaited me at the hospital. I watched the worn luggage circle around the carousel at baggage claim. Part of me wished that Derek were here to comfort me, while the other part of me wanted to land a smack across his face and ask him if he'd had a good laugh. I pushed those thoughts away. I had other priorities.

I hate hospitals. A young woman in a wheelchair rolled by. An elderly lady struggled with a walker. An entire family huddled together, crying. I expected the worst and feared my reaction. I arrived at the information desk.

"Hello, I'm looking for Mr. Swan's room, Frank Swan. He's my father."

The receptionist turned to her computer and typed in the name. She was courteous and prompt, but I couldn't help but feel like it took forever, when she finally told me, "He's in ICU, seventh floor. When you get off the elevator, go to the right. You'll see the ICU entrance."

"Thank you," I replied, dragging my poorly packed suitcase behind me.

Even the elevator shook my memory. Derek hopping on one foot as I stretched likes a ballerina to grab my belongings. I felt stronger. I didn't like that the thought of Derek made me this way, but at the same time, I needed to be strong now. How I built my strength was irrelevant. The doors of the elevator slid open and I walked in, pushed seven and stood quietly as it lifted me up.

I tiptoed down the corridor but stopped when I noticed a woman sitting along the wall. Her head hung in her hands. Used tissues piled around her. *Is this the other woman? Is this Sabra?* I tried to imagine our first words, whether we would get along and how I'd explain her looks and personality to my mother.

"Excuse, me?" I asked, as I approached. The lady glanced up and ran her fingers, which were clutching her head, through her hair. She snatched a tissue and dabbed falling tears. She was attractive with olive skin and short dark brown choppy locks. Her eyes were puffy and bloodshot. "Yes?" she sniffled.

"Are you Sabra?"

"Uh, no," wiping more tears, "I'm not." The young lady blew her nose fiercely and grabbed another tissue.

"Oh." My focus darted from one point to another wondering where the mysterious Sabra was hiding. "I'm sorry," I said, turning away. I walked up to the entrance of the ICU. An intercom hung next to the door with a sign that read,

Entrance Permitted To Immediate Family ONLY.

Please press TALK to request admittance.

I buzzed.

"Yes?"

"Hi. I am Natalie Swan, Frank Swan's daughter."

The door clicked. I pushed it open. My palms turned clammy as I breathed in the sterile air. Looking like a spooked cat, I peered down the corridor.

The nurses zoomed like hornets. Patients, confined to their beds, flanked both sides of the walls and down the center. Four private rooms lined the far wall. I remembered the time I visited my grandmother in the hospital, all the faces, waiting for an answer, hoping for something to happen, good or bad. Today was no different. The air was thin and cold. It smelled damp. *How does anyone get better in this place?*

"Are you Natalie Swan?" the nurse asked, as she approached, checking a list on her flip chart.

"Yes. My father had surgery during the night. Is he alright?"

"You should talk with the doctor about the specifics, but at the moment he is stable. He's been sleeping since the surgery. You are welcome to sit with him. He is the second to the last patient on the right side," the nurse pointed.

"Has anyone else visited him?" I asked.

"I didn't get to talk to her. It was before my shift. But apparently, a lady did come in. She told the nurses she was his fiancé. Only family members are allowed in, so she was denied access." The nurse rolled her eyes and continued, "I know it's crazy, but hospital policy. From what I heard, she left in quite a huff."

The nurse patted my shoulder, "Your father's condition will improve." She headed off in the opposite direction. I took a deep breath and stepped forward, as if I had been asked to lead a march on the Capitol.

I ambled through the sea of sickness, people lying on each side of me. One after the other, until I reached him.

At the corner of his bed, I hovered, trying to see his face. A moan escaped my lips. His skin was darker, rougher. His lips were pinkish and dry. A deep purple vein protruded irregularly across his forehead. His breathing sounded shallow, but steady.

My guilt intensified. I felt horrible for being cross with him. I wished that my mother and father would have stayed together. Standing at his bedside, I realized that their divorce impacted me more than I acknowledged. My life with them made me vulnerable, self-conscious and scared. Afraid to be committed to someone else, to believe in myself, to take a risk. *Everything is so hard.*

So many thoughts zoomed in and out of my mind, like firecrackers being shot into the air, yet my body remained frozen. *Why does life come to this, lying in a bed in ICU struggling to hold on?*

I wanted to say so much to him. Tell him I loved him. I was proud to be his daughter. I was sorry for what I said. All I could do was sit in the chair next to his bed, watch, listen and think. Tears would not even come. I was sure that my tear ducts were clogged with so many years of grief, that allowing any more pain through them would surely stop my own heart.

Ticks from the clock echoed throughout the room as the hours passed. Other families came and went as I prayed he would wake. Nurses traveled from bed to bed, checking on patients and taking vitals. Almost every bed was full. I tried not to look around. I couldn't bear the desperate faces of the sick and those visiting. I had enough sadness to contend with right in front of me.

The uncomfortable tan chair numbed my bottom. I wondered, contemplating the meaning of the world and why we're all here. The longer I waited the more tired I became. I leaned my head back.

***

Running through the woods, a thorny bush ensnared me, my white glowing dress flowing behind as I forced my way free. Pieces of white lace and chiffon hooked on the protruding skeletal arms of brittle trees as I past. I tried to dodge them. I was sure the little boy had slipped into the woods. Although the trees were thick, this path, winding through its overgrown obstacles, had seen visitors before. Breath escaped my heaving chest, my bosom rising and falling. Abruptly, my run became a walk. A stitch in my side slowed me even more, as I clutched my body. I bent over to ease the pain.

Holding my side, the ache penetrated me. I finally lifted my head. A few feet beyond the woods, an endless field appeared. Green grass rose up like a blanket of mossy satin, rolling up and down. The grass glimmered in the sun's reflected glow. Each blade was distinct, yet all flowed together as one, like crystal waters.

I stepped onto the endless lawn, looking down at my torn and tattered gown now spoiled with the earth's dirt and mutilated by the claws of the wilderness.

On the top of a hill, stood a small figure. I squinted, focusing on the dot rising up from the vast landscape. It was him, the little boy, who had told me to leave, but then mischievously led me into this adventure. I sprinted toward him just as he ducked out of sight. Once I reached the hill, he was nowhere to be found. I twirled in the grass, searching the horizon for a glimpse of the peculiar boy.

There was no sign of him. In defeat, I sighed and looked up to the sky. It opened up, rain drenching me, like Heaven's grief flooding the valley. Newly formed lakes replaced the grass.

A tug on my dress pulled my attention. The small boy looked at me with his knowing eyes. He grabbed my hand and ran. I trailed behind him. Where was he leading me? I wanted to know. Would I finally find out the mystery that plagued me?

I followed him for what seemed like hours. We left the wet grassy field and stumbled upon a small pebbled road. As our pace slowed, the little boy spied on me, his eyes narrowing.

"Why did you decide to visit?" he asked.

"I didn't know I did. I just appeared here."

"It's a dream," he said defiantly, as though he knew more than a boy his age should.

"Yes, I know, but it seems so real. Who are you?"

He did not answer, but started to skip down the path. I couldn't help myself. I followed him.

Moments later, the skipping stopped. The little boy's expression changed as we arrived at the dilapidated gate. I recognized it right away. He pushed it open and meandered toward the farthest point of the cemetery, jumping over roots and kicking fist-sized stones.

I stopped. The familiar sickened feeling erupted in my stomach. Whatever lay beyond the gate was something I did not want to face, but I knew I had to.

I entered and followed the boy's path. When I reached the corner, he had vanished. A small concrete bench sat covered in vines. I pushed a few aside and sat on the edge. My head sank into my hands.

Distracted by a rustle among the trees and ivy, I looked up. In front of me sat a worn crumpling headstone. The boy's arm hung over the decaying stone. His face appeared gaunt and stressed. And, then it all became clear. It was his. He was leaning against his own grave.

"Are you, um, a ghost?" I reached out my hand to him, as

he dissolved in front of me. "No!" I screamed and fell to my knees, my arms outstretched toward the disappearing figure.

CHAPTER 29

"Nat, Nat I'm here. Honey?" A voice yelled. Hands shook my shoulders. When I opened my eyes, my mother's solemn expression stared at me. I jumped from my seat and hugged her. *Thank God she is here.* I gestured for her to take a seat, which she did.

"I am so glad you came." I gaped at my father, who was still resting. "He's been sleeping ever since I arrived. I wish he would wake up, just for a minute so he knows we are here."

"He knows. He stirred right when I walked up to the bed. He must have sensed danger had arrived," she smiled, an unfamiliar glow radiated from her. For a second, I experienced a peacefulness, as if all my worries were washed away. Her smile served like armor, protecting me from the stress and illness stretching beyond her protection.

"He looked at me squarely," she explained, "as if to ask where the hell am I and then he realized it. He grinned his crooked mouth when he saw you. He tried to mumble something and lift his arm, but drifted off to sleep again."

"I can't believe I missed him awake!" As the disappointment settled at the bottom of my stomach, I remembered part of the dream. I was reaching out for the boy. The grave belongs to the boy. *Why is he leading me there?*

"Don't feel bad. You are here and he knows it. That's all the matters."

"Yeah, but, oh, I said some pretty cruel things to him. I'm not sure if he'll be able to forgive me."

"Natalie, your father loves you. You're upset about the marriage. It's normal. Believe me. Nothing you said could come close to my vindictive behavior since he told me."

"What changed your mind? I mean, why did you decide to come?" She closed her eyes, and leaned back in the chair.

"I was sitting on the floor in the living room, looking at old pictures of you and Frank and me. Some of them were when you were first born. We were so happy. Those pictures showed the spark your father once had, his vigor and spirit. In the end, he could be a real ass, but those photos reminded me of what we had together and how much I loved him. I thought, I don't want the last thing I said to him to be, 'Go to hell, you selfish bastard.' Wonder if that was the last time we talked? I didn't want it to end that way. And, I realized that if you and I were together, we could work through this and help support him, and Sabra, if we have to. I decided on the flight here that if she makes him happy, that's all that matters. I need to move on and maybe this is a sign. It sounds like both of us have some moving on to do."

"Yes. You're right. I'm really proud of you. He wants you here. I know I'm glad you're came."

"Speaking of Sabra, any sign of her?" mom asked, inspecting the area.

"No. I spoke to one of the nurses when I first arrived and asked her if he had any visitors. She said a lady came, but was not permitted because she wasn't family."

"I don't think that's very nice. I mean they are engaged. They should let her in. Did they say where she went?"

"No. I doubt she's still in the hospital. That was hours ago."

"I am going to take a look around, get us some Cokes. I'll be back." I hugged her again as she got up to leave. I sat down and wiggled my fingers under my father's hand.

"Daddy, I am so sorry that this happened to you, to us. I hope more than anything you will be okay. I shouldn't have been mad at you. The things I said, the way I acted, was unacceptable, disrespectful. Not me." I paused. "I never wanted you and mom to divorce. I realize you didn't get along and, in the long run, it's probably better this way. But, it hurts. Still. Like it was my fault and that you didn't love us anymore. I know that's not true. But, then, I blamed myself for everything and blocked you out. We've missed some precious years because I was so stubborn, or too ashamed to admit that part of the problem of us, was me. I don't know. I just want you to know, I love you. And, I am so sorry for the terrible, spiteful things I said. I didn't mean them. If Sabra makes you happy, then I'll be happy."

"I'm glad to hear that," he mumbled.

"Daddy?" I got up and moved to the railing, holding his hand firm this time. "Did you hear what I said?"

"The part about loving me. That's all I needed."

"Oh, daddy. How do you feel?"

"Horrible. But, I guess that's normal."

"Uh, Sabra was here. I didn't get to see her, but she did try. She couldn't come in yet. Cause you're not married. She's not, um," I stopped, trying hard to hide my discomfort. *Maybe if I say it fast.* "Family."

"Your mother came. Good, I'm glad she's here," he said, as I lifted his hand up to my mouth and kissed his dry worn knuckles.

"Nat, I am sleepy. I think I will nap. Okay?" He yawned.

"Yes, daddy, anything you want." I placed his hand on the white barren sheets and sat back down in the chair.

When my mother finally returned, she was not alone. A young woman walked with her. It was just how I pictured her. Dirty blonde hair. Big green eyes. Flawless and fair skin, like freshly fallen snow. I noticed her small waist and petite frame and compared it to my mother's plump figure and graying hair. Distressed myself, I hoped my mother was not analyzing the situation too much.

Reaching her hand, she said, "Hi, Natalie. I'm Sabra. It's a pleasure to meet you, even under these circumstances. Your father talks about you all the time."

"Natalie," my mother began, "Sabra was sitting in the waiting room on the other side of the nurses' desk down the hall. They would not let her visit Frank. I spoke to them, well, argued. You know me. Anyway, I pleaded with them to please make an exception. They agreed, but only two of us can be here at the same time. So, I will step outside and let you and Sabra visit for a while, perhaps we can take turns."

I had no desire to sit with Sabra in silence as we watched my father sleep. Searching for a reason to sneak out I asked, "Mom, did you bring us drinks?"

"Oh, no. I got completely wrapped up when I found Sabra."

"Well, I've been here all day and haven't left. So, why don't I get us some drinks and take a break. You stay." My mother looked a bit grim about camping out with Sabra. But, I hadn't left my father's side since I arrived.

When I reached the outside of the ICU doorway, I sighed, the world adding pressure to my tense and aching shoulders. *Sabra. Daddy's wife-to-be. Ugh.* It was like looking at a younger, more attractive sister, with a better body and more confidence. I walked aimlessly down the hall toward the elevators. I drifted along the cold depressing hallway like a ship off course. My mind filled with questions—questions of doubt, guilt, loyalty and love.

Mortality. My parents are getting old. I had always been concerned about them getting sick or having an accident. But, old and dying? I had blocked it out. *What about me? My mortality?* The oddest sensation came over me. I slowed my pace and stopped in the middle of the hallway. The thought of no longer existing, not waking up each morning. To not be whole, a being, that sits and eats and laughs. And cries. *What have I accomplished? Who have I thanked? Who have I loved? Did I tell them? Derek. Why does he keep creeping into my thoughts when I am trying so hard to forget him?*

I reached the elevators and waited. The doors opened and as I started to enter, I collided with a young man. *I should start taking the stairs.*

CHAPTER 30

It was Scott. *WTF!*

"What are you doing here?" I exclaimed, walking right by him. He turned around and followed me into the elevator.

"I found out about your father." I must have shot a suspicious smirk, because he quickly continued, "Your mother told someone at her church, who told one of my mother's friends who told my mother. Anyway, I just moved here, and thought I would stop by to let you know that I'm sorry. And, if there's anything you need while you're here, just let me know."

"I appreciate that but I think we're fine," I said, like the old 'it' Natalie. *Mr. Beatler would be proud.*

Scott and I stood in the elevator alone stuck in heavy, thick, uncomfortable silence, until the doors opened again. I didn't believe I was nervous but my palms began to seep with a warm wetness. I maintained my composure and walked out of the elevator with my head held high. Scott followed.

"Natalie," he called after me, but I did not respond. "Natalie! Nat! Please!"

"What, Scott?" I demanded, stopping. "What do you want? Why are you here?"

"I wanted to be with you. I'm so sorry for, for your family.

Really, my intentions are completely honorable." *Hmm... I've heard that line before.*

"Okay, thank you. We are all doing fine. You can go." I turned away.

"Nat, I know you're still mad at—"

"Don't call me Nat!" My mouth distorted when I screamed at him, like a cherry had been stuck deep in my throat, dried up and lodged permanently.

"Okay, I'm sorry," Scott implored. I resumed my walk.

We reached the vending machines, and I pulled a dollar out of my pocket. I shoved it into the slot over and over, unsuccessfully. It looked like a miniature accordion easing in and out of itself.

"Here, let me help you," Scott offered, moving closer.

"Oh. You're still here?" I snapped. "Don't touch me! Don't help me! You can go," I ordered. "We're fine."

"Natalie, please. I just—"

"What?" I screamed. A family sat at a table next to the vending machines. They stared at me like an animal in a zoo. I straightened my posture and reduced the volume of my voice, "What?" I repeated.

He studied the clock hanging crooked above the doorway. "Well, there's something else."

I glared at him, recalling the overwhelming pain that swelled within me the day he threw me away like a used tissue. I could not relive that torment and humiliation. Not now. I had other things to take care of in my life and he was not part of my new world.

"Look, Scott. I am tired and can't think straight. My father's in ICU, his fiancé is here, my mother's here and work sucks. I'm being pulled in a hundred different directions, and," I shoved the dollar into the slot, "if I can't get this damn dollar in here, I'm gonna explode! I'm not sure how to handle all this. I can't talk right now." I pulled out a different dollar and tried to jostle it through the narrow slot of the vending machine.

"I wanted to tell you, I've missed you, missed us, and," he

hesitated. "I'm sorry."

His words didn't matter. I had given my heart to someone else, more than I ever had to Scott. Scott had hurt me. Derek humiliated me. *Shit, this sucks.*

One person more important than either of them lay in a bed on the seventh floor, one man that loved me more than both Scott and Derek put together. My father.

"Scott. Things change. I've changed and I have different, more important things to worry about now. I just can't talk. I've got to go to my father."

"I know. I'm sorry. Hey, here is my business card. If you need anything, call me. Even if you, um, want to vent." He handed me the card. I took it hoping that the gesture would make him leave. But, after I grabbed it from him, he went to give me a hug.

Backing away, I advised, "If I have any problems or need something, I'll call you. Thanks." I yanked the sodas from the mouth of the machine and walked briskly down the hall.

CHAPTER 31

People occupied ever corner of the waiting room. *Sardines*. I found a sliver of space at the end of a couch and seized it. The egg colored walls, dreary furniture and musty smell added to the melancholy atmosphere. I put my Diet Coke on the modest side table and observed the others in the room. Faces, like blank canvases, stared, consumed by internal anger, sadness and frustration.

The tension of twenty personal traumas unfolded around me. Every eye in the room, glassy. Through the hollowness of the air, lay an unruly desire to scream, to pull down the paisley curtains and rip the peach-colored couch to shreds. Instead, families huddled in corners, arm over arm, silent. The only movement was an occasional reach for Kleenex, and the only sound, a sniffle. I watched young and old come and go until I was alone.

I eased into the couch and swung one leg over the other. Leaning my head back I stared at the yellowish ceiling. *What on earth did Scott think, coming here, now? Throttling him—that sounded fun*. Sitting in the middle of the waiting room crying—that was reality. My eyes flickered under the dull fluorescent light and grew weary.

"Hi," someone said. Out of the corner of my eye, I saw

Sabra's head come around the French doors.

I straightened up and asked, "How is he doing?"

"Fine. Fine. He's sleeping. I thought I would walk a little bit. I'm not too good with hospitals." Sabra sat at the far end of the couch, balancing on the edge of the flimsy cushion. I had grown accustom to the odd silence in the room, but the silence that followed was different, as if I stood on a bare stage in front of thousands of people, waiting for my dramatic statement that would change the world. A deep, intimidating stillness fell around us. Sprinting out the door to the nearest bar seemed like a reasonable resolution to this awkward moment. Sabra shifted toward me and freed a defeated sigh.

"I have to tell you," she said. "I was nervous about meeting you."

Caught off guard by the comment, my eyebrows rose, becoming one with my forehead.

"Why?" I asked.

"Well, I guess, partially because of the unknown. I mean your father talks about you all the time, you know? And, well, I guess I was concerned about what you would think of me." Sabra picked her cuticles, searching for a rough part to tug at. *I do that.*

"Um, so you were worried I thought you were the wicked witch, stealing my father from us." I smiled, keeping my lips tight together.

"Us?" Sabra prodded.

"I meant my mother and me."

"Oh, yes. He talks about Sybil every day." She got up, walked to the window and gazed up to the gray and cloudy sky. I was certain that at any moment, it would crack open and shower the earth with tears.

"Well, anyway, I was worried about meeting you and your mother. Like I said, he talks about both of you all the time. I'm not sure how to compete with that."

"Why compete?" My interest piqued. "I mean, there's not a reason to believe a competition is in order. Daddy loves you and wants to marry you." I shrugged my shoulders, in resignation, and leaned my head back on the couch.

"Oh, I don't think it's that easy." A bubble of blood erupted at the corner of Sabra's ring finger. I felt guilty for enjoying her pain. I wondered if she was experiencing the same emotional roller coaster I did the night Scott tossed me away. Pain was better than feeling nothing. Sabra continued, "See, your mother still loves Frank. I can tell. And, well—"

"What?" I asked, draining the last bit of Diet Coke.

Sabra moved closer to the window, her eyes misty. She seemed confused, straining to find the right words. "Sometimes," she finally murmured, "I think he still has feelings for her."

My mother never stopped loving my father, but I was convinced that he had not loved her since before my birth. Which always made me wonder why I was conceived in the first place. Tension and bitterness served as a staple in our house. This new information sparked my curiosity.

"Well," I started, thinking it best to play this conversation out, "they were married a long time. I am sure they both will always care for each other. That doesn't mean they can't have someone else in their life."

"You're right. I've tried to ask him about it, and he tends to change the subject. I do love him. But I don't want to marry him if he still loves your mother."

My brain froze. My heart constricted. A tunnel closed in on my thoughts, focusing only on what she just said, "If he still loves your mother." *Did this woman just confide in me? Could I use this information to get my parents back together?* My head spun with ideas, contemplating the next move. Evil thoughts entered my mind. I decided to remain neutral for now, and try not to show emotion either way.

Before I responded, Sabra continued, "I have to be honest, this heart attack thing has been horrific for me." Sabra reached up to her eye to catch a tear. "My father died of a heart attack when he was forty-two, looking at Buicks with my Uncle Bob. It destroyed our whole family. I can't go through that again." Sabra collapsed on the couch and sobbed uncontrollably.

I moved closer to her. Although this woman planned on stealing my father from us, I recognized desperation. Sabras face showed genuine fluster and confusion. I tried to comfort her, placing my hand on her shoulder and padding her gently.

"Sabra, everything works out for a reason. Something brought you and my father together. I know it's cliché, but if it's meant to be, it will. I'm no expert in romance, believe me. When it comes right down to it, when you find him, hold onto him. Together you can get through anything."

Oh, my God. What am I saying? Where are these words coming from? I sound like a damn psychologist, and I need one more than all these people put together.

"I know you're right, Natalie. I'm just scared. I'm not as strong as everyone thinks. I just put on a good cover."

"We all do." I was a professional at playing the game. Yet underneath, I was clueless on how to get what I wanted, like Dorothy in Oz searching for a way home.

"Thank you," Sabra said.

My potential stepmother and I had bonded. *Wow! This is baffling.* I wasn't fond of giving Sabra advice about my father, but we seemed like two long lost sisters, realizing how alike we were. *I'm going crazy.*

Sabra reached for another Kleenex. "I think I will head back and check on him." She sauntered out of the room, leaving me alone, again.

Within a split second, my mother appeared in the doorway.

Is this a waiting room or my office? It's like a parade of troubled women. Am I a therapist, or a marketing executive? What is going on?

Mom rubbed her hands nervously. She always seemed on edge—on the brink of a breakdown. She would smile, but behind the turned up corners of her mocha colored lips hid a trembling fragile woman. I believed that my mother's smile vanished when she was alone. *Everyone plays a part.*

When she walked into the room, her brows narrowed and her crow's feet deepened, reaching down into her cheeks. Yet, a smile was affixed on her face, ready to enter the masquerade.

A clear defiant gaze penetrated from her eyes.

"Hi, mom." A chill swept through the room as my mother entered. "How is daddy?" I asked, my teeth on the verge of chattering.

"Fine," she said, in a whisper.

"What's wrong?" She crossed her arms and sat in the chair in the far corner.

What's going on? Did Sabra upset her? Did something happen to daddy? What?

"I've been sitting in that claustrophobia-inducing space with your father and I've been thinking, a lot. Probably too much and I've decided something." My mother looked at me as if it might be for the last time. Her faced changed. The fake happiness usually concealing her stress transformed into a serious hardened expression, as if she were walking into the court to receive the jury's judgment. The transition of her face revealed even more wrinkles and lines. I'd never noticed them before. She had aged more than I wanted to believe.

"Natalie, there's something I need to tell you. I'm not sure how to say it or how to explain it all, really. And I will probably forget parts, but it's been eating at me for...well, I can't remember how long."

I arched my back, stiffening as if a needle prickled over my sensitive skin. Uneasy air seemed to escape my lungs.

There are no secrets between us. Or, are there?

"Mom, you're scaring me. What on earth are you talking about?"

"Before you were born, I did something."

"What? What do you mean?" I asked, between stolen breaths.

"And," mom continued, ignoring me, "we've never told you. As a matter of fact, nobody knows, except your father of course. Well, no one that's still alive, anyway. This is the reason, one of the reasons, why my relationship with your dad is, different."

"Okay. Mom, I'm not sure where this is going, but I am starting to feel like I'm in the Twilight Zone."

"I'm sorry. I'm not sure how to begin. I guess the first thing I should do is tell you," she paused, "you had a, oh how do I say this?" Mom's eyes darted around the room as if she was searching for someone to help her. Nothing offered any comfort, for either of us.

"You have," she struggled, "a brother."

CHAPTER 32

"A brother? What? What the hell are you talking about?"

For the first time since I planted myself on the couch, I got up and walked to the center of the room. When I turned around, my mother's strained face, pointed lips and narrowed eyes, convinced me she was not joking. This was serious. *Can this be happening? A therapist. As soon as I get home.*

"Oh, my God! It's true! I, I can't believe this. A brother?" I—I don't understand. You've never—daddy never mentioned…"

"Some things you'd rather forget, my sweet girl." With unsteady footing, she got up and walked towards me.

"Wait, this is— Why didn't you tell me? What's his name? What happened to him? Where is he?" I ranted like an auctioneer, trying desperately to find a bid in the sea of unknown faces.

"You have a lot of questions. This is confusing and upsetting. I realize this is a shock, for you and me. Let me explain, okay." She grabbed my hand, squeezed it tightly and led me back to the couch. I followed like a scared lost child, in an enchanted forest, a storm brewing in the distance.

"His name was Caleb. And, he was perfect. His hair was rich, golden and shiny. He had deep toffee eyes, with flecks of gold, and the softest olive skin. The cutest thing though, was his nose. It turned up slightly and rounded at the tip. When your daddy and Caleb would sit next to each other, their noses were identical. Just like yours." I reached up and caressed the bridge of my nose, remembering how I would stare at my father as a child, and hope to be just like him.

My mother continued, "And, Caleb loved your father. He followed him all around the house. When your dad came home from work, Caleb's eyes grew so big as if he were opening a shiny red toy truck on Christmas morning. He loved his daddy. And, your father was captivated by everything Caleb did. Caleb was his pride. No matter what the conversation was about, eventually it would turn to Caleb—the new word he said, a food he decided he liked. The smallest things were exaggerated and told to as many people who would listen."

I wondered for a moment whether we were in the ICU or in the psychiatric ward. Maybe I had come to visit my mother. I wasn't able to comprehend the words that were leaving her mouth. They certainly could not be real, not from the world I was living in. So, my mother must have lost her mind, my father's heart attack was a dream and I was sitting in the ward listening to my mother blabber on about a fantasy life. I turned away from her and clutched desperately to the table to stop my dizziness, trying to rationalize this peculiar conversation.

"Natalie, are you paying attention?" I heard her ask. I snapped back. *Oh, no, damn! We aren't in the psychiatric ward. We aren't even in social services.* The reality of the situation came flooding into me like a dam breaking, water gushing in and flattening the trees and homes, and people.

My head drooped like a wilted flower. The blood in my body began to boil. "So, mom," I swallowed, "I have a brother, Caleb. Where is he? How could you never speak of him? No pictures? How?" I questioned the truth of the story. *The stress of daddy's illness, meeting Sabra and coming to California is finally erupting. Maybe she was going mad.*

"Natalie, Caleb was killed when he was four years old."

This news did not change my face. I watched my reflection deep in my mother's eyes. Not saying a word, I continued to stare at her mystified, as if I were looking at a strobe light in a rave club. My head whirled and a booming ache landed in my temple. Finally, I awoke from my trance.

"What? Killed?" I asked, as if the word was foreign to me. "What, what happened?" My emotions hurled through a killer ride, up and down, like a yo-yo. Mom sat back in her chair and reached up with her shaking hand to rub her forehead. Mist covered her eyes. Her face tensed. Her top lip quivered.

"Caleb is not with us today because of me. Caleb is dead because of me."

The wall she had hidden behind for so many years crumbled. Tears welled in her eyes and exploded through the cracks of her past. "I have not said those words out loud in almost 40 years. I buried the memory far in the back of my mind. I shut out every emotion associated with Caleb, but I can't anymore." Tears gushed down her cheeks and neck, absorbing into the fabric of her collar. She made no attempt to wipe them away. She let them drown her.

After a few minutes, I moved from the couch, using the armchair to assist me. I wasn't sure what to do or say. It was like reading someone's diary, but half the pages had been ripped out. A mixture of intrigue, bewilderment and fear commingled within me. *This life-jolting story will change me forever.*

The one thing I did realize was that my mother was in extreme pain. Not physical pain, but emotional pain as if her heart had been clawed from her chest. I had never seen her in this state. No matter what may have happened in the past, she did not deserve this.

I made my way to the side table, picked up the box of tissues and knelt on the floor next to my mother. I yanked a tissue and offered it to her as I rubbed her back.

"Mommy. I hate seeing you like this. Please, what can I do? I, just, I don't know."

"There is nothing you can do," she conceded. I've done it

all to myself, to your father and to you." She regained some composure, "I must find the courage to tell you the rest." She sighed deeply and continued, "Natalie, Caleb died because of my negligence. Nothing more. Nothing less."

"That's impossible."

She put her hand up, squashing my words. "I have to finish what I started, and continue revealing my precious little secret." She took a deep breath, and after a moment, proceeded, "Caleb and I went to Woolworth's. It was Saturday. I was excited because I was going to drive Frank's truck. The car was in the shop. He wanted to watch a football game and had no desire to go to Woolworth's. I remember he asked me to get him some shaving cream. I hadn't driven the truck much, but liked it because it was higher than the rest of the cars on the road. Anyway, Caleb and I piled into the truck and headed to Woolworths."

Seeing the anguish building in my mother's face, I said, "You don't have to go on if you don't—"

"No, I do," she demanded. "We shopped. Got all we needed, including the shaving cream. In front of the checkout were some of those small plastic pools for kids. Caleb went crazy over them. He kept asking over and over if he could have one. I said no about a thousand times and started to pay the cashier. When I glanced over my shoulder, he was sitting in the middle of one of the pools, his legs criss-crossed and his arms folded in front of his chest. Kind of like you did when you didn't get your way. He's green overall strap had fallen off his shoulder and he's bottom lip was pulled over his top. You would have thought he'd lost his best friend."

Nostalgia resonated in her voice. Her story transported me back in time. As she described the events, I played this horror movie in my head, watching it unfold. Afraid of what was coming next.

"I turned back to the cashier. 'I'll take one of those kiddy pools, too,' I said." Mom choked on her words. She rolled her eyes up. Mine followed. Water stains darkened the ceiling. She shook her head and shrugged her shoulders. "Why did I buy that damn pool?"

"You wanted to make him happy," I said, trying to find words to comfort her.

"Yeah, right. Well, the pool was really light and small. I carried it to the truck along with the other stuff. I put it in the back of the truck and thought, wow this is great, I have the truck. The pool fits perfectly. Then, Caleb tugged on my skirt. 'Momma,' he said, 'can I sit in the pool?' I guess it didn't register in my head. I mean, I thought he would be fine. The house was only a couple of blocks away. I said, 'Okay, but be careful.' His eyes lit up. We got out on the road, not too much traffic. It was a beautiful day. Sunny. Not too hot, just pleasant. A breeze cooled the air." Mom stared at her left hand, rubbing the permanent indention where her wedding ring had sat for so many years.

"I remember waiting at the stop light. Daydreaming about something, probably your father. Then, the car behind me honked. The light had turned green so I stepped on the gas. Of course, the car behind me started to speed up as well. A few yards or so later, I checked the rearview mirror." Every line on her face deepened. She forced the words from her lips, "Caleb and the pool were gone."

My heart sank listening to the story leave my mother's lips.

"I slammed on the brakes," she continued, "and jumped out of the car. When I took off at the light, the wind and the acceleration of the truck lifted the pool out of the back bed. Caleb's weight wasn't enough to hold it down. The gust carried the pool through the air, landing on top of Caleb. The car that was behind me had no time to react. The man tried to stop. He swerved but he still could not avoid missing the pool.

"I don't think at first, he realized a little boy's body lay helpless, covered by that flimsy pool. Because he got out of his car and came over to me apologizing, promising he would buy me a new pool. I pushed right past him. I scanned the street looking for Caleb. The pool was wedged under the tire of the man's car. I heard my screams. The sun turned black. I remember waking up in the hospital. A police officer and a doctor were in the room. They told me that Caleb was dead."

This was too much to absorb. I struggled to keep focus. The room became fuzzy, and I felt faint. The chill that had cut through me earlier was replaced with droplets of sweat.

I had always known something was missing, but maybe it wasn't something, maybe it wasn't something at all, but instead, someone. *Could the missing link in my life be this little boy, my brother?*

After a few moments, my mother continued, "It was like a brick wall had been built around me. My vision become fuzzy, my mind crowded. I cried so many tears I could have filled a swimming pool double the size of what I purchased that morning. It was a dream, I decided. A nightmare. A reminder from God. A warning to be a better mother and wife. To be responsible. To be loving and kind. To not take life and those you love for granted." She paused, wiping a tear.

"When the door of the hospital room opened and your father walked in," she struggled, "I realized it was not a dream. It was real. Your dad's skin was pale, as if all his blood had been drained. White as the snow that covered the highest peak. And, it seemed as if he was trying to breath in that same icy cold air. He did not say a word. He sat in a chair in the corner of the room. Hours passed in complete silence." I reached up and placed my arms around my mother, kissing her gently on the cheek.

"What happened?" I asked.

"We came home. We had dinner. We went to bed. We didn't sleep. We didn't talk. Three days later, we were getting ready for the funeral. My parents were there. Obviously, devastated. The coffin was so tiny. So innocent. We had cried so much, we had no energy to cry anymore. We sat at the service like two empty vessels, wishing more than anything that we were in that coffin, instead of our child. I was so engrossed in my own thoughts, I couldn't even tell you what the preacher said."

I kept reminding myself, that this was not a dream, like so many I had suffered through in the dead of night. *Mother is not crazy. This is real. And, maybe, I'm not crazy either. Is the little boy that had led me through the midnight journeys trying to tell me something, trying to reach me?* My head tingled as though a thousand buzzing bees were trapped.

"After the service," she continued, "we went to my parent's house. I don't know why we thought this was the right setting, but we finally talked. I told your father what happened, from what I remembered. Disappointment filled his eyes. Then anger. He said, "You stupid ignorant bitch! You killed my son." He got up and left. I don't know where he went. I still don't. To a bar. To a woman. I don't know.

"I was curled on the couch, considering whether I could go on. Caleb was gone. Frank was gone. It was my fault. The house was so quite and still. Finally, the door lock clicked. An eye-popping squeak echoed from the foyer, then his clunky footsteps. He came back. I shot out of the couch and faced him. Seconds later, we ran to each other. We fell to the floor, clutching each other and cried. For hours we sat in the middle of the hallway. We talked. I was so relieved he came back. I was sure he had left me to sit alone in this terror, to relive that day over and over in my head for eternity until I reached the grave myself. We both wanted to make things better, to try to move on. We decided to block it out, to remove the entire event from our life. I know now that was the wrong thing to do."

She looked at me, right in the eyes. "Two years later, we had you. I was not about to go back to work. You would not leave my sight. I remember holding you so tight. Your father would say, 'You're smothering her.' I loved, love, you more than anything. I had another chance." Mom rubbed my cheek with the back of her hand and stared at me. "Your our first tooth, step, word, tantrum, your first day of school." I smiled, remembering that day too.

"Things seemed to be going fine," she continued, "but then it all changed. When you were about ten, your father and I were up in the attic. I was in one corner, Frank in another. I'm not sure how he found it. I thought I had hid it well. I called his name, but he didn't answer. Out of the opposite corner, he walked straight toward me, holding an old cedar box. 'What is this?' he asked. I didn't answer. He knew. I couldn't destroy every picture. So, I put them in this keepsake box we had bought Caleb and hid it at the bottom of a trunk. Sometimes I would go up and look through the pictures. I'd cry as hard as the day he died. I buried my pain and secrets in that box."

Are the pictures still there? What would they have said if I had found them?

"What did he do?" I asked.

"He sat up all night, looking at those photos. I don't know what he was thinking. We had suppressed our feelings for so long that when they returned, the anger and regret and guilt were worse than ever, a fire that was never truly smothered. We should have known. Anyway," my mother continued, "after that, everything went downhill. He reminded me every day of how I lost Caleb, how you could have had a brother, how our family wasn't whole. We started to argue, daily. He would leave early and come home late. It started off he'd come home at ten, then midnight, then one, two. One night he didn't come home at all. That's when we decided it was time to separate and you know the rest."

Were they ever going to tell me all this? Why is she telling me now?

"I'm sure there's a lot I left out. The bottom line is your father blames me for Caleb's death, and he always has. He can't stand being around me because it reminds him of Caleb and all that happened between us. I have tried so hard to fix it, to mend our relationship. The more I tried, the more I pushed him away."

At the end of her confession, she appeared resolute, as if inch thick dust had finally been wiped clean. The sun peaked through the solemn clouds, and life began to flicker around us. A burden was lifted.

I heard voices, people moving around, nurses shoveling papers. A plump lady entered the waiting room, sat in front of the TV and sniffled as she flipped through a magazine. The bubble insulating us from the rest of the world stopped time even though it continued all around. It popped when a booming voice sounded, "Excuse me. I'm Dr. Martin. Ms. Swan?"

Both mom and I responded simultaneously.

"Mother and daughter, I presume." We nodded and I reached out my hand to greet him. He resembled a toad, gray and slimy.

With a raw voice, he explained, "Ladies, Mr. Swan is stable, but the surgery took a lot out of him. He needs rest. It would be fine for you to go home. You both need some sleep as well. In the morning, I will be back around to check on him."

"Doctor, when do you think he will be moved out of ICU or be released from the hospital?" I asked.

"Well, I'm not sure yet. If things go well tomorrow, he can probably be moved in a day or two. Leaving the hospital, well, um, I'll know more in the next couple of days. He really is doing fine. Get some rest." Dr. Martin turned to leave, but before he reached to doors, I yelled out a thank you.

"Well," I faced mom, "it sounds like daddy is going to be fine."

"I hope so. On the way here, I was certain I had killed your father, too. Sometimes, I think I'm just doomed."

"You are not doomed. And, mommy, I love you. I love you so much. I'm sorry this happened to you and to daddy. When you first started talking, I thought I had been shipped to another dimension. Maybe you, or me, or both of us, had gone nuts. But, now that you've told me all of this, things make more sense. I've always been missing something, now I know it was someone. Thank you for telling me."

We embraced, standing in the middle of the waiting room. We remained immersed in our private world, as a nurse pushed an older woman down the hall, a family waddled into the room and consumed the chairs, three interns scurried off holding a library of medical books, the phone rang unanswered at the nurses' station and a man in a brown trench coat banged his fist on the counter demanding to talk to a doctor. Among all that chaos, mom and I shared the most tender, genuine moment I had ever experienced, breathing in new knowledge and exhaling painful memories of the past.

CHAPTER 33

At the hotel, I fumbled for the room key. As I pulled out the rectangular plastic card from my purse, a business card fell to the floor. It was difficult picking it up, my back aching from sitting in the rigid hospital chairs. The card belonged the Scott. I flipped it over—Scott Fuller, Esquire.

Oh, God. I gripped the card with both hands ready to rip it to shreds. With my fingertips clutching the card, I raised my head, filled my lungs with air and closed my eyes. *This day has been unbelievable—the news of my father, meeting Sabra, learning about Caleb and the lingering thoughts of Derek. Treading water. I wonder if they will deliver wine to my room.* I loosened my hold on the card and turned toward the door.

I slid the key into the slot, while weighing the positives and negatives of calling Scott: *We dated for four years. He isn't a stranger. Talking to him might help. He seemed genuine when he spoke at the hospital. Then again, he said he missed me. I wonder if he's up to something? If so, does it really matter? Tell him what's going on and release your anxiety and emotion. Therapy. The therapy that I keep saying I need, and this session would be free, except for the wine of course. Unless he paid. Use him to empty your mind from the day's gut-splitting news, and wash yourself clean.*

I stepped through the door of the hotel room, flipping on

the light with my elbow. I threw the room key on the bed, eased my pumps off and tossed my purse on the small desk along the wall. I pulled the comforter back and plopped on the bed. *This mattress is a rock.* With my head sunk in the middle of the flimsy pillow, I closed my eyes and breathed deeply, trying to absorb the shock and awe of my mother's story. As if being in a coma, I had awakened to discover what had happened in the last thirty years. *Surreal.* I wondered when the tears would come, how the truth would unfold and weave itself into my life. This new knowledge made things make sense.

I turned on my side and closed my eyes. The bed might have been worse than a cot at Alcatraz, but it was quite and I was alone at last. Seconds before I felt myself ease into a nap, a buzzing startled me. *My phone. Crap!* I pulled myself up, stumbled to the desk and found my phone vibrating in my purse, reverberating against my sunglass case. I looked at the screen.

"Three messages?" *Fine.* I smashed the little arrow to play the first one.

"Natalie, it's mom. We were interrupted by the doctor today, and I didn't get to say everything I wanted. I am so sorry for not telling you. I thought it was for the best, but it wasn't. I've been selfish. Try to get some rest and I'll see you in the morning. I love you, Natalie."

I listened to the next message. "I know you know." *Derek.* "I understand that you don't want to hear from me right now. But, you need to know a couple things. First, I love you. Second, I hope your father is okay and that you and your family are hanging in there. I wish I were with you. Finally, Sara and I were wrong in how we handled this. Sara loves you. We were together a long time ago, but it wasn't right. You and me?" He paused. "Right—is NOT the right word? With you, I'm alive. Don't give up on me, Nat. I love you."

Finally, Scott.

"Hey, Nat. I'm sorry for surprising you at the hospital. I thought it was right when I headed out, but seeing your face, I felt sick. Like the day you left. One of the worst days in my life, but I only realized it when you were gone. I'm stupid. You are all that I ever wanted, and I threw what we had away. No need to call me back, just know I will always love you."

I started to dial Scott's number, but hesitated. *Will he interpret my call as an invitation for sex? I'm depressed, vulnerable and confused. He'd see straight through me and take advantage. Then again, so what?* I was lonely and angry with Derek, and mostly, I wanted to be held by someone.

In the middle of my chaotic thoughts, Scott's phone began to ring. *Damn!* Hanging up and abandoning the idea crossed my mind. It went to voicemail. *Good. I tried and he isn't picking up.* Suddenly, Scott's voice was interrupted by a bizarre beep.

"Hello." An awkward silence followed. "Hello?" he repeated, raising his voice.

"Um," I started, my voice shaky and regretful. My throat shriveled to a raisin.

"Natalie?" Scott asked. "Is that you?"

"Yeah, yes. It is," I responded cautiously. "Did I get you at a bad time?"

"Of course not. How's your father?"

"He's stable at the moment. They told us to go and get rest. I'll head back early tomorrow." As I finished my sentence, it hit me like a lead pipe. *God, why did I call him?* My reason and normally logical mind turned to slush, like melting snow pushed into a heaping pile, laden with dirt from the street. I clutched the bridge of my nose and squinted hard as though a wicked headache finally exploded.

"Are you okay?" he asked.

"Well, it's been a rough day. I'm also sorry. I was so short with you earlier. I mean, I really do appreciate you coming to the hospital. It's just been crazy, and I'm tired. I, I don't know."

"I completely understand. Remember, you sat with me all night during my mom's mastectomy. You cradled me like a baby. I will never forget the kindness and love you showed me. I want to be there for you, if you'll have me."

"I—, um. I'm not sure, Scott. I'd like to talk to you, but I can't, well, get involved. I've got too much going on. Not to mention, I buried those feelings when I left that night."

"I understand. I don't expect you to take me back or anything. I just feel miserable. I mean, that night at the pool, when you walked away. I was certain that I'd never see you again. Ever since, I have hoped that I would. Just to tell you how sorry I am for screwing it all up. We had something. Something. I deserve this. I had everything I could ever dream of right in front of me, and like a stupid ass, I threw it all away."

"It all works out, Scott. We weren't meant to be. I realize that now. Anyway, how is your mom doing?" I asked, trying to change the subject.

"She's okay. The cancer is in remission, but mostly, she's depressed."

"Yes. So is my mother. Wow, I learned a lot about my family today." I rubbed my aching eyes.

"What do you mean?"

"Well, apparently, I have a brother. His name is Caleb."

An unexpected sensation overcame me. *I'm nervous.* Saying the words out loud for the first time. *Caleb is my brother.* Sharing this new part of my life filled me with a thousand different emotions. I reached across the bed and grabbed a tissue from the nightstand right before a tear streamed down my cheek.

"Look, Natalie. Why don't I come over? We can talk. I want to hear all about this and everything that's going on in your life."

"I'm not sure. You don't have to do that."

"I don't mind, really."

"There's a lounge in the lobby," I said. "Meet me there."

"Okay. Where are you staying?" he asked.

"The Radisson. Close to the hospital."

"I'm on my way."

After hanging up, I questioned my decision to meet with Scott. But I needed to talk to someone. I crammed into the petite bathroom and judged my drained face. Mascara smudged the corners of my eyes and spread lines down my cheeks. I looked and felt like I had been run over by a truck. My appearance was unacceptable. *I couldn't go to the laundromat like this, let alone see Scott.* I grabbed my makeup case and revisited each crevice of my face until it was presentable.

Half an hour later, I had sunk into the red suede couch in the lounge. I had ordered a glass of wine, but it had not arrived yet. Within minutes, Scott walked through the revolving doors in the front lobby. He spotted me immediately and walked swiftly over.

I was certain my eyes revealed the pitiful soul hiding inside me. I looked like a kitten that had received its first bath, wet and desperate to run wild. Even with all the makeup I lathered on, my eyes remained puffy and red.

The stress that I had harbored since finding out about daddy's heart attack and learning about Caleb, surfaced and spurted out likes a broken water faucet. *Why did this river of tears decide to show up now?*

Before Scott arrived, I was confident that I would be able to maintain my composure. Maybe it was seeing someone I knew, someone I cared about. Maybe it was because I could release my feelings and then walk away.

We sat in the empty bar as I cried in the arms of my former lover. When the tears started to dissipate, I peered up at him and considered his warm brown eyes that in the past had been so loving, but also cruel.

For the next hour, I explained my personal soap opera. Scott listened intently, rubbing my back and occasionally, pushing my hair out of my eyes.

"I can't believe you have a brother and that your mother has kept it a secret for all these years. How did she keep it inside? I would have had to tell someone, do something." Scott stopped short. "I guess a lot of things make sense now, huh?"

"What do you mean?" I asked, startled at his revelation. I feared that he had discovered my secret. When we dated we rarely spoke of our inner battles, our lost goals or hopes. Our relationship was more business-like.

"I mean, sometimes when we were around your parents, there was this weird tension between them. Not like two people that had been married for years and knew all there was to know about each other, but rather two people that didn't know each other at all. And, well, I don't want you to take this the wrong way, but even with you, when we were together, sometimes I felt like I didn't know you. I mean, like there was more, but you wouldn't let me in."

I wiped away another tear using a cocktail napkin. These were not the same type of tears that I shed for my father or Caleb. Scott knew and he was right. I never let him in. I expected so much from him. I set him up to fail. *If he failed, then I didn't.*

"Scott, how can you understand me so well, now? I mean, you're right, everything was my fault."

"Wait, that's not what I'm saying. Nothing was your fault. I always thought our relationship only touched the surface. I had a lot to do with it failing. Our problems were my fault. I was a horrible listener. I was selfish. But, Natalie, I did love you."

"I know. And, I loved you, the way I thought love was supposed to be. Now I realize that there's more to love, than what we had. We weren't meant to be. Maybe," I hesitated, "we're meant for this." I reached over and took Scott's hand. "To be friends. You certainly have helped me tonight. I appreciate it."

He squeezed my hand gently.

"Did you ever hang up the pictures?"

"The pictures?" I asked.

"The paintings? My paintings of you?"

Embarrassed that I had not, I shook my head nimbly and released his hand.

"Oh," he said, sounding disappointed. "Do you still want them?"

"I don't know." Then, quickly, followed by saying, "Yes.

They were, they are, important to me." Scott smiled and we embraced for the first time as friends. "I'll put them up, when I get home. I guess they have reminded me too much of, well, our years together."

"Natalie, are you seeing anyone? I mean, it's not my business. But, I want you to be happy."

"Actually, I did meet someone, but it's crazy too. I guess I'm destined for complicated relationships. This one's a doozy."

"Tell me. I promise to listen."

"Well, long-story-short, my best friend secretly set me up to meet a man who ended up being a client. And then, after falling in love with him and handing all of myself over to him on a platter, I found out that he was her ex-husband."

"Wow. And, that goes against your stead-fast rules and nature."

"Exactly!"

"Do you love him?"

"It's complicated," I responded, knowing I did.

"You said it earlier, about us, it wasn't meant to be. Maybe it is with this guy. Don't let some childish game get in the way of your happiness. For us, my stupidity and immature behavior ruined our relationship. And you're thinking, 'not again.' Don't be afraid to explore this. Natalie, it might sound crazy, but I've learned a lot since we broke up. Mostly, about what an asshole I've been for my whole life. Life is weird. I have tried to change. So much has changed in my life. I'm different. God, I hope I'm different. Being a jerk doesn't help you win friends, not in the long run. I hurt you. I hurt others. I don't know why. There was no purpose. I guess the only thing it served was my ego. My need to be in control. Well, control is not all it's cracked up to be. Sometimes you've just gotta go for it."

"What do you mean?"

"Right after we broke up, I went on that business trip. The one Lisa was going to be on? We had spent a lot of time together, but not for work. Anyway, she told me she was pregnant. I didn't know what to do. Then, just like she had done before, she ran off and hooked up with some other guy. Shit. It's probably not even mine. All of this made me think of the games I've played with those I actually cared about the most. Sometimes, life has to kick you in the ass so you can get your shit together. I've started to play a different game. Try to live better, dream more, be grateful. So, I made a huge change and moved here. It's only been a short time, and I think things are better, but—", he paused, "Hey, I'm sorry. I'm hogging the conversation. We're supposed to be talking about you."

"The sad thing is, you are. What you're saying is true about me as well. I'm not living, and I'm certainly not grateful. Sometimes I'm like a broken pair of wings. One wing is strong, carrying me along each day being the perfect employee—professional, consistent, reliable. The perfect daughter—respectful, loving, accommodating. The other wing, the other side is waiting for me to fall and break, trying to figure out how to pick up the shattered shards. It's all just a bandage to cover my true self." *Where was this coming from, and why was I telling Scott?* I shook my head and continued, "You must think I am nuts."

"You're not nuts. We're all just trying to figure things out. Everyone needs a little help once in a while."

I moved to the edge of the couch. "You know, Scott, it's all whacked. If mom would have never told me about Caleb, I wouldn't know any better. Now that I do, I'm more complete. I've believed that a piece of me was missing. I never dreamed it was my own flesh and blood, a sibling. It sounds crazy, but I want to visit him, talk to him. When I get back home, I am going to go to the cemetery. Do you think that's a bad idea?"

"No, it will help bring closure to some things."

"Thanks again, Scott." We hugged and he gave me a soft kiss on the cheek. I pushed myself out of the couch. He followed my lead. We faced each other squarely, staring and smiling, analyzing the situation in silence. I started to rock back and forward awkwardly, like a defective pendulum. Finally, Scott wrapped his arms around me, giving me a final hug. My eyes and face were so worn-out, I couldn't bear to cry anymore.

The thumping of the revolving hotel door interrupted the peace. Someone flew in, their flat shoes clunking against the tile floor.

"May I help you, sir?" the attendant asked.

"Ah, yes," a man said, pulling the attention of everyone in the lobby. He bellowed as if talking into a microphone. "I'm trying to locate a guest."

I recognized the voice.

"Her name is Natalie Swan."

Oh my God. I whispered to Scott, "It's him."

Derek turned around precisely when Scott and I parted. His chest heaved up and down as if he'd run from New York to San Diego.

"Let me check for you. One moment, please." The front desk clerk replied.

His eyes locked on me, and mine on his.

"Miss." He turned to the young woman. "I found her." He left the counter and walked straight toward us. The sound of my heartbeat replaced the smacking of the revolving door. Derek appeared tired and worn, like leather that had sat unattended in the hot sun. His eyes were a stinging red. Every inch of his being seemed to tremble. I wondered if he felt as nervous as I did. Especially finding me in the arms of this stranger.

Derek slowed his pace, investigating us, landing his gaze on Scott. He was searching, perhaps running through all the names I had mentioned to him. His senses seemed to pique as his eyebrows lifted, widening his stare and exposing the red jagged vessels enveloping his eyes.

I wasn't sure whether it was his rage or my passion, but the heat of his body radiated outward. *I want to be with him. He should be the one holding and comforting me.*

Instantly, I felt ashamed, as if I had betrayed him. But, he was the one who had betrayed me. I glanced at Scott, who had been there when I needed someone. Where was Derek?

Having a laugh? God, why do I allow myself to seep into this madness of mind games?

Derek shook his head as if he was trying to jolt the blood in his veins that had temporarily stopped its fluid movement. He wrinkled his nose, batted his eyes and cleared his throat.

"Natalie!"

My blood moved faster as my heart rate accelerated. Confusion channeled through me. Everyone in the lobby turned and stared. An inquisition mounted against me. Aware of all the eyes on me, I walked closer to Derek, studying him.

"Dere—"

"So, I guess this is Scott," he interrupted. "Well, I came here to apologize and explain. I wanted to tell you that I love you and that I'm sorry. But, I can see," he glared at Scott, "I'm too late."

"Wait, Derek, no, I—" starting to approach him. "Listen, I—"

His words shut out my attempts to explain. "You think you were the fool. Well, maybe. But, it looks like I'm a fool too!" he shouted.

He shot Scott another deadly look and then strutted swiftly toward the revolving doors. I started after him, following him outside. Rain flowed down the sidewalk. I looked to the right, then left. Down the street, Derek stepped into a cab. I ran, calling his name, but seconds later, the door swung shut and the cab skirted out into traffic. I stood paralyzed on the sidewalk, watching the car until it was out of sight, the rain drenching my hair and clothes. No one on the street would have known the difference between the rain splattering against my face and the tears commingling with them.

This is the worst day ever.

From behind me, Scott clasped my dangling hand and pulled me under the awning of a café. My body shivered in his hold. We stood close for a long time until the trembling subsided and my breathing returned to normal.

The rain started to slow. He wiped my brow with the end of his cuff. "Natalie, I'm sorry. Derek, he seemed overwhelmed. He wouldn't even let you explain."

"Yeah," I said.

"Natalie," Scott paused, staring directly into my eyes. "He said he loved you. Do you love him?" Even with all that had happened, I could not bear never seeing or being with Derek again. *How can I reconcile my love and anger for him? How do I forgive him?*

"Yes, I do," I told Scott. "I love him."

No matter what Scott thought his chances were, his face showed it all. He realized he had none. "Why don't I take you back to the hotel? You need some rest before heading to the hospital in the morning. I'm sure that once Derek settles down, he'll realize he was being overly dramatic."

Scott walked me to my room. After a friendly hug, I said, "Thank you, Scott." I pretended to be better but I ached inside reliving Derek's abrupt disappearance.

"No, thank you, Natalie. I'm glad that we had this time, and I'm sorry about Derek. He'll come around."

"Goodbye, Scott." I forced a smile and kissed his cheek softly. I left him in the hallway.

Two lost people, alone again.

CHAPTER 34

The hotel room served as a silent sanctuary for my thoughts and me. Although my bottom felt numb from sitting on the edge of the bed, I remained balanced on the mattress thinking about the evening's events. A picture formed in my mind of a small innocent boy, tugging on his mother's skirt, looking up at her with wide longing eyes.

I grabbed my purse from the nightstand and pulled out my wallet. Inside was a picture of my mother and me when I was only five years old. I yanked the photo out of the plastic compartment. It stuck slightly. With my thumbs, I covered my long pigtails and tried to imagine what my brother may have looked like. The glossy paper became damp with tears.

My childhood fantasies, loneliness and inadequacies—all the feelings I had placed high on a shelf—roared down the tracks like a steam engine winding through rural America on its way to an unknown destination. *What would be next? How would life unfold? Did more secrets exist?*

I began to replay the secret plot set up by my best friend to meet her ex-husband. The man I knew, in my heart, that I loved. *What does he think now? That I'm back with Scott? That our relationship was so petty to me that I would jump in the sack with an old lover? He didn't even let me explain. I'm the one who is angry at him.*

Disappointed in him. I'm the one who's the fool, not him. I haven't done anything wrong.

After storing the picture back in my wallet and tossing my purse on the floor, I raised my arms above my head and stretched. "Ah," I said out loud. I pushed myself up from the bed, unzipped my pants and let them fall to the floor, untouched.

I crawled into bed and plunged my aching tired head onto the pulpy pillow. I stared at the creamy blank ceiling, until my eyes hurt. Finally, they narrowed, closing into darkness.

***

The blackness hijacked my mind, sweeping me back to the old cemetery. Although it was a dream, I knew where I was and why I was there. To find out the truth.

There was no shifting ground or endless plain of green hills. No wedding party, no parents or friends. No faceless lover. No one. Just me, wearing faded blue jeans and a white button down cotton shirt. My tennis shoes were worn, covered in red clay and dust.

The iron gate sat directly in my path. Instead of the rundown one I had seen in previous dreams, this gate was new, shiny and well kept. I unlatched it and pushed it open, easily swinging on its hinges. Inside, the endless graves still cast a sense of sadness, but the grass was a perfect emerald green, and thousands of cherry blossoms floated in the air, landing around my feet. The sky rained pink and ruby snowflakes. Beyond the trees, the garnet moon hung, shining through, glowing like an amber pendant hanging in front of the sun.

I pushed the tentacles of a huge weeping willow aside, exposing a pebbled path. I journeyed through the manicured graveyard, skipped over a rambling creek and listened to the peaceful quiet. I was lured to the corner of the cemetery, where the mysterious tombstone lay directly in front of me. Its granite stone twinkled in the sun's light. I was ready to face him.

"Caleb?" I called, hoping he would respond. "Caleb? It's

you, isn't it?" I searched the grounds, peeked around the headstone and glanced back toward the gate, trying to find him. "Please come out."

From behind a small bush, the little boy emerged. He wore his green overalls. Rich blonde locks swung in his face, covering his knowing eyes.

"Caleb?" I asked, lowering my chin and inspecting him like I had never seen him before. Now, I could see it. His eyes matched mine. His nose was a twin of dad's, just as my mother had described. Clearly, we shared a family tree.

"Yes," the boy answered, staying at a distance.

"I'm Natalie."

"I know."

"I'm sorry. I didn't listen. I mean, I assumed that these dreams were just that, dreams. But, I understand now. They are so much more. They define me, my life." I stepped closer toward Caleb, but he ducked under a tree. "Mommy told me what happened. Caleb," I continued, moving in slow motion to his hiding spot. "She is so sorry."

Poking his head out from behind the branches, he asked, "She told you?"

"Yes. Finally. She has been living with this for decades. It was difficult to listen to the story as she explained it. But, now things make sense."

Caleb crouched under the tree, looking up at me through the leaves. "She really told you?" he considered. "Finally. I've begged her to forgive herself. It wasn't her fault." He paused, tucking his thumbs in his pockets. "Would you believe me, if I told you that I asked her to?"

"What?" I asked. "What do you mean, asked her to?"

Caleb stepped from behind the tree, landing directly parallel to me. "I've been asking her to tell you for a long time."

"You have?"

"Yes. She is so unhappy and so is daddy."

The smile erased from my face. "You visit them too?"

Caleb remained quiet. He shifted his feet along the top of the grass. "Sometimes," he whispered. "But I don't think they understand. Like you do. Now, anyway."

"I'm sure they do."

"It really doesn't matter. As long as everyone knows, I can go on. I couldn't leave without mommy, you and daddy, being okay and without you knowing about me." Caleb started to cross in front of his tombstone that now clearly read, "Caleb Swan."

"Where are you going?" I asked.

Caleb stopped, sighed and gazed up toward the sky.

"How will I visit you if you're up there?" My face tightened, realizing that he was leaving me, disappearing in front of my eyes. Vanishing from my dreams. *How could this be? Now that everything is so clear. My brother. He's helped me understand who I am. Our first and last time together with the truth. It's not fair.*

"Please don't go Caleb."

"I'll always be here. With you." He leaned against the stone.

"Wait!" I screamed. "I wish we had more time together."

"Yeah, me too. It's important to spend time with those you love. Remember that. I love you. Goodbye Natalie."

He smiled, winked and disappeared.

***

When I woke, I sat in my bed, legs criss-crossed, and wept.

CHAPTER 35

With my father's barely audible snores, a gentle rhythm sung in the air. I watched his chest rise and fall as he healed, beneath the white cocoon of cotton linens. The ICU was still and quiet. The occasional murmurs of the nurses behind the counter interrupted the silence. I positioned myself in the rigid chair. For the moment, I tried to block out the confusion, and focus on the issue that mattered most—making sure my father got better.

I hung my head toward the floor, my eyes turning glassy like still, smooth waters. I ran my hand through my disheveled blonde strands.

Footsteps tapped on the floor. Glancing to the side, I saw a pair of patent leather Bellini Pumps approaching. It wasn't my mother, since she only wore these certain tennis shoes from Walmart.

I flipped my hair back, and turned around. Sabra stood timidly with her arms folded tightly in front of her bosom. She acknowledged me with a curt bob of her head.

Sabra walked toward dad's bed, twitching as if worms slithered along the sides of her body. Her eyes drilled into him as she reached the side of the bed. She shuddered. It seemed hard for her to look at him. For an instant, I thought that we may have had more in common than I realized. Like me, she kept her eyes smooth as a calm ocean, hiding the choppy waters churning behind them. I glanced around awkwardly to locate the closest escape. *Maybe Sabra reconsidered sharing her thoughts and feelings with me yesterday.*

A doctor broke the stillness between us. He was a tall, robust young man, with brownish hair and green eyes. A stethoscope hung around his neck. He wore a short white coat. The length of the arms barely reached his wrists. It seemed as if he had squeezed into a one-size-fits-all that just didn't fit *all*. His movements were jerky and uncomfortable. He spoke phonetically, like an old model robot. I guessed he was young, in his mid-thirties, but his dark, thick-rimmed glasses and fine, narrow lips made him seem much older.

"Good morning, ladies. I'm Dr. Long," he greeted us, as he walked toward my father's bed, with a spastic ambling. "It seems," he continued, "that Mr. Swan is doing well at the moment. His vitals are good, strong. Has he been up this morning?" He lifted the clipboard off the hook at the foot of the bed and began flipping the pages. I was confident Dr. Long did not read a word.

"Not since I've been here," I responded. "He seems to be resting a bit more soundly than yesterday. How long will he be in the hospital?"

"Well, we'll have to wait and see." Dr. Long seemed agitated with the question, as if he was supposed to pinpoint exactly the date and time to release a patient. He nodded abruptly toward me, and Sabra, and then moved on to another patient on the other side of the room.

Sabra's breathing grew labored. She did not say a word during Dr. Long's visit. No questions. She barely acknowledged him. Not that he would have answered.

Sabra's condition concerned me. Lines cut into her paled face making her appear much older. I worried that deep within her elegant frame hid an insecure, scared girl.

Compelled to comfort her, I searched for something to say. But it was hard. I expected more out of her. *How weak. What type of wife is Sabra going to be if she isn't strong enough to support daddy. I shouldn't be judgmental.* I didn't understand all that Sabra had been through. *Everyone's level of stress is different.*

Yet, her eyes appeared void of emotion. An empty vessel drifting off course toward a cliff. I prayed that love, respect and hope filled her otherwise hollow shell. Here was my dad, recovering from a massive heart attack and invasive surgery, and Sabra—a toddler lost in a store, searching for her mother.

"Sabra," I struggled to sound reassuring, "um, I think he's going to be fine. He's a trooper."

This is ridiculous. I'm trying to find a way to comfort a woman who I barely know and who plans to whisk my father away. I had plenty on my own plate. Serving as BFF and therapist to Ms.-Younger-than-me was not on my list of priorities.

Derek's abrupt departure left me torn and confused. I loved him, but wanted him to experience pain. He didn't understand why I had left his calls unanswered or why I went to Scott for comfort. Sara's plot had broken my spirit. Derek walking away punctured my heart. Caleb disappearing tortured my thoughts. He may be gone from my dreams forever. The next time I would talk to him would be at a real cemetery. No little boy would lead me. He would be in the ground. Or, in the heavens. No matter where he was, he was now in my life.

These feelings nauseated me. Sabra's temporary insanity frustrated me. *Why does everything always seem to be about someone else?*

As though I was not in the room, Sabra stared at dad. Her face revealed a troubled person. She thought hard, as if contemplating the next move in a never-ending war. An extraordinarily large tear rolled down her face. She made no attempt to wipe it away. No additional tears followed. Just one.

"Well," I continued. "I'm going to, um, get some coffee."

I waited, but Sabra provided no response or reaction, just a minor twinge. I wondered whether it was safe to leave my father with this brainless twit. *What if something happens and he needs help? Will she be able to call someone or will she stare like some freaked out kid who just smoked her first joint?* I checked out the surroundings. Two nurses stood close by, one at the nurse's station and one tending to an elderly woman three beds over.

I lifted myself out of the mammoth chair. I took one more inquisitive look at Sabra and walked to the nurses' station, far enough away to give her space, but well within sight, in case she went postal. I leaned on the counter and watched.

Sabra remained immobilized, hovering over dad like a bee examining a flower. I wondered what she could be thinking. "Take the nectar or move on to the next bud?" *Could she, like me, be reflecting on her life and her decisions? If I were Sabra, I would regret divulging my feelings and fears to my soon-to-be stepdaughter.*

Moments later, Sabra hobbled to the guest chair and fell into it like it was a pile of soft down pillows instead of the hard straight seat. In this state, she seemed like a child in a giant's chair. Her face etched with desperation, longing and silent discomfort. I had seen this expression before—in the face of Scott weeks ago at the pool. She wanted out. Guilt had kept her here.

Dad's eyes open. He appeared confused, as if he wasn't sure where he was. I wanted to run over to him, but decided to wait and give them space. Dad and Sabra smiled at each other. Her grin slowly faded. Dad shifted painfully in the bed.

"Sabra, honey," I heard. His words were strained. Even from this distance, the physical and emotional pain resonated as he spoke. His eyes showed his perseverance.

"Yes, Frank," Sabra said. Mechanically, she got up from the chair and walked to the edge of dad's bed, reaching for his hand.

"Sabra, I guess I really did it this time, huh?" He swallowed a chuckle. Sabra seemed disconnected from the rest of her body. I almost felt the boulder that balanced on her chest. The air thinned.

"You know, you've given me such happiness. I have enjoyed," his voice broke with a feeble cough. "Everything. You have been the light in my life these many months and I want," he continued to wrestle with his words, "to let you know that I love you."

"Why are you saying this? You're going to be fine," she said.

"Yes, well, maybe. But, how are you? I know what happened with your father, how hard it," he coughed, "was, especially as an only child." Under his breath, he forced, "you look sad."

Sabra did not answer. Her stare fell to the cold floor.

"I see it in your eyes," he continued. "You've wanted to go for a while." His forehead strained, as if the pain showing on Sabra's face penetrated straight through him and collided with the anguish already brewing inside his body. He fought to continue, "I mean, I'm fine. We both need different things. I don't want to put you through this. You're young. You don't need me holding you back," he finished, running out of air.

"You are not holding me back. I wanted to take this journey with you," Sabra came alive, like she had woken from a terrible dream.

"So did I. Now things are different. This heart of mine's the icing on the cake. It's too much and we're not enough. I can tell in your eyes, in your body and in the absence of your smile. I feel it in this clunker of a body I have. You can go. No regrets."

He tried to lift his lethargic hand, to touch her cheek, but he was weak and it fell deflated on the bed. "I'm tired." He turned toward her and looked her straight in the eyes and said, "Let me look at you." He stared at her, analyzing her face.

"I am sad," he muttered. "But, I'm not sure if it's because you're leaving or I wish Sybil was here. Hell, it might be because I'm pissed that I'm lying in this hospital. Maybe its everything." He attempted to adjust his head on the pillow, but he couldn't move. Defeated, he yawned meagerly and drifted off.

I found myself wanting to cry for them. For myself. I needed to live my life. To take the words he just said and do that too. "No regrets." *I've got to start living and not just breathing.*

Freedom radiated from Sabra. She wanted to walk out

those ICU doors and never look back. *Doesn't she feel guilty at all?*

Moments later, she straightened her Liz Claiborne skirt, smoothed back her hair and walked like a bride down the aisle, one step at a time. She slowed only to say, in my direction, "Sorry." She did not look at me. The ICU door clicked shut.

It's the three of us again.

CHAPTER 36

When my father woke hours later, he saw our eager faces, those of me and my mother. We were both grabbing on to the bed as if it were a raft in the middle of the ocean. I knew in that moment that everything was going to be okay. That we had what we wanted.

My mother grabbed his hand and started to interrogate him as usual. "How do you feel? Did you get some rest? Do you want something to eat, drink, ice chips?"

Dad did not respond right away. He kept staring at us. Even though we were confined in this sterile and depressing place, we were the perfect picture. This time, when dad reached his hand, he stretched with more determination than ever and touched my face with his fingertips.

With the slightest whisper he said, "I'm fine. My family is here."

The days passed, dad grew stronger. As his heart healed, so did the bond he had lost with mom many years ago.

One evening, late, after I had returned to the hotel, mom confessed to dad that she had told me about Caleb. Mom explained that dad was resistant at first, but after hearing my reaction and how she could finally move on, he realized the significance of bringing the situation into the open. Now, they could work to mend their heartache, whether or not they were together as man and wife. *Could they be friends?*

Three weeks later, I approached my parents, who were sitting in dad's room laughing. An energy I had not felt in years burst inside me. I couldn't remember the last time my parents had laughed together. *Maybe more than friends?* I hoped more than anything this was a start, a new chapter in their odd and complex lives. They deserved happiness.

After taking in the vigor of the sounds of their laughter, I started, "Mom, dad. The last thing I want to do is go back to Miami, but I've got clients and things to work out. I need to go home, find out what's happening at work."

"We completely understand, Nat. You've got a job and a life," mom said. "Your dad," she leaned over and planted a kiss on his forehead, "is doing fine. I'm going to stay until they say he can come home."

I bent down and kissed my father on the cheek and hugged my mother. I realized how lucky I was. No matter what might be waiting for me at home, I had two people who loved me regardless of what I did. I also had Caleb, at least in my heart, to carry me forward.

I caught the next available flight back to Miami. On the way to my apartment, I stopped at a liquor store, and bought a bottle of Merlot, determined to drink the whole thing.

When I walked through my front door, my feet were cramping. A single pain shot from my back down my right leg. I lay down on the hard floor and stretched my arms and legs as far as I could, like DaVinci's Vitruvian Man. I stayed there for about fifteen minutes. My muscles relaxed and the pain started to ease.

Investigating my home, like a curious cat, I visited each nook and cranny of my miniature abode, passing the kitchen frequently to refill my wine glass.

Everything remained the same. Laundry sat piled in the closet. The refrigerator could have doubled as a storage unit. Pillows lay in disarray on the couch and floor. None of this mattered. I was home. I missed it more than I realized. It was mine, a place for me to daydream, fantasize, hope and cry. If I wanted. Distant from the world, anonymous.

After a thorough review, I fell on the couch, exhausted. I rubbed my aching feet and swallowed the ruby liquid. The bottle sat half empty when I snuggled my head on the throw pillow.

The light on the answering machine blinked wildly. I knew it was Derek, or Sara, or Scott, or someone I didn't want to talk to. I ignored them, for now.

For the first time in weeks, I didn't have a care in the world. The wine clouded my thoughts. I gulped another mouthful, the heat of the wine filling my veins. My eyes rolled back and fluttered as I inched my hand down to my slacks, unbuttoned the clasp and pulled the zipper down. I reached under my panties, my palm sweeping across my soft hairs. Inching further, a warm wetness lubricated my fingers. I daydreamed about the night Derek and I made love in Saint Augustine. *I wish I could feel Derek inside me, loving me, making me whole.*

The empty bottle lay on its side, a small puddle of wine seeping into the coffee table. My body lay limp and satisfied.

When I woke the next morning, I was still lying on the couch, my legs spread, the left one hanging over the side. My head was spinning. *No way I'm going to work.* No one knew I was back in town, and I needed a day for me.

I dragged myself to the bathroom. Since I heard about my father's heart attack, I thoroughly inspected myself in the mirror. A deep jagged wrinkle had formed right between my eyebrows. *That wasn't there before!* I stared at it, rubbing it, hoping that enough massage would erase it from my face, but to no avail. A permanent reminder of the last few weeks.

I puttered around the apartment, picking up things, cleaning the kitchen counter and coffee table, tossing a load of laundry in the washer. I passed them about four times before finally deciding to do something I had been ignoring. I picked up one of Scott's paintings leaning against the wall. The face of a gentle loving woman served as the focal point. Her eyes were full of life and spirit, her face was smooth and innocent.

I held the painting in my hands, looking into a mirror of the past. The young vibrant woman was me, but I didn't feel like the girl in the painting. I felt older.

After hanging the painting on the bedroom wall, I sat on the floor, looking up at the spinning fan, the blades cutting through the light. I lost at least an hour, reliving the conversation with my mother, flashing imaginary family photos in my head.

The phone startled me when it rang its familiar tone. I uncrossed my legs and pushed myself up.

"Hi, mommy," I said. "How is daddy?"

"He's doing fine. I wanted to make sure you got home all right. Are you at work?"

"Well, my intention was to get up and go, but that was before many drinks."

"I hope you didn't drive anywhere."

"No. No. I laid here and thought about everything. I'm fine," I hesitated. "I appreciate you telling me, about Caleb."

"It wasn't as bad as I had feared. I guess I thought the world would explode or something if I revealed my little secret. Actually, a lot of good has come from it."

"I agree. Mommy, I need to tell you something too. It's not a big deal, but in the middle of daddy and Caleb, I've been struggling with another situation. I wasn't sure whether to go into it all, and it wasn't really appropriate to discuss at the hospital."

"Tell me," she prodded.

"It's about a man. Or men, I suppose."

"Yes, those can create problems," she remarked.

"Well," I stopped, trying to decide whether to say the words. "I'm in love."

"That's wonderful news. I've been waiting for this phone call for years," mom said, sounding elated and relieved. But I didn't respond. "Okay," she continued, "something's wrong. Why is that not great?"

"It's a long story. Needless to say, I fell in love with a guy who happens to be a client, which is against all my rules. Sara, my so-called best friend, set me up to meet him. I hate games. Then I found out that she is his ex-wife. He knew all about the set up, which to me means he has no integrity. Then the other night, in California, he came to the hotel. He said he loved me."

"Okay. So you love him and he loves you?"

"Yes," I replied.

"That's sounds perfect to me, Natalie."

"Yes, but he saw me with Scott," I added.

"What? Scott? I'm confused. I thought you two were through."

"We are. It's just, he found out about daddy. He lives in San Diego now, and came to the hospital. He was someone to talk to. Nothing happened."

"Call this other guy. Tell him how you feel," she urged.

"I am so mad. He betrayed me."

"Oh, Nat. Has my story not taught you anything? Don't live in the should'a, could'a, would'a world. Seize what is in front of you. You don't like games? Then don't play any. If you love him, you should tell him. Now! If it doesn't work out down the road, at least you can say you were true to yourself."

"Yes. You're right," I conceded. "Courage is want I need."

"You have it. Call him. I'd better go and get back to your dad."

"Okay. Wait! You're not gonna like this, but I need to know. Where is Caleb buried?"

"Why?" she asked.

"I'm going to visit him." I responded, trying to convince myself too.

"Is that a good idea?"

"Yes. He's waiting for me."

"What?" mom asked.

"That's also a long story. I'll explain later. Visiting Caleb is the right thing to do, for me. Please tell me," I pleaded.

"He's at Woodland Park. Are you going alone?"

"Yes. Alone." I confirmed.

"When?" she asked, sounding concerned and confused.

"Today. Later this afternoon."

"Oh, so soon? Why don't you wait and we can go together, when your father and I get back," she said, as though she was hiding something.

"Are you okay, mom? You sound a little stressed."

"No, I'm fine. I just need to go. Your father wants some, um, water. I'll talk to you later. I love you."

"I love you, too."

CHAPTER 37

I drove to the cemetery, parked at the curator's building and asked the fidgety little man where, specifically, Caleb's grave was located. Minutes later, I stood at the entrance of the section reserved for children. I recognized it immediately. The iron gate welcomed me.

I mustered a half smile when I arrived at Caleb's marker.

It was tiny like the poor body that lay beneath it. I knelt beside the grave, totally alone. Yet, sounds of life flourished beyond the iron fence—the chirp of a cardinal, cars rushing by on the road, a plane flying overhead, the gentle shuffling of leaves. Across the street, kids were playing basketball and cheering each other on. *How ironic.* Life blossomed in every direction.

The few square feet I occupied held two beings—the body of my brother and me. Peace softened my mind.

"Caleb," I conjured up the courage to speak. "I didn't know that you existed until a couple of weeks ago. I'm sorry I've never been to visit you. I would have. Now, I will. Mom told me what happened. She's lived with that guilt for most of her life. But, now, I think she has set herself free, and I understand a little more about myself too. You would have been a wonderful brother. I wish we'd had the opportunity to grow up together. You are the piece of the puzzle that I needed to find."

I'm talking to a grave. "Wow, I really do need a therapist," I said, laughing at myself. *Whatever! I want to talk to him.* I continued, "Caleb. I've been dreaming about you and other things. You know that, don't you? I'm afraid I won't be seeing you any more—in my dreams. I guess that means you are free too. Maybe you'll visit me again, someday, somewhere. I hope."

I took a deep breath, looking around. Leaves danced from their branches as the wind blew. Beams from the sun peeked through the clouds, warming my skin. I detached from the world. Just Caleb and I existed.

I placed my hand on his tombstone and said, "Caleb, thank you. You saved me." Deep within the ground, Caleb rested. A piece of my past, now a part of my future.

Kneeling, the ground's dampness seeped through my pants. My legs shook. I pushed myself up and stared at the bright green blades of grass. I shifted and straightened the drab and sun-drained flower arrangement. I noticed a piece of paper stuck between the petals. Upon closer inspection, I realized it was an envelope.

"What is this?" I asked. I carefully picked up the envelope by its corner and examined it, back and front, but there was no address, no name, just blank. I tucked it in my pocket, thinking I would deal with it later. Right now, I wanted to say goodbye to my brother.

"Caleb. Rest peacefully. I'll be back soon. I love you."

I strolled around the cemetery for another hour or so, reading each gravestone, saddened at how young the occupants were. I peered at the massive trees rising up from the earth, hanging over the shaded plots, comforting and protecting the cemetery's inhabitants. It reminded me of looking up through the soaring branches of the redwoods at Muir Woods—the overwhelming magnitude of the earth's beauty and strength.

All of a sudden, I had a desire to seize the day.

I returned to my apartment and buzzed around with a

renewed energy. I played the messages on the machine, at work and on my cell phone. Most were from Derek, begging me to call him. Some were from before he went to San Diego, others were after. His voice seemed strained and confused.

He kept repeating how he didn't mean to hurt me and that he wanted to be with me and *blah, blah, blah.* The last one from Derek sounded different. His tone had changed. He sounded irritated, on edge. This message was left a few days after our blow up at the hotel.

"I know I didn't handle seeing you with Scott well. I didn't let you explain and I jumped to conclusions. I was surprised. I had envisioned you sitting, crying your eyes out, stressed and alone. Which is wrong of me because you're strong. And, when I saw you with him, jealousy took over. I hope that you can forgive me, now for three things. For acting foolish, for agreeing to Sara's childish plot, and for being an asshole about Scott. Please call me. I love you. I really, really love you. No games. Just me."

I played the message three times before deleting it.

Wow. Maybe I should call him.

I listened to the other messages. One was from Scott. He wanted to be sure I was all right. Maybe he really had changed, but I didn't love him anymore. I loved Derek. I had to fix everything, somehow. I wasn't sure where to begin, where to peel the Band-Aid away and let things heal.

I stumbled to the bedroom, unzipping my slacks. The corner of the envelope was sticking out of my pocket. I had forgotten about it.

I slipped it out and held it, contemplating. *Should I open it? It's probably someone's bill they forgot to pay or some weird love letter.*

I stuck my index finger under the corner and broke the seal. Inside was a note addressed to me. I dropped it and backed away as soon as I saw my name. *It can't be.*

After a few cloudy moments, I inched over toward the paper and reluctantly picked it up, my hand shaking. There was no name or signature, but I recognized the handwriting. I went to the beginning and started to read,

Dear Natalie,

    If you are reading this letter, then I finally have your attention. Don't be mad. Your mother told me of your plan to come here, and since you won't talk to me, I thought this might be a way to share with you how I feel. First, I love you. I am dying with the thought that you hate me. I know this won't make everything better, but I hope that it will at least make you happy. Go to 2112 W. Flagler.

"Mom?" *That's why she sounded so nervous on the phone. Now SHE is serving as matchmaker? Super.*

"Go to W. Flagler? What on earth?"

Early the next morning, I drove to the address. I pulled up to the building and opened the car door, when I noticed the most amazing sign I had ever seen. It read, "The Caleb Swan Academy. A Place for All Children."

I could not believe my eyes. I stood in front of the building, staring at the sign contemplating why, who, how could this be. A family coming out of the door with two small children interrupted my gawking.

What is going on?

As I entered, a lady at the front desk said, "Ms. Swan. Hello. We're so glad you're here."

I'm sure my face looked alien, lost from an unknown planet.

"How do you—" I stopped, as the woman pointed to a picture of the entire Swan family, including Caleb. The photo had obviously been photoshopped but we were all together—mom, dad, Caleb and me. Our family.

"Wait," I started. "Who would have—" The woman stopped me in mid-question and said, "Mr. Voeltgin says hello."

I leaned against the wall and slowly slid down on the floor, as I watched the children play and laugh.

"I can't believe it."

CHAPTER 38

Today, I have to go to work. Around noon, I headed to the office. Sara was not at her desk. I had tried to figure out how I would face her, or anyone, for that matter. From one moment to the next, my thoughts flipped from not caring at all, to caring more than anything.

The day passed rapidly while I sat confined in my office, trying desperately not to speak to anyone. Around 4 p.m., I walked down the hallway to Mr. Beatler's office and poked my head through his partially closed door.

"Ah, Natalie. I was wondering when I'd see you. How is your father?"

"He's doing fine. Thanks, John."

"I know it's tough. I lost my dad when I was twenty-two. You never get over it. You cope. So, I'm glad to hear he is doing better. Cherish that, Nat."

"Thanks. I appreciate your support and for letting me stay for as long as I did."

"Family, first. Why don't you head home? Get some rest."

"Good night," I said, as I left his office.

On the drive, my thoughts were consumed with Caleb's Center and how Derek had orchestrated the whole thing.

At home, I admired the other paintings from Scott. They

were good. Two were of me. The three others were abstracts, Picasso-like. I studied them for a while, and then walked into the kitchen, pulled the hammer and nails from the drawer next to the refrigerator and spent the next hour hanging the rest of the pictures. Once they were up, I stood back, pleased with the work and with finally deciding to hang them. I could not believe I'd waited this long to make them part of my home. The colors alone brightened the bleak walls and lifted my spirit.

That evening I received another message from Derek. Just the sound of his desperation made me wants him more. *Sex is exactly what I need right now.* All the tension in my body had built up like a cement bunker, ready to split open.

"I hope you were pleased yesterday. Please call!" he pleaded.

Instead of acting on my desire to call and beg him to fly to Miami and whisk me away, I took a long shower. With the towel tightly wrapped around me, I opened the dresser drawer that hid my precious pink nightie. I had not worn it since my trip to St. Augustine. I dropped the towel onto the floor, picked up the delicate garment and slipped it on. *I love how I feel in this.* I sauntered over to my bed, lay down, covered myself with the silky white sheets and fantasized about Derek.

I twisted my back deep into the mattress, my skin rubbing against the fabric. Just thinking about him, touching and kissing me, made me swell. My sensitive breasts were aroused. The soft cloth tickled my nipples. I rolled my head from side to side dreamily. Under the covers, I reached down between my legs. Memories of our night together at the Dixie Cottage played in my mind. My desire for him erupted, but I was only partially satisfied.

I have to figure how out to make this better. I need him.

The next day, I worked diligently to catch up. Sara called in sick. *Thank God. Another day to put off the agony of dealing with her.* I had not been able to finish the Voeltgin marketing plan before my father's heart attack. I was totally focused on completing it, presenting the plan to Mr. Beatler in the morning and getting it off my plate. I planned to suggest that someone else manage the account. There wasn't any way I could keep my personal and professional lives separate. Not in this case.

Night settled on the city. Stars lit up the sky beyond my window. In addition to the marketing strategy, I printed my résumé. I planned to send it to a couple of firms. I shut down my computer at about 8 p.m. I assumed that everyone else had left the building hours ago. A soft buzzing vibrated within the walls.

I walked the halls for a while, the Voeltgin proposal tucked under my arm. I reminisced about my time at Jameson. I recalled my first day on the job, frightened at the thought of dropping a sheet of paper or not answering the phone by the second ring. When I stood up to Mr. Beatler and persuaded him that the Mason Account was a bad business decision and how Jameson's involvement would be detrimental to the company's reputation. The time when my first real client complimented my work in front of Jameson's CEO. The massive window in my office, where the sun would pour in, and where tomorrow was defined.

I had given so much of myself, of my life and talent, to this company. I hated to think that giving all my 'it' was for nothing.

Then, I remembered the moment I realized my best friend toyed with all I had, my life. *I suppose it's all a learning process, the good and the bad.*

My stroll through memory lane brought me to Mr. Beatler's office.

People were laughing. *I can't believe someone is still here this late. Past nine?*

As I approached the door, the laughter grew louder. Then I heard sounds of passion and moaning, and then laughter again. A struggle for air, and then silence. A slight whimper, and a sigh.

What the hell?

Mr. Beatler's door was closed, but clearly the noise came

from inside. I knocked and pushed the door open. "Mr. Beatler?" I asked, trying to make sure he was in the room. As I entered, the Voeltgin proposal dropped to the floor. My hands clasped the sides of my head and I gasped. There, on the desk, locked in a passionate embrace, Mr. Beatler and Ms. Messer were sprawled out, naked, exposing every wrinkle, bulge and scar. Mr. Beatler's pants lay deposited around his ankles.

Ms. Messer screamed. I screamed. *This cannot be happening! What the fuck! I did NOT need to see that!* I studied the disturbing scene. A sickness, filled with disappointment, entered my stomach, rose up and landed in my throat. *Let down again.* Anger and resentment had become commonplace. I felt betrayed, but I wasn't the one flapping my ass on a twenty-five year old desk.

"I've felt sorry for you." I said to Ms. Messer, shaking my head. "I guess you're doing better than I thought. Please carry on. This isn't a place of business or anything. I'm sure Mr. Beatler's wife and three children wouldn't mind at all."

"Natalie," Mr. Beatler started apologetically, as he grabbed his pants and fumbled to zip them up. I picked up the proposal and turned to leave, but quickly glanced over my shoulder and said, "You should be ashamed." I sprinted down the hallway. Mr. Beatler followed. When I reached my office, I grabbed my purse and left immediately. By the time Mr. Beatler's choppy body caught up with me, the elevator doors were closing.

"Unbelievable!" That was it. *I'm quitting.*

I paced in my apartment for three hours, struggling to comprehend Mr. Beatler and Ms. Messer's affair. *I wish I could just block it out.* If I had not been so stressed and on verge of throwing everything I'd worked for up in the air, I might have been able to muster a snicker. *Shit! What a sight.*

CHAPTER 39

The next morning, I dreaded what lay ahead. I wore the most comfortable clothes I had that were clean—cropped slinky pants, a tank and sheer cover. I didn't bother applying makeup.

In the parking lot, I stayed in my car staring at the building, cringing at the thought of walking those halls, seeing those people. I wanted to mail in my notice and never return, but I needed another job. *Two weeks. That was professional.* I would have to try to survive until my last day arrived.

I snuck up the back stairs to my office. Signs of Sara were scattered around her workstation—her purse, cell phone, lip-gloss and keys. *Her coffee cup is missing. Probably getting a refill.*

My top priority was to craft a resignation letter.

Sara returned, but did not bother me. I sat at my desk and typed.

I printed out the document. With it in hand, I was ready to waltz down to Mr. Beatler's office. When I started to get up, the phone rang.

"Hello," I answered irritated.

"Ms. Swan?" a spirited man's voice inquired.

"Yes."

"Ms. Swan. I am Jonathan Long with the American Heart

Association. I just wanted to call and thank you."

"Thank me for what?"

"You don't know?" He asked, sounding confused.

"No, I'm sorry." I replied.

"Oh, well. A donation was made in your father's name. A substantial donation. You were listed as the donor. I wanted to personally thank you."

"I think you have the wrong person." *What is this about? Probably wants me to buy something. How did he get my work number? For goodness sake!*

"You are Natalie Swan, daughter of Frank Swan?" he probed.

"Yes, but—"

"Thank you," he interrupted. "The money will be extremely helpful to our organization."

We hung up. I still held the phone to my ear, stunned.

Suddenly, it dawned on me. The pieces began to crystalize. *Derek. What is he trying to do? The school and now this?*

I wanted to wallow in the moment and consider his actions, but I did not have time. The letter was still clutched in my grasp. *Stick to your top priority, Nat. Get it over with.*

I returned my focus to the matter at hand. I got up, nodded to myself and stepped into the hall. Sara had left her desk, but her coffee cup sat next to her keyboard, red lipstick smearing the rim. I sighed and walked toward Mr. Beatler's office, with my head held high. *This is the right decision.*

Mr. Beatler was behind his desk, his head slumped over. *Did he sleep the night here?* I felt sorry for him, but I could not let those feelings interfere with what I had to do. I stood in front of his desk and he looked up lazily. His eyes filled with shame, scanning me. He searched for something to say, but could not find the words.

"Mr. Beatler," I started. "Last night, I was shocked and appalled. I have looked up to and admired you. You've been my mentor. I am so confused about what happened last night, but none of that matters. The last few weeks have changed me. I don't know how to trust anymore," I explained.

"Nat—"

"You're a liar," I interrupted. "God, John, you're married. You have children. I mean, doesn't trust and marriage and love mean anything anymore? Is it all a game?"

"Come on, Nat. Life isn't easy. We've all got our issues. Vices."

"We're not talking about a little fault like running late to work or forgetting to pay a bill. We're talking about fundamental traits. Loyalty? Respect? You don't have either of those. I don't even know what you're about. What do you stand for?" I asked.

"I'm not sure what you want me to say."

"There's nothing for you to say. Nothing would be good enough." I paused, letting the finality of it all settle, and then continued, "How dare you put the company, our livelihood at risk, knowing that we've already had to overcome one employee scandal with Barry. I'd have thought you would've learned after dealing with that."

"You don't even know what happened, Nat."

"You told me. Barry had an affair with a subordinate. Sounds familiar," I barked. "I'm forced to witness the demise of the man that has helped shape me professionally." I stumbled. My stomach rose up, landing like a rock in my chest. "I can't work here anymore. I haven't been happy for a long time. I need a change. And now with this and…" My thoughts turned to Derek and Sara. "…the people I trusted the most," I struggled, "have completely disappointed me."

"Nat. You can't quit. We—I, need you. Don't leave based on my actions," he begged.

"Mr. Beatler, you need more than me. You need help. Be honest with your wife, your family and yourself. I can't work in this environment anymore. I realized it a while ago. It just became truly clear to me over the last several weeks." I laid the resignation letter on his desk. "I emailed you the Voeltgin proposal," I said flatly. "Hopefully, 'it' will be exactly what you hoped for." I left.

News travels fast.

I reached my office. Sara sat at her desk. She had already heard. I marched into my office and closed the door. *Only a couple more hours and I can escape from this place.* As soon the clock struck 5, I was out of there.

On the way home, I drove by Caleb's center, slowing down for a moment to watch the children inside. Seeing those lit-up faces made me think about being a mother. *I wonder, would I be a good mom? I know I'd never keep any secrets from my children. Would I?*

CHAPTER 40

The next few days were hard, but I was comfortable with my decision. One week before my last day, Sara tottered into my office and counted the number of boxes piled along the walls. Each containing memories of the past eight years. We made eye contact, but did not speak. I glared at her until she finally whipped her hair around and stormed out of the office. I figured Sara had convinced herself that my departure directly linked to what happened between us. That was only part of the puzzle.

On my last day, I waited for five o'clock to arrive. My computer account had been disabled. *Things change so fast. Maybe, sometimes, it's out of our hands.*

Sara paced outside of my door. She was getting on my nerves.

"What do you want?" I asked.

Sara stopped abruptly, poked her head in through the door frame and replied, "Don't leave on account of me. I'm sorry. Tell me what I can do to make it up to you," she pleaded.

"Guess what? I'm not leaving because of you," I confessed. "All that's happened," I said, looking around my office, "has taught me a lot, about me. Oh, and by the way, you may want to ask Mr. Beatler about his extracurricular activities."

"What are you talking about?" she asked.

"He seems to be a bit preoccupied if you know what I mean." I started to pack the last books from my credenza as if it was the most important task of my life.

"So you found out, huh?" Sara placed her hands on her hips and gawked at me as if I were a clawless crab, searching the sand for a hiding spot, limping along. *Maybe I am when it comes to life, sex, men, people.*

"You knew?" I looked up from the half-filled box.

After a few seconds, Sara admitted, "Of course. Mr. Beatler's secretary is the biggest gossip in the building. How do you think I got him to ask you to go to San Francisco?"

"What the fuck are you talking about Sara?"

"Language! Miss-potty-mouth!" she yelled. "The thing is," Sara continued, "I don't think his wife would care. From my understanding, she's been sighted with some young blonde hunk from the club she goes to."

"What is the world coming too?" I shook my head disapprovingly.

"Natalie, do what you want, but lighten up. Not everyone is perfect and pristine like some," she said, raising an eyebrow.

"I can't believe this. For God's sake. Does everyone have secrets around here? Am I the only one who doesn't? You, Mr. Beatler, my parents, Derek. Who the hell am I supposed to trust? Who?" I demanded. "No one. All these damn secrets. You, everyone, disgust me!"

"You! You, need to look at yourself in the mirror, missy. You think I've got secrets? Your parents? Derek? Big deal. We all have secrets. Shit. Even you, Nat."

"I don't have any—" I resumed putting books in the box.

"Oh, God, Nat! You've got the worst secret of all of us." Sara walked toward me and ripped the book out of my hands, throwing it on the floor. My mouth dropped. "What are you doing?" I screamed.

"You need a wakeup call, Nat."

"What are you talking about?" I stood face-to-face with

her.

"I don't understand how someone can be so smart and so fucking clueless at the same time. How is that possible, Nat?"

"Are you implying that I'm clueless?" I crossed my arms in front of my chest and shifted my weight uncomfortably.

"Yes."

"How dare you—" I began.

"Don't you dare me anything, Ms. Non-risk-taker. Ms. I'm-perfect-the-way-I-am. Ms. I'm-afraid-of-everything-around-of-me. My God, Nat, what *is* so frightening *is* your secret, your dirty little secret. The only one who doesn't know what 'it' is, is you."

"What?" I swallowed hard, as the fear within me began to rise up. Scott and now Sara. *Does everyone know?*

"Well, I guess I'm the one that's going to have to tell you." In some deep, dark way, I figured Sara was pleased to be the messenger. But I already knew. I was not the perfect little model for the world to admire. What Sara did not realize was that I discovered more about myself over the last few weeks than I had my entire life. I understood what I needed to do and leaving Jameson was just the first step.

"You have a false impression of yourself," she started. "You can't read yourself or those closest to you. You have a major character flaw and that, my friend, is self-doubt, self-pity and an overall lack of knowledge of who you are. You need to figure it out, time's a wastin'. Look. I may not be the smartest. I might just be a secretary forever and work for people like you and Mr. Beatler, who think they are better than everyone else, but guess what? News flash! You're not. You're in worse shape than I am. At least I'm grounded in some reality. I know where I stand. Nat, figure out what you're about and what you want out of life. It's short. You watched it with your dad. Without a moment's notice, 'it' can all be sucked away. No warning. No time to plan or research, which you always love to fall back on. 'I need to research this,' you say.

"You hate me," she continued. "And, you know what? I don't care. Regardless if you think I'm a heartless little bitch, I would do it again. I would. Because I love you, my friend. A friend that needed a push. That needed some leverage. Sure, yeah, I could have done things differently. But, so could you. So—could—you! Grow up Nat, people don't like pansies. Shit! You need to start believing in yourself and stop worrying so much about everyone else's opinions. There's a man out there that loves you. He's in love with you. He would do anything for you. He didn't love me like that. We made a mistake. We wanted to get out of the world we were bound by, by the lives our parents expected us to live, so we escaped by getting married and running away. It was stupid and childish. Don't make a mistake. Don't let him pass by. The time is right, now, for you."

"But, Victor—"

"I love Victor. He was right for me, and Derek's is right for you. Damn, Natalie. You need to decide what you want."

"Alright, already. You're right. I'm working on it."

"Really? How?" she jabbed.

"I'm leaving. The rest I'll figure out as I go. What else do you want me to say?"

"We've said enough. It's time for you to think. Face your fears. Your secrets. Life. Nat, do it, before it's gone. Before you truly are alone." She placed her hands on top of her head and continued, "I never meant to hurt you. You are my best friend and I'm sorry. I should have been honest with you."

The words, "you are my best friend," lingered in my ears.

"I've been unhappy for a long time. Change will be good for me. Isn't this a risk?"

"Yeah, I guess. So is Derek. But isn't it worth it? Taking a risk, than to do nothing." She paused. "Where will you go?"

"I've got some leads."

"Good. I hope everything works out for you. And, that someday you'll be able to forgive me."

Sara picked up the book that she had thrown on the floor and handed it to me. Then left the office, wiping a tear away.

CHAPTER 41

My eyes darted to the ceiling, the door, the desk and the books tucked neatly in their boxes. *Order and control. That's what I have created for myself.*

My heart sank seeing the Dali leaning against the wall. As if I'd never examined it before, a new meaning of the piece emerged. For so long, I hid from the world around me, not even learning from the painting that hung above me all these years. Today, not only did it reveal secret meanings, I recognized myself in its landscape. *The truth hidden beneath everyone's skin is more complex than what the surface suggests.* That applies to everyone. Derek. Sara. Mr. Beatler. Mom and dad. Me. I inspected every inch of the Dali, its layers peeling away before my eager eyes. Something I had not sensed in a long time rose up within me—gratitude. I was thankful for my recent experiences. I had grown and matured.

Back in San Diego, Scott explained how he was different, but I didn't understand how his experience had changed him so quickly and so radically. *I do now.* I was different, too.

Regardless of what Sara thought, today I stood proud and confident. The marathon would be long, but at least I started the run.

After I retrieved my Monet umbrella from the coat rack

and leaned it against one of the boxes, I sat behind my desk with my feet up. *Change is going to be hard.* And a lot of change waited for me, right around the corner.

Later that evening, I lounged on my couch, hidden like a mini-fort, behind a wall of brown cardboard boxes, duct tape and black magic marker.

Would I find another job? Was it too late to change fields? What did I want? Where was I going? Could I fix things with Derek?

The unknown defined my future. My life with Jameson lay behind me, and I grew more satisfied with my decision especially after Sara's diatribe. I could not meet with those people anymore or brief Mr. Beatler in his office after what I witnessed. The memory of Mr. Beatler and Ms. Messer stretched out on his desk flashed in my mind. I swallowed a laugh, finally, as I remembered Mr. Beatler's love handles flapping away.

I turned back to the job at hand—opening boxes and sorting through all the pieces and parts of my office. Before I ripped the tape off of the first box, the phone rang.

As usual, the phone hid under the cushions or under the couch. I immediately started my search. I pulled the phone from underneath a stack of magazines, the display said, "No Data," again. Reluctantly, I answered, afraid that silence may be on the other end like before.

"Hello," I whispered and a weak, "Natalie?" responded. I recognized the voice. My blood pumped like a steam engine, chugging away from the station. I had not spoken with him since the night at the hotel. The sound of his voice was like hearing the words of a lost, but loved, friend. The oxygen running through my body coursed with a level of satisfaction.

"Derek," I said faintly.

"Hey, wow, you answered. I've tried to call your cell and work, I can't remember how many times. Have you gotten any of my messages?" Derek sounded relieved.

"Yes. Well, um—"

"Why haven't you called me back?" His voice was soft, genuine.

"Why do you think?" Before he could answer, I continued, "I need to go."

"No, wait. Please? Please! I need to talk to you. I have to explain." The pain in his voice ripped open my heart. This call served as the last attempt to reconcile and, in truth, I wanted to talk to him too. I wished I could pull him close so that his strong arms would protect me. *He can help me find my way.*

"Okay," I said firmly.

"You're mad about Sara. Rightfully so. I, we, both should have been upfront with everything. She thought you wouldn't agree to meet me."

"And she was right, obviously."

"I disagree. It was meant to be. Us meeting."

"Really?" I questioned.

"Yes. Natalie. I need you, like air itself. You make me want to do and be better. When I'm with you, I can do anything, conquer the world. My brother told me before he died, to seize life, to love life to the fullest. I am full of life and spirit when I'm with you. I need you."

My core melted, seeping out of my body, slipping under the door and dripping down the stairs. I remembered our conversation the second night we were together. Derek said then that life was unpredictable, that the future was a mystery. My mother's words echoed in my head. All the signs were there. I loved Derek, more than anything. But my stubbornness and pride built walls around me, killing my chances of being with him. I was so afraid of appearing weak or vulnerable. Sara's words stopped my self-deprecation and I realized what I was doing. *Forgive him and give this a try.*

"This is hard," Derek continued. "But the thought of not seeing you, of not talking to you, makes me empty inside. I blew it in San Diego. I have never been such an idiot in my life. I want to see you," he demanded.

"Oh," I snapped out of my dream. "I'm not sure if that's a good idea." *Don't be too easy.*

"Nat, it is. I'll be in Miami on Thursday for business.

Please have dinner with me."

"I'm not sure about—"

"We could meet after work," he pleaded.

"Oh, I guess Sara didn't tell you. I quit."

"What? Why?" He sounded shocked.

"Well, it's a long story. Needless to say, I'm glad I'm gone."

"What are you going to do?" he asked.

"I'm not sure yet. It doesn't matter right now." I hoped he would say his offer was still good, even though I had no intention of working for him.

"Okay, how about lunch? Breakfast? Coffee?" he continued. "Nat, just tell me what to do, and I'll do it."

There wasn't anything for him to do. I equally wanted to be with him. A man never talked to me as if his life depended on it. In the past, I was the one begging or being used, leaving broken-hearted. This case, however, was different. Two people were heartbroken.

"I know it was you," I declared.

"What?" he asked.

"The school for children, Caleb's school. The donation for dad. It was you." I repeated. Like the phone line had lost its pulse, he did not answer. "Okay, fine. Thursday at 6:30 p.m.," I suggested. I tried to sound impervious, but secretly under my skin, the heat of my body anticipated his arrival.

"Thank you, Natalie. I'll text you when and where. I love you."

"Bye, Derek."

I called my mother. I had no one else to confide in.

"Mommy, there's something I want to share with you." I proceeded to explain the whole story from the beginning—when I first met Derek, finding about Sara, Mr. Beatler, knowing she had talked with Derek, Caleb's school and our Thursday meeting—everything.

"Okay, now I'm gonna talk and don't interrupt," she began. "I love you more than anything in the world. I'm proud of you. You make me laugh. You listen to me, even when you don't have time and have other things to do. You're smart, gorgeous and funny. I wish I were more like you. You can do anything. But, you cover up your frustration and apprehension. You secretly question everything. I know this 'cause I am like that too. If you think too hard and too long, you'll make yourself crazy. I've tried to balance on that wire, and eventually, you fall. What you've got to do is forget about what everybody else thinks. Stop dwelling on the petty and take charge. You have control over your life. You decided to quit. Fine. Do something different. You love Derek. Tell him. Don't wait for it to come to you. Life is too short. You should live to the fullest and not settle for anything less."

"I guess I'm still just a little girl." I paused, considering what my mother had said. "I need to refocus. Find my spirit."

"Don't be so stubborn. Don't shoot for perfection. For yourself or for those around you. You'll only get disappointed. Trust me. It's also okay to let your guard down sometimes. If you keep building up that wall, it's worse when it finally crumbles."

"Yes. You're right. Everyone is right." Although I already knew the answer, I asked, "Mommy, how did Derek know about Caleb?"

"The secrets are deep and immense. I'll say only this. I like him."

"Thanks, mommy. I understand. I love you, too."

We hung up. I stared at the boxes. My past was locked in cardboard, but for the moment, I was content. Derek and I would be together in two days.

CHAPTER 42

Rain drizzled down outside the shower window. On my tiptoes, I could see steam rising from the asphalt. The sun burst through the dark clouds, hitting the pavement and grass. The low, curly clouds masked the endless sky. Floating past, like elegant dancers, the tips of their toes barely touching the surface. I stepped out of the shower and wiped away a portion of the steam from the mirror, so I could admire the clean canvas of my face.

Tell him how you feel. Put the past behind and move on. I nodded, working to convince myself.

Derek texted directions to our meeting place. It did not include an address, just turn here and there. Based on the treasure hunt in St. Augustine, I was not surprised, but wondered what he was up to.

Usually, I got dressed within thirty minutes. That evening I took my time. I had a little getting-ready wine and gave special care to my hair and makeup. My black dress with the red trim hung on the door and for the first time, I pulled out the shoebox labeled "Red Satin Heels." Looking into the full-length mirror, someone different stared back. A happy, confident, me. I liked it.

The directions had to be wrong. There were no buildings

or restaurants, just a narrow road leading to the beach. I kept driving, slow and steady, searching for a sign of life or a clue as to what might lie ahead. After a few more minutes, the path turned rocky and then sandy. It was a dead end. The open ocean stretched before me. My immediate thought was to drive away. *I must have made a wrong turn.* But something pulled at me.

Before I realized it, I had parked, opened the door and stood outside the car. Waves crashed against the russet pebble beach and wind echoed in my ears. The rich sea air filled my chest. As if a magnet were pulling me, I walked closer toward the sand and scanned up and down the coast. *What is that?* To my right, about ten or fifteen yards away there was a wooden platform, encroaching on the ocean's edge. A figure sat hunched over a table. I squinted. The moonlight's glow revealed a familiar face—Derek.

I took a few more steps but stopped short of the sinking sand. Derek searched the horizon. His hands sat locked in his lap. A thoughtful, yet serious, expression painted his face. Time disappeared as I watched him. The soft waves calmed my nerves.

My foot did not want to move forward, uneasy in the three-inch heels. I bent over and started to yank my right shoe off, but tripped. Derek must have heard me. He turned toward my direction. "Natalie? Is that you?" He called.

"Yes. It's me." Derek seemed to fly from the platform. He stood by me within seconds.

"Here, let me help you." I slipped off the other shoe and took Derek's outstretched hand. His touch was just as I remembered. He escorted me to the small raised area, dodging small rocks and a pool of trapped water. On my tippy toes, I stumbled up the stairs to the private deck.

White linen cloths and stunning china, bone colored with a single gold line running along the edge, decorated the table. A vast and fragrant bouquet of lilies, tied in a purple satin ribbon, sat in the middle. Derek pulled the seat out and tucked me in under the table.

Although I didn't see any kitchen, I smelled roasted pork, potatoes and grilled vegetables mingling in the salt air. My nose rose as freshly baked bread seduced my senses. Derek popped a cork and poured each of us a glass of Shiraz.

"You look beautiful," Derek commented, as he handed me the wine. My hands turned cold. I breathed deep and held the cool air in my chest as I reached for the salvation swimming in the crystal goblet. Trying without success to keep a steady hand, I took a large gulp.

"Thank you. You're quite handsome, yourself." He wore a linen jacket, with matching tie-string pants. My dress seemed out of place next to his cruise-like attire.

"Good evening, Natalie. Do you remember me?" JJ, the driver from New York, walked onto the platform, wearing a tuxedo.

"Well, of course I do, JJ."

"I've brought you some freshly baked sourdough rolls. I'll be back with your salads shortly. Enjoy."

"What is going on?" I asked.

"Oh. JJ is going to take care of us tonight."

"Really? Is that part of the other 5% assigned duties?"

"He's a fantastic cook. Had some formal training even."

A chuckle rose up in me picturing JJ somewhere on the beach, sand in his shoes, his tux flapping in the wind, chopping carrots. JJ arrived with the salads, romaine and arugula piled high, topped with fresh strawberries, gorgonzola, candied walnuts and a rich vinaigrette. I grabbed the spotless fork, and began picking at the salad, hating to destroy the display.

After JJ left, Derek and I sat quietly for a long time, waiting for someone to make the first move. Tension grew like boats in choppy waters. We were like awkward teenagers, realizing that we liked each other. The bread melted in my mouth. JJ's sculptured salad tasted divine, but I was preoccupied, analyzing everything in my life, drunk with new knowledge and self-discovery.

As my head fell back and the wine traveled down my throat, the moon captivated me. I was sure it studied me too, with its knowing face and wise grin. In that moment, I realized everything works out in the end, even when the trip is filled with unknown faces, rough terrains and hidden messages. With rocky paths or sinking sands, the journey is the most important part.

Sara, Derek, mom—they were not the enemy. *I am my own enemy.* Dragging myself down, beating myself to the ground, on every issue, every breath. *I'm tired of feeling inadequate. It is not everyone else's responsibility to make me happy. I have to find happiness on my own.* My future, my life and all the joy that I so desired, sat in front of me. If only I would open that old rickety gate and let him enter.

Derek cleared his throat, looked up and said, "Natalie, thank you for agreeing to meet me. I've played this conversation over in my head so much I can't say how many times. And now here we are, and suddenly I am at a loss for words."

"Me too," I added, relieved that he brought the issue up. I quickly continued, "Derek, I want to thank you too."

"For what?" he asked, as JJ returned with the main course.

"What you did. The school, the heart association, and well," I peered out at the water and then at the spray of lilies on the table. *Just as I dreamed it.* "This, this amazing dinner. I—"

"Excuse me, miss. Are you done?" JJ asked. I nodded. He replaced the empty salad plate with another filled of sliced roast pork tenderloin. After serving Derek, JJ said, "the pork has a garlic and rosemary marinade. The new potatoes have been slightly tossed in butter and dill, and the vegetables have been grilled over open flame with olive oil, fresh cracked pepper and a touch of my special sauce. Enjoy." JJ smiled, seeming pleased with his creation, and left the platform.

"Special sauce?" I questioned.

"I have no idea what is in it, but it's like crack. Not that I would know, I mean. It's addictive is all I'm trying say."

"A place back home has this amazing macaroni with white truffle cheese sauce. On the menu, they call it 'Crack-in-a-

Crock.' So my expectations are high," I teased.

"I know." He winked. We both reached for our knife and fork and dug into the entree.

"I'm sorry. Honestly. It was not my or Sara's intention to hurt you. She was really just trying to help two friends."

"I don't like being played, Derek. I'm a 'what you see is what you get' kinda person. Sara knows that." I scooped up a helping of potatoes.

"I think we should forget about how we met and under what circumstances. And care only about the fact that we met."

A devilish smile invaded Derek's gentle face. He cut his pork and stabbed a grilled carrot, washing it down with the wine.

"Are you happy we met?" he asked.

"Yes. I just don't understand how it all happened. I mean you and Sara. I thought Victor was her only husband. She never mentioned a previous marriage."

"Sara and I got married right after high school. Everyone, our parents and siblings, they were all telling us what we 'should do' and its like we rebelled or something. Got married and left, thinking we would conquer the world. Show them. We were stupid and too young. Everyone said it wouldn't last and they were right. We just didn't have a clue. So we ended it, on good terms and have stayed friends. I think now that's all we ever were, more like brother and sister. Anyway, yes, I knew you were coming to San Francisco and I was excited about it." He paused, swirled the wine and gulped it like he was drinking water. "I've been thinking. We really met on our own, without anyone's help."

As we polished off the last morsels of JJ's perfectly cooked food, Derek reached for my hand. I brought it up from my lap and took his.

"What are you talking about?" I asked, pushing my plate away defeated. *I hope JJ has a crane ready to lift me out of this chair and carry me to the car, because I am stuffed.*

JJ arrived with a colossal dessert. *Oh my.* Vanilla ice cream, drenched in chocolate sauce, nuts and whipped cream filled the rim of a margarita glass. A perfectly positioned cherry balanced on top of the sinful mountain. It was an edible piece of art. JJ seemed to magically remove our empty plates and sit the concoction in front of us. I was still staring, thinking there was no way I could eat another thing. Meanwhile, Derek took his spoon and dug into the delightful mountain of ice cream.

With a little bit of vanilla ice cream at the corner of his mouth, Derek said, "I know you know."

I analyzed him, trying to recall what he was referring to, while piling a huge helping of ice cream and chocolate on top of my spoon.

"Come on, Natalie. You remember." The cool vanilla wrapped his tongue. "The elevator incident when you almost broke my foot with those evil shoes."

"I did not almost break your foot! You're being overdramatic. And, yes. I remember." I wanted to laugh thinking about Derek hobbling on one foot, but choked my giggle and continued, "And, that you spruced up a bit before we met at the tiki-bar."

"I'm saying for the record. It hurt. Okay? And, you got that silly mark off your shirt and put some earrings on." *How did he remember that?* "Anyway," he continued, "we had a connection then. Right when I looked you in the eyes. I knew." His tone grew serious and he narrowed his gaze. "We didn't know each other. I had no idea you were Natalie Swan. I mean, Sara had described you, but it's not the same. I didn't know who you were. But, I knew I wanted to." He dug his spoon into the dripping ice cream. "Didn't you feel the same way?"

I remembered exactly how I felt when Derek first looked at me in that hallway. It was the same warmth and passion I had sitting next to him now. Emotions I never wanted to forget, or to lose. Like a bird, soaring high, with no inhibitions. Or, a candle's flame dancing in the dark, lighting the way. A focus so strong that buildings could fall into the ocean, the moon could explode and the world could disappear, but we would survive. And making it all even stronger was the fact that Derek was right. I didn't know he was Derek Voeltgin when we first bumped into each other.

Finally, I admitted, "You're right, Derek. I did feel a connection. I wanted to go down to the bar and talk with you." He smiled. I figured he was pleased with himself, accomplishing his first goal—to convince me we met by chance.

Derek glanced down toward the floor and reached for a package, which he unwrapped. He eased out what appeared to be a book and laid it on the table in front of me.

"Sir, can I take this?" JJ asked. Only a bit of melted ice cream lay at the bottom of the immense glass.

"Yes, JJ. Thank you." JJ carried all the dishes away. I studied the cover of the book—a picture of a man and woman. Their faces were downcast and seemed depressed, like two people carrying broken hearts in search of repair.

"The picture—it's a Dali. Couple Near the Fortress." Derek pointed out.

"A Dali, really?" *Unbelievable.*

Although the moonlight reflected against the water and illuminated the landscape, JJ floated from one corner to the other, lighting dozens of candles. *What is this about?*

"Open it," Derek urged.

My hand crawled across the table, pulled the book closer and slowly opened the cover to reveal the first page, which read, "If a fortress can fall, so can the walls we create today. For you, Natalie Swan." *Okay. So, this is a bit whacko-mungo.*

"Go, ahead and turn the page." He seemed eager for me to go on.

The next page, on the left hand side, was a picture of me as a baby, maybe a month old. *A photo album? Thank God it's not a naked baby picture.* After accepting the fact that I'd have to endure pictures of myself, I studied the photos.

On the right side, was a picture of another infant? I did not recognize the child. It wasn't me. I studied it for a moment and then read the caption—Derek, 5 weeks old. I looked back at the caption under my picture—Natalie, 4 weeks old. I chuckled, as though I was a parent myself remembering an innocent time.

"Go ahead." Derek acted like a little boy opening presents on his birthday.

On the next pages were a photo of me at one year old and a photo of Derek at the same age. The next showed each of us at five, then at ten. I laughed out loud when I turned the page again. A picture of Derek entering high school. *What a geek!* He was nothing like the dashing man he transformed into. His hair stuck up all over, like he had been electrocuted and his clothes were sloppy and out of place.

My picture wasn't much better with long pigtails and shiny braces peeking through my shy smile. We filled out a bit in the pictures of prom and graduation. *My hair was so much lighter than it is now.* The photos continued for pages, from our college years, at twenty-five and thirty. Each had a caption explaining the photo.

I started to turn the next page, but stopped and studied Derek. "How did you get all these pictures?"

"I have my sources," he said, as he raised a brow. Of course, he worked with my parents. My mother must have had a ball picking just the right photos.

"Do you like it?" he asked, as he placed his rugged palm atop my soft gentle fingertips, which were teasing the pages in the album.

"I love it," I said, looking down where he touched me. I couldn't help detect the electricity running through me.

"I'm glad. I wanted to show you how much we have in common and that we are meant to be together."

I tried hard to absorb all of the surroundings, the amount of effort and time he'd put into this evening. He was right.

Derek pulled his hand away and reached toward the album, "There are a couple more pictures you haven't seen yet."

He turned the page to reveal a photo, both of us together from one of our romantic nights together in St. Augustine.

"I thought this picture was perfect. You were so happy."

The feelings I had during that trip flooded my veins. The night we made love. The moment I discovered I had found the one.

"There's still another picture," Derek said. Something in his voice made me look up at him. "Go on!" he could barely contain himself. He had seemed to get more and more fidgety as we made our way through the photos. I slid my finger underneath the page and slowly flipped it over.

Tears began to leak down my cheeks like a burst pipe. On the left was a picture of me standing on the dock in St. Augustine. On the right was a picture of Derek in a tuxedo, kneeling. His right hand cupped a small midnight blue velvet box that he held up toward my photo. Underneath, in large letters, the caption read,

WILL YOU MARRY ME?

Derek pulled from his pocket the same elegant box from the picture, opened it to reveal a diamond ring and asked, "Will you marry me?"

I scooted my chair back a foot, gasping. Everything that had happened seemed to be sucked down into the floor, caught by the sand and swept out to sea. The ring dazzled against the candlelight, sparkling like a massive glass boulder shining under the squinting sky.

I couldn't swallow. My voice ceased to function. I nodded awkwardly and accepted the ring on my finger.

"I love you, Natalie," Derek whispered.

Staring at the engagement ring, I said, "I love you, too."

This was the beginning of the new Natalie, a new way of living and loving, not only loving Derek, but also myself. Forgiveness seemed to lift the stress from my shoulders and leave me renewed.

"I have another surprise for you." Derek reached up with his fingertips to wipe the tears from my eyes. *What else could there possibly be?* He picked up the photo album and grabbed my hand.

We walked down the stairs of the secret get-away and strolled until we reached a dock where a sailboat sat tied. JJ nodded as we crossed the small walkway to the boat. On the other side stood my mother and father.

"So, are we planning a wedding or what?" mom screamed.

I hugged her and squealed, "Yes."

JJ carried a tray of champagne, and we spent the evening toasting.

By the time we found our way to the bedroom, deep in the gut of the boat, I felt exhausted. I had missed Derek and now he was mine.

He kissed the edges of my face and toyed with the strands of my hair. I wanted so much to make love to him, but before I realized it, my eyelids had closed and I drifted off to sleep.

***

Looking like a princess, I wore the white satin gown, which flowed over the floor. Derek stood next to me, the man that I loved, my groom. No fuzzy faces, no disappearing tents, no graveyards. My father leaned over giving my mother a kiss on the cheek. Sara and Victor sat at the wedding party's table, talking infectiously. Friends and family filled the dance floor.

Among the crowd of dancers, a little boy in green overalls walked through in slow motion. He stopped in the middle of the dance floor. Our eyes met. He smiled and winked.

It was the best dream I ever had.

ACKNOWLEDGEMENTS

There were many friends and family members that helped me during the creation of *Precious little Secrets*. First, I want to thank my parents, Idi and Phil. They inspired and encouraged me to express myself and be creative. Although they aren't with me to see this book completed, I am so grateful that my mother got a chance to read a very early draft. I hope she would have enjoyed the final product.

Also, I want to thank my wonderful husband, Kevin. He has been extremely supportive during this process and has helped me enormously. Not only has he helped with all the technical aspects of this venture, he also served as the primary editor of this book. His ability to see things and connect all the pieces and parts astounds me, and I am very grateful. He helped make this book so much better than I would have imagined.

I've also been fortunate to have an amazing friend to guide me along this journey, Bev DeMello. We are each other's accountability partners, meeting frequently to discuss our writing goals, exchange ideas and information, offer feedback, and cheer each other on with a glass of wine and a toast. Thank you, Bev.

I would also like to thank my friends and family who read drafts of this book, especially my sister-in-law, Connie Crawford. Your insight and spirit are inspirational.

It has been a long road and I wondered if the gate would ever open for me. Now it finally has, and I am thrilled and anxious to continue my passion for writing and telling stories.

ABOUT THE AUTHOR

Visit www.michellenickens.com.

Follow Michelle on Twitter @PWTallyGirl

"Like" Michelle's page at
www.facebook.com/MichelleNickensAuthor

Made in the USA
Columbia, SC
01 May 2017